"For Gaitskill, the solutions to loneliness and the cruelty it so often prompts are honesty, vulnerability, and recognition; this is the underlying moral vision that courses through her fiction. Gaitskill may be a secular writer, but there is something almost religious in the way she depicts human frailty. It's common—indeed, inevitable—and cannot be barred or banned or legislated away; it can only be viewed, unblinkingly . . . Whereas others might only judge, she attends, as artists are meant to do."

—Maggie Doherty, *The Nation*

"Ms. Gaitskill writes with such authority, such radar-perfect detail, that she is able to make even the most extreme situations seem real . . . and she displays a reportorial candor, uncompromised by sentimentality or voyeuristic charm."

—Michiko Kakutani, *New York Times*

"Gaitskill's work feels more real than real life, and reading her leads to a place that feels like a sacred space."

—Priscilla Gilman, *Boston Globe*

"Gaitskill's style is gorgeously caustic . . . Her ability to capture abstract feelings and sensations with a precise and unexpected metaphor is a squirmy delight to encounter in such abundance."

—Heidi Julavits, *Publishers Weekly*

"Throughout [her] astonishing essays about literature, music and more, she seems to be circling the notion that curiosity—embracing the muddle—is the path to empathy for sick, sad creatures like us."

—Ann Manov, *UnHerd*

"After setting characters in perilous or caustic sexual terrain, Gaitskill always orients the reader on their minute, often uncertain movements of mind through which an acute vulnerability is exposed. Despite claims made for her fixations, what *New York* magazine recently called her 'predilection for tales of kink,' Gaitskill's art is about nothing so transgressive as the confusion to which much modern living tends."

—Wyatt Mason, *Harper's*

"[Gaitskill's fiction] creates an atmosphere, provokes a response, and suffuses us with an emotion that we can easily, all too easily, summon up. It's art that you can continue to see even with your eyes closed."

—Francine Prose, *Slate*

THE DEVIL'S TREASURE

THE DEVIL'S TREASURE

A BOOK OF STORIES AND DREAMS

MARY GAITSKILL

McNally Editions

New York

McNally Editions
52 Prince St., New York 10012

Originally published in hardcover in 2021 by ZE Books, Houston.
First McNally Editions paperback, 2023

Portions of three previously published novels by Mary
Gaitskill were used by the author for the creation of this work:
The Mare (Pantheon, 2015); *Two Girls, Fat and Thin* (Simon &
Schuster, 1991); and *Veronica* (Pantheon, 2005; and in the UK
and Commonwealth territories, Serpent's Tail). Portions of this
work have also appeared in a somewhat different form in the
introduction to the British edition of *Veronica* (Serpent's Tail,
2016) and in an essay by Mary Gaitskill titled "Learning to
Ride at 56" (*Vogue*, 2015).

ISBN: 978-1-946022-82-0
E-book: 978-1-946022-83-7

Designed by Jonathan Lippincott

1   3   5   7   9   10   8   6   4   2

For Sharon Hanson

CONTENTS

AUTHOR'S NOTE

The Devil's Treasure: A Book of Stories and Dreams is a collage made from the fragments of my own work (novels, essays, memoir, and critical writing) connected by a single story. I hope you enjoy it.

Reprised Works

Two Girls, Fat and Thin, a novel in two voices, first and third person

Veronica, a novel in single voice, first person

Lost Cat, a memoir

The Mare, a novel in six voices

The End of Seasons, a novel in the third person

THE DEVIL'S TREASURE

When Ginger was seven she went to Hell. She'd first heard of it because her father said "What the hell!" when something was funny. Then one day he came out of his bedroom shouting, "This is hell!" while her mother cried behind the door and it was not funny. His eyes were staring and he was showing his teeth like a scared dog. When she asked, her grandmother told her Hell was a made-up place underground where people went to be tortured forever. Then she saw a cartoon in which the Devil sat on a pile of treasure and laughed while demons poked dancing people in the behind with pitchforks. It did not look like torture. It looked scary but interesting too.

The night she went to Hell, Ginger went to sleep in the bedroom she shared with her sister. They laid their heads on their pillows and their mother sang them "Tender Shepherd."

> One say your prayers and
> Two close your eyes and
> Three safe and happily fall asleep.

And then Ginger went looking for Hell. She didn't have to look far. Her spirit rose from her and walked through the house. The furniture watched her kindly. The only thing that called her was the sugar bowl, from which she liked to sneak spoonfuls during the day. But her spirit didn't stop even for that. She went straight to the backyard and found the trapdoor that led to Hell. It wasn't hard to open.

The stairway down was clean and well lit. She thought, *I will steal the Devil's treasure and put it under my bed so I'll have it in the morning!*

As she ran down the stairs in her nightie, she noticed pictures on the walls. They showed faces and scenes, and they moved as she went past. In one picture naked people were being driven up a great stone stair by powerful men with no faces. It reminded her of the cartoon and so she stopped to look at it. And then she was in it.

TWO GIRLS, FAT AND THIN

Whenever I think of the house I grew up in, in Painesville, Pennsylvania, I think of the entire structure enveloped in, oppressed by, and exuding a dark, dank purple. Even when I don't think of it, it lurks in miniature form, a malignant dollhouse, tumbling weightless through the horror movie of my subconscious, waiting to tumble into conscious thought and sit there exuding darkness.

Objectively, it was a nice little house. It was a good size for three people; it had a slanting roof, cunning shutters, lovable old doorknobs that came off in your hands, a breakfast nook, an ache of dingy carpets, and faded wallpaper. It was our fifth house, the one we collapsed in after a series of frantic moves that were the result of my father's belief that wherever he lived was hell. Eventually he became too exhausted to move again and made our sedentary status a virtue, gloating as he gazed out through the cracked shutters at the arrivals and departures of several sets of neighbors on both sides: the Whites, the Calefs, and the Hazens on the left, and the Wapshots, the Rizzos, and the morose, relatively stationary old Angrods on the right. "We live in a society of cockroaches," he said, "scurrying all over the face of the map with no thought of community or family, nothing."

The Painesville house was the most significant point of my upbringing, and it unfolds from its predecessors with the minor inevitability of an origami puzzle in several pieces. With each house the puzzle becomes more sinister, then more sad, then simply strange, the final piece made from a grainy photograph of Anna Granite's face. I imagine Justine Shade picking up the various paper constructions to examine them, furrowing her brow, tapping her lip with her pen.

I was born in Blossom, Tennessee. I think of grape arbors, trellises clotted with magnolias, the store downtown that sold white bags of candy. (There actually was a grape arbor in our backyard in Blossom, but our second, more lived-in Tennessee house near Nashville had a square back-yard full of short grass and festering sunlight.)

One of my succession of therapists used to say that "the body remembers everything," meaning that on some level so deep you don't even know about it, you've stored compressed yet vivid details of everything that's ever hap-pened to you, including, she was later to assert, everything in your past lives. This could be true, I guess, but these bodily memories are so unevenly submerged and revealed, so distorted—as the deficient yard is garnished with imag-inary arbors and trellises—that they may as well be com-pletely invented.

My mother, whose name was Blanche, came from a poor but respectable matriarchal farm family. She was the oldest of three girls, but she was the shortest, the shyest, the one most likely to be teased. As the oldest she was responsible for taking care of her sisters, Camilla and Martha, when there was no school and their mother went into town to clean rich people's houses. This was a hopeless arrangement, as Camilla and Martha were strong, boisterous girls who banded against their sister, barred her from their games, and ridiculed her. They refused to get up to eat her carefully prepared breakfasts, they wouldn't help her with the dishes, they ran around the house like cats, knocking things down while she tried to clean. The sole factor that enabled the harried girl to maintain any order at all was her intense and agitated seriousness. Her idea of the world was a pretty picture of shiny pink faces and friendly animals in nature scenes, of dulcet conversations and gestures—a lively but always gentle and harmonious world that could not accommodate (and could be totally undone by) sarcasm or cruelty. Out of the need to impress a lacelike pattern on brutishness came her unshakable determination to clean and sew and mop the floor. She got up before sunrise to get cream and eggs. She wreathed her table settings with clover and daisies. She made jam and arranged the jars so that their colors complemented one another: mint, plum, cherry, apple. Her sisters' jeering hurt her, but it also roused and locked into position a surprising element of strength that dignified her melancholy zeal, which caused her unkind sisters to remember her, in their broken-down middle years, with pathos and respect.

The same frantic need to prettify informed her mothering. We spent a lot of time together when I was five, more than I spent with other children. On Saturdays, we sat at the kitchen table, intently drawing crayon animals in their jungles or under cloud-blotched skies. We made up stories illustrated by pink-eared families of mice. We built homes for my animals that ranged across rooms, and my mother always consented to "hold" the wicked frog who lived in a penthouse atop my dresser. Or my mother would read *The Wizard of Oz* aloud. Other times we would sit on the couch and my mother would show me art books and prints, inviting me to invent stories about the little boy in red and ruffles standing alone with a bird on a leash. And at night, she would sit on my bed and tell stories of her girlhood. I would hold her hand as she constructed airy balloons that floated by in the dark, bearing glowing pictures of her and my father holding hands on the porch swing, or of her lying in a meadow of clover, dreaming and looking for fairies while horrible Camilla called her home.

My father entered this magic world in the evening, when he returned home from work in grandness, and our phantasms and elves stood at attention to receive his directions. He would put on one of his records—opera, marching music, or jazz—and turn up the volume so that it trumpeted aggressively through the house, ramming his personality into every corner. My mother worked in the kitchen, stirring a big pot of chili or peeling potatoes, and my father would pace excitedly between kitchen and living room, drinking beer after beer and eating the dry roasted peanuts, sliced Polish sausage, and hot green peppers that my mother had arranged in little dishes as, against a thundering sound track, he expounded upon his day. He was a manager in the clerical department of a sales firm in Nashville. He would talk about the office intrigue as though it were symbolic of all human activity, as though he were enacting daily the drama of good versus evil, of weakness versus strength, of the fatal flaws that cause otherwise able men to fail, of the mysterious ways of the universe that make the rise of "bastards" possible. He would start on some incident—how "that socialist shit-ass Greenburger" had tried to undermine the unfortunate clubfoot Miss Onderdonk in order to cast favor on a pretty new typist, and how he was publicly exposed and deplored—and then link this to some greater abstract principle, cross-referencing it to events in his childhood or his stint in the army, as though one had led, inexorably and triumphantly, to the other. The room filled with overlapping scenarios from the past (his past, as created by me) that appeared in a sweet-smelling, melancholy wave of events—picnics, days at school, and old ladies who had clasped him in their perfumed arms before slipping away forever—carrying on its crest and depositing safely in our living room the scene now transpiring.

He paced as he talked, now and then walking close to the windows to peer out, rubbing his fingers together as though grinding something to powder, nibbling zestfully at the snacks that occasionally dropped down his shirtfront, and drinking beer. My mother moved about the kitchen in a frilly apron, her hair bound into a ponytail with a rubber band garnished with large plastic flowers. She listened enthralled to the stories of betrayal and redemption, nodding vigorously, shaking her head in disapproval or agreeing, "Absolutely! That's right!" as the music under-scored her husband's stirring rendition of his eventual tri-umph. "You can't throw your weight around like that in my office, buddy. It's okay to be a tough guy, but you'd better be sure I'm not tougher. And nine times out of ten I am." I would listen gravely as they talked. It seemed as though they were arranging the world, making everything safe and understood.

By the time we sat down to dinner, life was friendly and orderly, and we could regally feast on chili over spaghetti noodles, with chocolate ice cream in little ceramic cups for dessert. Then there would be TV—soldiers winning, dogs rescuing children, criminals going to jail, women finding love—and then my mother would carry me to bed singing,

> Up the magic mountain, one, two, three.
> Up the magic mountain, yessiree.

This and every other image from that time is faded, small and surrounded by a thick border of fuzzy, quavering black-ness. The images aren't connected; there are large spaces between them filled with the incoherent blackness. The emotions belonging to the images are even more unclear; they seem a slur of abnormal happiness, as if my childhood were characterized by the cartoons I watched on TV. This is probably because the adults around me, believing child-hood to be a pretty thing, encouraged me to feel that way, talking to me in baby talk, singing about itsy-bitsy spiders and farmers in the dell, laying an oil slick of jollity over the feelings that have stayed lodged in my memory, becoming more and more grotesque as time goes on. But the feelings continue to lurk, dim but persistent, like a crippled servant, faithfully, almost imbecilically, trying to tell me something in the language of my childhood, my own most intimate language, which has become an indecipherable code.

An indecipherable code. I wrote that sentence thirty years ago in the voice of a fictional character named Dorothy Never, the heroine of a novel titled *Two Girls, Fat and Thin*. It is more real to me now, more real than I understood then. It describes the subtext under much of my writing and my experience of the world, primarily the social world, but even my inner world. It describes something I don't understand. At the same time, I don't think it describes anything especially strange; almost anyone can be baffled by an image from a dream, or a sudden intense feeling, or a realization that they completely misunderstood someone they thought they knew well because that person stopped conforming to a cherished (or despised) inner picture. Then there is the realization that you've completely misunderstood yourself, a self that is so shaped by events, context, time, and immediate requirements.

A terrible and wonderful example: Before my father died in 2001, I knew that I loved him but only dimly. I didn't really feel it, and to the extent that I did, I experienced it as painful. When he was dying I almost didn't go to him. When I was trying to decide whether to go, someone asked me, "Do you want to see him?" And I said, "That's hard to say. Because when you're with him you don't see him. He doesn't show himself. He shows a grid of traits but not himself." Still, I decided to go. The death was prolonged. It was painful. Because of the pain, the "grid" that I referred to—my father's style of presentation—could not be maintained. A few days after I arrived my father lost the ability to speak more than a few words at a time. But his eyes and his face spoke profoundly. I saw him and I felt him, and I loved him more than I thought possible. I was stunned by both the strength of my feeling and my previous obliviousness to it, and my realization that, if I had not come to see him, I would never have known how real my feeling was or how beautiful it was to say it and to hear it said.

I recall that, at the time, I had a mental picture of this experience that looked like one of those practical joke containers disguised as a can of nuts or something; you open the lid and a coiled cloth-covered spring leaps out at you—it felt that startling. This image was followed by another mental picture, an image of human beings as containers that hold layers and layers of thought, feeling, and experience so densely packed ("the body remembers everything") that the (human) container can be aware of only a few layers at a time, usually the first few at the top, until and unless an unexpectedly powerful event makes something deep suddenly pop out, throwing some elements of the "self" into high relief and disordering others, hinting at a different, truer order that was there all along.

Such ordered disorder informs the mosaic of these novel excerpts, which are linked together not sequentially, but by the feel of subjective connections between them. The characters who speak are very different in age and circumstance. In *Two Girls* they are women comically misshapen by brutal and ridiculous childhoods lived in externally decent, even beautiful American neighborhoods. In *Veronica* they are a model and a middle-aged proofreader, both bruised and bewildered by life, but subliminally joined by their belief in synthetic ideals through which they try to find reality in various indecipherable codes primarily expressed as style. In *The Mare* they are a lost middle-aged White woman who can feel reality only through an imaginary "radio signal" and a loving Dominican girl living through the distortions of poverty, inequity, and abuse. When I read through these books, I had a strong double sense of my simultaneous acuity and lack of understanding of the worlds I was trying to represent, putting everything I had into the attempt to create a version of these realities on the page, stumbling as the characters do, trying to find the essence in the confusion. It was humbling and even a little frightening.

I remember the time a kid fell off our porch and cracked his skull. It was Halloween, and I wasn't allowed to go out because my mother thought that, at five, I was too young. My mother dressed for the occasion in her red terry-cloth robe that reached the floor and made her look thick and imposing. The ordinary packaged candy looked special in a large crystal punch bowl. She handed it out with a gently officious air, enjoying herself as my father sat quietly in the shadows of the dim, radio-mumbling house. Most of the kids in our neighborhood were close to my age, and they stood bashful and ungainly in their monstrous wings and clown feet, incredulous and feeling slightly guilty that a stranger had put on a ceremonial robe to give them handfuls of candy. Sometimes a crowd of big kids would come and bellow "trick or treat" like a threat or thrust their masked faces into our living room to scream right at my mother, who screamed in return and hurriedly thrust the candy at them. It was during one of these screaming moments that we heard the real screams of a small child who had just fallen off the porch. There was a scramble of movement amid masked children in the dark, and then the boy was in our bright kitchen, sitting on a stool, bundled in a blanket, sucking his thumb. Probably his parents were there some- where, but I don't remember them. My mother was on the phone to the hospital, picking her nails while my father paced in and out of the room, coughing and wiping his mouth. He said something that made me think we could get into trouble because the boy fell off our porch.

I was frightened and fascinated by the boy. It terrified me to think that you could be standing on a porch, my porch, receiving official candy in a spirit of goodwill, and then, with one wrong movement, be pitched into darkness, cracking your head in a way that could kill you. I stared at his face. It was a garish painted mask of red and blue, his sole costume. His lashes were long and beautiful, his eyes serene and wide, completely undisturbed by the large red gash in his head. I stared at the gash and at the brown hairs mashed around in the blood. I thought I was looking right into his brain. It seemed glowing and wonderfully mysterious. I felt very close to him. I wanted to put my hand in his head. *We could get into trouble for this.*

I ran out of the kitchen and got my stuffed animal, a little limp dog named Greenie. I thrust it at the boy and said, "Take Greenie." He did. He held Greenie tightly with one arm, sucking his thumb, quiet again, his beautiful eyes looking at me with what seemed like curiosity. I stared into his deep red brain until my mother bundled him in her sweater and took him to the hospital.

I let him take my toy. I felt that Greenie had helped him in some way, and it made me feel good to think that I could help a person, especially a person whose brain I'd seen. When I got Greenie back the following week, I valued him all the more as a healer and personal emissary of my goodwill.

When it was over, my father held me on his lap. He held me as though he was frightened of what had happened to the boy and thought I must be frightened too. The house was dark, the radio was singing to us in the background. His hands encircled the ankle of one of my legs and the knee of the other, and I rested in his body as though it were infinite. He said, "Daddy will never let anyone hurt his little girl." He said it as though the sentence itself was grand, as though saying it turned him into a stone lion, immobile but internally watchful and fierce.

•

Once my father took me with him to watch a basketball game. These were the games he talked about when he walked around the house, rubbing his fingers together and saying, "The Mighty Reds," or "Hey hey! What do you say? Get that ball the other way!" as though the words were inflatable cushions of safety and familiarity with which he could pad himself. The Reds were clearly one of the good forces in life, playing basketball against bastards and viciousness. Even my mother said their name in the way people talk about doing right; it wasn't fun, but you had to admit it was important.

The game wasn't fun either. The auditorium was hot and muggy, full of muffled, senseless noise and strangers with invulnerable gum-chewing faces. Sweating men ran with meaningless urgency, straining to prevent each other from doing something that changed from moment to moment. Strangers sat on benches roaring at intervals. My father sat with his neck stretched forward, his face set in the expectant, placated look he had when the world was forming a pattern he approved of.

When it was over we walked home in the dark. "The old Reds won," said my father. "Don't you want to cheer?"

I cheered into the damp night as I ran up the sidewalk. The houses and trees were remote and strange in the dark, the mailboxes lonely and disoriented on their corners. Cars swished by in mournful sweeps of light, and we walked in triumph.

At home there was cinnamon toast and hot chocolate and my mother in her special white Chinese robe with black dragons on it. We marched into the rec room, Daddy carrying me on his shoulders, my legs dangling down his chest. Fat old Walnut the cat thumped behind us, his tail low and steady. My father put Carmen on the record player, and I darted around the room, swirling in an invisible lavender skirt. Daddy and Mother kissed on the blue flowered sofa. Mother's legs were folded and tucked against her body like the wings of a plump bird, and I saw the jagged shred of toenail and the hard little callus on her pink incurved baby toe. Her husband's hands covered her face as he kissed her. "Olé, olé!" shouted prancing me. Scornful Carmen, with an aquiline nose and a rose in her teeth, silently leered from the velvety dark of her album cover where she sat propped sideways against a tall blue lamp. She had been stabbed to death by the time Daddy swung me into his arms.

Up the magic mountain, one, two, three.
Up the magic mountain, yessiree.

We left Walnut curled beside the heat vent. Mother followed behind, smiling at my head as it rested on Daddy's shoulder, hitting light switches as we passed from room to hall to room to staircase. "She's going to sleep with Mama and Daddy tonight because the Reds won and because she is such a good girl."

My memory of that night is a swollen, rose-colored blur that shades every thought venturing near it. The pink bed was massive. The quilts and blankets were rumpled into low mountain ranges with frowning eyes and brow indentations that stretched and melted when Daddy pulled the blankets over me. Tiny curls of hair and granules were the worms and earth of the pink bed world. The smell of Daddy's hair oil and Mama's perfume penetrated me like a drug too strong for my system to metabolize.

I lay cuddled in the arms of my softly pajamaed father, waiting for Mama, who was lazily brushing her hair at the vanity table. The rest of the room, with its furniture, curtains, glimmering bottles, and snakes of Mama's jewelry, was a dream of objects that claimed to be familiar but weren't. Then the light went off, and Mama slid between the sheets, her fragrant body heat lilting from the open space between nightgown and skin, and there was no longer any world outside the bed. When my eyes adjusted to see the gray squares of window and the trees beyond, they were as far away as stars, and the lumbering furniture was ephemeral as the half-dreams that bother you when you're trying to wake up.

1979: That was the year I began to wake up not knowing who I was or where I was. I was twenty-three and I was taking classes at the University of Michigan. I had not graduated from high school; I could be at the university because I had taken an equivalency test and then gone to community college for a year and a half. I did not go directly to college. I instead lived on my own between the ages of sixteen and twenty-one, mostly hand to mouth, going from one provisional job to the next. I had started writing then and decided to go to college because I realized that my skill level was not adequate for what I wanted to achieve.

At the university I met people my age who were in graduate school or who had stayed in Ann Arbor after graduating. I was not fully at ease with these people, though, because most of them were not only better educated, they were culturally far more sophisticated and confident than I was—and yet at the same time they were also far more viscerally and experientially naive. I did not know where to put myself in this environment, and I began to lose my sense of . . . everything. In this environment I started waking up in the morning with no idea of who I was or where I was. I had to remind myself, and it took several minutes. I would call up images, pictures of myself doing things: walking to class, in a restaurant drinking tea, talking to someone. At first the pictures were bizarre and alien, then neutral, then I'd say, "Oh, right," and get out of bed. My self, it seemed, had broken, and something unfamiliar was trying to emerge. It was scary, but it was powerful too. I wanted to know who it was that was looking at the pictures before I said "oh, right."

When Justine was seven, she ordered the Catholic boy down the street to tie her to his swing set and pretend to brand her, as she had seen Brutus do to Olive Oyl on TV. Sometimes she made him chase her around the yard with a slender branch, whipping her legs. His name was Richie, and she remembers he was Catholic because his mother, faceless in memory, told her that if she lied there'd be a sin on her soul and she'd have to go to Hell.

"Mrs. Slutsky is a good woman, but she is ignorant," said Justine's mother. "You must be kind and respectful to her, but don't listen to anything she says."

But Justine liked listening to Mrs. Slutsky talk about Hell and encouraged her to do so every Saturday morning when she went to play with Richie. The Slutskys' apartment was close and ramshackle. Once Justine put her finger on the wall and dirt came off on it; she felt like she was in a story about poor people. She loved the picture of the beautiful doe-eyed Jesus with a dimly flaming purple heart wrapped in thorns adorning the middle of his chest that hung in Mrs. Slutsky's bedroom. She loved the ornately written prayer to the saints in the den. She loved to stand in the kitchen, which smelled of old tea bags and carrot peels, and question Mrs. Slutsky about Hell.

"What if you do something bad but you believe in God? What if you believe in God but you're always doing really bad things? What if you do something bad but you're sorry?"

Mrs. Slutsky would explain everything as she did the dishes or ironed or smoked, expansively delineating the various levels of Hell and purgatory. Sometimes Justine and Richie would sit at the kitchen table and draw pictures of a smoking red Hell with the victims' snarled-up arms writhing skyward. Justine liked to draw angels floating at the top of the page, looking down in sorrow and raining pink tears of pity into Hell.

She and Richie spent hours watching Saturday morning cartoons on the Slutskys' sagging, loamy-smelling green couch. She wanted to be tied up and whipped after watching cartoon characters being beaten and tortured by other characters for the viewers' amusement. She watched the animated violence with queasy fascination, feeling frightened and exposed. It was the same feeling she had when Dr. Norris touched her, and she felt a bond with docile, daydreaming Richie, simply because he was near her while she was having this feeling.

When she began making him tie her up, she couldn't tell if he wanted to do it or if he was passively following her lead. She recalls his face as furtive and vaguely ashamed, as though he were picking his nose in public.

We watched *Combat!* every Tuesday. I loved the theme song from *Combat!* and can remember the final bars even today. The theme was about fighting and winning, but it was also about something more subtle and intimate, something voluptuous. I didn't know exactly what this something was, but it had a lot to do with Lieutenant Hanley. Lieutenant Hanley was a slim, boyish person with large, flowerlike eyes. He was always getting captured or wounded. Even when he wasn't getting captured, there was something about him that made his capture seem imminent. Episode after episode featured Lieutenant Hanley bound on the floor or to a chair while a large German stood over him, arrogantly resting his jackbooted foot on a table or something. ("Why does he put his foot there?" I asked. "Because Germans love their boots," said my mother. "They love to show them off.") Of course, Sergeant Saunders, a grizzled, stocky man, would come rescue him, and they would go on with the plot, but there was always a small moment when it was so nice to have Lieutenant Hanley tied up and looking at his captor with those brave, flowerlike eyes, and somehow the music referred to that moment. It was a very human theme song, I guess.

When I started the sixth grade, our neighborhood was rezoned, and now my best friend had to take a bus to a school half an hour away, and I was transferred to yet another school. The new school was filled with crowds of strangers with ratted nests of bleached hair, makeup, and breasts. The girls wore pointy boots and stood with their legs apart and their hips thrust out; the boys wore cleats and had faces like knives. I once saw two boys standing in the hall by their lockers, one boy passive and expectant, the other gently holding the passive one's face with his palm, and then, with a sudden movement, the touch turned to a slap, leaving the slapped face hot red. This caress/slap was repeated again and again, with varying gradations separating the caress from the slap, on one cheek and then the next. The slapped boy's expression remained impassive, even insolent.

Both boys and girls covered their notebooks with drawings in hot Magic Marker and decals. Their drawings were of monsters with dripping fangs; long, roiling tongues; bugged-out, veiny eyes; and short hairs all over them. The monsters were surrounded by Magic Marker words in huge, ornate Gothic letters: "Cool," "Eat Me," and "Suck." Almost everyone drew, with the same ornamental flourish and precision, a huge swastika or Maltese cross in some central place on his or her notebook.

It was pretty much the same situation as the last school, except this one had more audiovisual aids, and instead of the teacher giving the usual talk during science period, she'd have one of the boys wheel in a television, and we'd watch a program called *Adventures in Science*. It was awful, and during the first week, a girl behind me said, "I'd rather fart than watch *Adventures in Science*."

There were race riots in Detroit that summer and there was a lot of talk about that. Darcy Guido stood up to imitate Martin Luther King Jr., tap dancing, rolling her eyes, and pulling her lower lip down and sticking her tongue up to make weird wet lips that looked like the genitals of an orangutan. The day the National Guard flew over their roof-tops in helicopters, all the neighbors stood in the streets and cheered. Even Pat Brasier's mother came out on her concrete slab and said, "That'll teach those animals!" Other people just yelled, "Kill them! Kill them!"

For days the riots were on television. At dinner, Justine and her parents would sit at the table, eating and watching the dark figures run around on the screen while flames flickered in the blackened buildings. Her father would speak on the reprehensibility of rioting and violence, smartly wielding his utensils, the very posture of his haunches expressing the rightness of his disapproval. Her mother would agree, adding praise for Martin Luther King Jr. The people who ran the TV apparently felt the same way; after showing clips of rioting or angry Black spokespeople, they would console their viewers with old footage of Dr. King giving his famous "dream" speech. Justine became tired of seeing him and of hearing him and of hearing him praised. She didn't see what was so great about him.

•

This fictional place is based on a real suburb in
Michigan, outside of Detroit. The events set in this
particular neighborhood are real, or at least real-ish.
It's the point of view that is mostly imagined, and the
tones and textures are just slightly elevated, the reds,
for example, brought up feverishly high. In retrospect
that technique seems crude—and it is. But it also
seems like a truthful way to write about the place. It
was a nice enough place materially. But it was brutal.
Not physically. Psychologically. I felt it as soon as we
arrived, felt violence in the people's eyes, their voices,
the way they held their bodies. The little girl crudely
mocking Martin Luther King Jr. stood out in my
memory not because it was unique in its careless,
gleeful cruelty but because it was not directed at
another child or something else in the usual realm
of children. It was directed at someone engaged in
a life-and-death fight and this girl, "Darcy," surely
knew that. We all knew it. But it was nothing to her
or to her crowd of friends who laughed and joined
in her clowning. Or rather it was something to be
mocked. This mockery felt reflexive and mysterious.
In this case it was racial; it was very acceptable for it
to be racial. But it was also generic; sometimes it was
both. I remember being called a "Jew-bag" at ten. I
didn't know for sure what a Jew was and I doubt the
girl who called me the word knew either. (I asked
my mother and she said, "It's what the Kleins are,"
which I did not find illuminating.) I didn't doubt the
people who screamed "Kill them!" would've killed
Black people; I also thought that under the right

circumstances they might kill me. I wasn't so much morally outraged as I was bewildered and afraid. I was so afraid of my neighbors that I didn't go outside unless I absolutely had to. I went to school and came back and otherwise refused to go outside. This was one reason that my parents considered me mentally ill. I understand why they thought that. But I think they were wrong. About that part anyway.

Then the riots were over and it was time to go to the Wonderland Mall for clothes. Justine loved Wonderland. It was dotted with shrubs and waste containers; there was a fountain with a rusting cube placed in the center of it. Muzak rolled over everything, decorously muffling sound and movement. Huge square portals led into great tiled expanses lined with row upon dizzying row of racks hung with clothes. Signs that said JUNIOR MISS, COOL TEEN, or LITTLE MISS GO-GO in fat round letters protruded from the tops of the racks, some of them illustrated with teenage cartoon girls with incredibly frail bodies, enormous staring eyes, tiny O-shaped mouths, and large round heads with long, straight swatches of brown or yellow hair.

The dresses on the COOL TEEN racks seemed to have been manufactured in a country where no one sat at home waiting for her mother: it seemed that in wearing the hot orange-and-yellow polka-dotted "hip-hugger" skirt with matching vinyl belt, the paisley jumper with purple pockets, or the high-collared chartreuse dress, Justine would suddenly occupy a place in which her mother didn't even exist.

She did real shopping, ironically, with her mother, but what she loved best was to go with Mrs. Bernard and Edie and Pam all the way to Wonderland. She and her friends would lounge all over the back seat, giggling about pubic hair or how stupid somebody was, while Mrs. Bernard, a strangely thin woman with a face that seemed held in place with tacks, talked to herself in a low, not unattractive mutter. (Edie said her mother had a mustache that she tore off with hot wax, but Justine didn't believe it.) Once at the mall, the four of them would comb the grounds like a gang of cats, riffling the racks, plunging into dressing rooms, snacking savagely between shops. Mrs. Bernard would wander ahead and be continually bushwhacked by salespeople who thought her mutter was addressed to them, leaving the girls to stare and giggle and to furtively admire the groups of tough older kids lounging on the public benches, smoking cigarettes and sneering. Sometimes glamorous older boys would follow them, saying, "I'd like to pet your pussy," and other dirty things; this was exciting, like the poem about the crucified man, only it made Justine feel queasier as it was real and in public. It was horrible to be in front of people having the same feeling that she had while masturbating and thinking about torture. She was sure that Edie and Pam didn't have feelings like that; probably they didn't even masturbate. They blushed and giggled and said, "You guys better stop it," but they swung their purses and arched their backs, their eyes half closed and their lips set in lewd, malicious smiles. Justine would imitate them, and when she did, sometimes a door would open and she'd step into a world where it was really very chic to walk around in public with wet underpants, giggling while strange boys in leather jackets and pointed shoes called you a slut. The world of Justine alone under the covers with her own smells, her fingers at her wet crotch, was now the world of the mall filled with fat, ugly people walking around eating and staring. It was a huge world without boundaries; the clothes and record and ice-cream stores seemed like cardboard houses she could knock down, the waddling mothers and pimple-faced loners like dazed pedestrians she was passing on a motorcycle.

Once, at Sears, she was sullenly picking through the dressing rooms, trying to find a vacant stall, when she flipped back a scratchy yellow curtain and saw a strange person. She was about Justine's age and weird looking, Justine thought, ugly, with pale cold skin, a huge, exposed forehead, and blue plastic glasses on her face. She was fully dressed and slumped on the floor in a position of utter passivity and defeat, right against the mirror, staring at herself with the lack of expression that comes from extreme mental pain. Their eyes met for seconds—the stranger's faintly reflecting embarrassed humanity—and then Justine backed out. The sight of such mute, frozen pain was stunning and fascinating. Justine had never seen such a naked expression on her parents' faces, let alone on the face of a stranger. It made her feel queasiness and fear; it also made her want to poke at the queasiness and fear so she could feel them all the more. To see and feel something so raw in the mall was obscene, much more obscene than the whispering boys. She went to get Edie and Pam.

"Come and see," she said. "There's a drooling retard in the dressing room."

Naturally they hurried back. Justine had imitated the girl's deranged slump with embellishments of jaw and eyeballs, and they approached the dressing room with a sense of cruel, illicit excitement. But when they got to the dressing stall and flung the curtain back, there was no one there. They sighed with disappointment and turned to go, and there was the girl again, standing up and peeping at them from behind the curtain of another dressing stall. Her face was accusing and almost snotty. Edie and Pam knew it was her, but somehow they couldn't make fun of her, even though they would've liked to; her staring face made them feel caught.

"God, what a queer," said Pam as they left the dressing room.

They found Edie's mother eating candy necklaces at the coffee counter of Woolworth's and left.

The thing about the heightened color, the loud, gaudy shapes and voices—that style revealed what was perversely great about the children of that place as well as what was ugly; it revealed the nasty vitality that was squeezed into such ridiculous shapes (*large round heads with long, straight swatches of brown or yellow hair; tiny O-shaped mouths*) and yet found ways to assert itself with strutting sexual postures and pointed shoes. That was great, and as scared as I was, I could appreciate it. The ugliest things were "cute" and "sexy," and anything that didn't fit was screamed at and humiliated. It felt horrible, but it was just so *warped* that it was also funny. I appreciated the warped funniness too, which was confusing; it made my own humiliation vaguely funny to me.

And I *was* humiliated in that place; I actually was the queer in the dressing room. ("Queer" was meant as a general insult; I don't think any of these kids knew what the word really meant.) I did actually slump against the dressing room mirror during yet another dismal shopping trip, for some perverse reason exaggerating my unpleasant misery for my own strange edification, when someone spied me and then brought back her eager friends, whom I then embarrassed by spying at them from behind another curtain. Everyone was so afraid of being embarrassed or caught somehow, even by the class queer! In fact there was a reason I was afraid to go out; every time I did, which was only when I had to go to school, I was ferociously jeered at by groups of kids, most of whom I didn't even know. I eventually got out of this bad position by taking advantage of yet another neighborhood rezoning, which placed me in a school where I was with a completely new set of kids. I avoided ostracization there by pretending, to the best of my ability, to speak and act and dress as much like everyone else as possible—by resolutely *not* being myself. It actually worked. I had very few friends and no real friends, but no one bothered me either. And from my camouflaged place, I was painfully aware of the cruelty directed at other kids who had also failed to thrive in this weirdly hostile place—cruelty that was sometimes even directed at a reasonably popular kid who for some reason slipped up and did or said something that was mysteriously queer. The energy of it was like a malevolent swarm that continually roved, intent on locating and attacking anything that wasn't exactly like itself. And there was such terrible joy in it, this impulse to discover and attack! There was a *Simpsons* episode I saw years back, so long ago that I can't remember the plotline. Homer's neighbors suddenly turn on him as he sinks into the ground where they can't attack him, except the crown of his head shows and someone screams, "There's his head! Claw it!" And everybody claws his head! That's what it was like, this spastic, communal urge to claw somebody's head while it sinks into the ground.

VERONICA

When I was young, my mother read me a story about a wicked little girl. She read it to me and my two sisters. We sat curled against her on the couch and she read from the book on her lap. The lamp shone on us and there was a blanket over us. The girl in the story was beautiful and cruel. Because her mother was poor, she sent her daughter to work for rich people, who spoiled and petted her. The rich people told her she had to visit her mother. But the girl felt she was too good and went merely to show herself. One day, the rich people sent her home with a loaf of bread for her mother. But when the little girl came to a muddy bog, rather than ruin her shoes, she threw down the bread and stepped on it. It sank into the bog and she sank with it. She sank into a world of demons and deformed creatures.

Because she was beautiful, the demon queen made her into a statue as a gift for her great-grandson. The girl was covered in snakes and slime and surrounded by the hate of every creature trapped like she was. She was starving but couldn't eat the bread still welded to her feet. She could hear what people were saying about her; a boy passing by saw what had happened to her and told everyone, and they all said she deserved it. Even her mother said she deserved it. The girl couldn't move, but if she could have, she would've twisted with rage.

"'It isn't fair!'" cried my mother, and her voice mocked the wicked girl.

Because I sat against my mother when she told this story, I did not hear it in words only. I felt it in her body. I felt a girl who wanted to be too beautiful. I felt a mother who wanted to love her. I felt a demon who wanted to torture her. I felt them mixed together so you couldn't tell them apart. The story scared me and I cried. My mother put her arms around me. "Wait," she said. "It's not over yet. She's going to be saved by the tears of an innocent girl. Like you." My mother kissed the top of my head and finished the story. And I forgot about it for a long time.

There were good people in that suburb too, of course there were; people who weren't out on their stoops screaming. They were actually *humble* people who did not expect or want much of life—even *I* wanted and expected more than they did, and I remember the nervous laughter when I told grown-ups that I wanted to be a writer or a spy. They were mostly blue-collar autoworkers who had saved enough money to move out of the city to a coveted all-White suburb where they might live what they considered decent lives. But as I perceived it, this decency was weak, blinkered, and resigned. It was, apparently, what it meant to be adult. It wasn't my decent adult neighbors who yelled "Kill them!" at the sky as the National Guard flew overhead. It was their teenage sons. Part of my fear was that my parents didn't condemn the shouting, in public or even inside our house—possibly because to them the boys were just kids and not to be taken seriously. But to me those boys were the real force of the neighborhood—not weak, not resigned, not decent, and not merely blinkered but terrifyingly blind. Terrifying, but complicated too.

Maybe a year after some kid called me a Jew-bag there was an explosion of TV specials about the Holocaust and Anne Frank; at the same time there was also an explosion of kids drawing Maltese crosses and swastikas on their notebooks and desks and whatever else it was possible to draw on. The Maltese crosses were connected to drag racing (which was huge in the area) and the funny car artist Ed Roth. But they were also German, and the swastika seemed a natural step up into cool badness—that is, ferocious allegiance with ruthless power that was also defiance against the sanctimony of the Holocaust specials and, even more, defiance against the life of dull decency that had been planned and was waiting for them.

I wonder if what I'm describing is what some people mean now when they refer to the nature of "Whiteness." The people in that suburb were very White and they guarded it jealously, strenuously rejecting anything that wasn't *them*— including other White people. But something else was happening too, something that could happily use racism as a means of expression but was actually bigger than racism and harder to define, something you could not mount a social movement against because there's just too much of it in too many forms: call it unstoppable human shittiness.

TWO GIRLS, FAT AND THIN

At the beginning of October a new kid entered Justine's class. Her name was Cheryl Thomson. She was big, she had acne, and she wore old plaid skirts that were obviously not from Sears or Wards. This could've been all right; some very cool kids—Dody among them—dressed this way. But they had a sloppy panache, a loose-limbed grace that made their flapping shirttails and shifting skirts seem sassy; halting, thick-bodied Cheryl did not. She sat in her seat with her stubby hands in her lap, talking to people politely before class, a dull, dreamy look coating her gray eyes. Then the teacher came in and, in an innocent effort to help everyone get to know the new student, opened class by asking Cheryl questions meant to gently reveal her; for example, "What is your favorite food?" Cheryl did all right with that, but when asked about music, instead of saying "the Monkees" or "the Beatles," she answered with "country music," causing a ripple of disbelief to alert the room. From that point on, every answer she gave confirmed her to be a hopeless alien in the world of primary-colored surfaces. She wanted to be a firefighter when she grew up! Her favorite TV show was *Andy Griffith*! She liked to go fishing! Every answer seemed to come out of some horrible complex individuality reeking with humanity. The clarity and trust in her soft voice made them squirm with discomfort.

In the lunchroom, everyone was talking about how queer she was. Her second day at school somebody tripped her in the hall; the following week somebody put a tack on her seat. When she sat on it, she cried, and little Marla Jacob sneered, "God, what an emotional!" From that day on, she was known as "Emotional," the worst insult imaginable.

Her presence changed the whole composition of the class, uniting everyone, even other unpopular kids, against her. Everything she said became further proof of her stupidity, her social failure. Every ugly and ridiculous thing introduced into any discussion in the classroom, on the playground, or at the mall was "like Emotional." She was most often taunted verbally, but there was also physical abuse: a shower of orchestrated spitballs, an ambush by a dozen or so boys and girls who struck at her legs and arms with their belts.

Emotional's reaction was by turns angry, hurt, bewildered, but her most constant expression was one of helpless good nature. She was too even-tempered to remain angry or brooding; she always tried to reverse the tide against her, to make jokes, to be positive, to join in. Once Justine saw a smiley face drawn in Magic Marker on her note-book with the words "Happy-Go-Lucky" written underneath and knew, sickeningly, that it was true, in spite of everything.

The story of Emotional is also real. I changed only the point of view. I feel almost like I shouldn't admit it, though I'm not sure why. Maybe because it makes it seem like I have no imagination. But how could I not write that story? I cannot forget that girl and what happened to her; most particularly, I can't forget the obscenity of what her haters chose to call her and why: her peers, at *thirteen years old*, had such contempt for natural emotion that to call someone "Emotional" was the worst thing they could think of. It's true, that is beyond my imagination. I realize that worse things have happened to many, many people. I read Ta-Nehisi Coates's memoir of growing up in Baltimore, where he endured fear of literally being destroyed—killed—by gun-wielding kids his own age who wielded guns because they were afraid of being destroyed, possibly by the police. In comparison, it seems ludicrous to talk about this girl being destroyed by being merely verbally humiliated, physically tormented, and rejected every day by her peers. And perhaps she was not destroyed; I don't know what happened to her. But I am sure that she was damaged, as sure as if she were physically beaten. The kind of violence (or the threat of it) that Coates suffered was by any reasonable measure worse. But he had one big advantage that Emotional did not have.

He had a posse. In his memoir he speaks eloquently of the need for boys in his neighborhood to have a group of friends to physically enlarge their presence, to make them appear more formidable whenever they appeared in the world; even a posse of nerds is better than no posse at all. Emotional had no posse. I'm guessing that her ability to ever form a posse was probably compromised for the rest of her life. But maybe that's not true. Maybe she was stronger than I think. Maybe she was lucky. I turned out to be stronger than I thought and I was lucky. But even so, I had no posse then and I still look at groups—any groups of any kind—with a degree of unease that has made posse formation difficult.

Sometimes when I came downstairs for dinner, my father would be resting in his black leather armchair; he would raise his eyebrows in greeting as I stumped down the stairs. I would set the table and talk to my mother. Dinner would be accompanied by television voices and the sound of my father gnawing his steak bone. During warm weather, we would sit at the table long after we'd finished eating, with our chairs pushed out and our legs comfortably extended, drinking iced tea and watching television. I stirred so much sugar into my tea that it went to the bottom of my glass in a grainy swirl and sat there; I fished it out with a spoon and ate it when I had finished drinking. Newscasters would talk to us, and my father would translate, commenting on the bastards who were trying to undermine the United States in its fight to protect Vietnam from communism.

Sometimes he would ask my opinion on what the news-caster said; I would give it and he would say, "Good comprehension. You're following it pretty well," and lean back in his chair, his mouth a satisfied line.

There were other evenings, though, when I lay upstairs trying to read while my parents' voices floated up through the floor. I would visualize a part of my mind separating from my body like a cartoon character, tiptoeing away from the rest of me to listen at the door with a cupped ear, and then hurrying back to tap the complacent corporeal reader on the shoulder, gesticulating wildly. They were talking about me. My mother was telling my father how rudely I had greeted her that afternoon, or how I had told her to shut up that morning. The cartoon character reported sentences in scraps: ". . . it's got to stop . . ." "What are we going to do?" "I just don't know." Soon my father would be pacing the living room to the martial bagpipes of the Coldstream Guards, ranting about "little shits" who deliberately rejected everything good and decent in favor of ugliness, who selfishly disregarded the feelings of those who'd sacrificed for them.

When my mother called me for dinner, the table would already be set, and my father would be sitting at its head, watching me as I entered the room. His face was bitterly red, his eyes glassy, and his hair stood away from his head in an oily halo gone askew. "There she is," he might say. "The one who doesn't want to be a part of her family. The one who ignores her mother and tells her to shut up." We would eat silently, my mother consuming tiny forkfuls, my father noiselessly, but violently, chewing, squeezing his napkin into a shredded ball with his free hand. Slowly, starting first with veiled attacks on "selfish turds" and "fat slobs," he began to tell me how awful I was. Soon he would be leaning toward me on his elbows, his mouth forming his words so vehemently that he showed his teeth. "You sit there on your fat butt night after night wearing the clothes I bought you, stuffing your face with my food, stupid and ugly, contributing nothing." He paused to study me as I chewed. Tears ran down my face and over my lips as I ate, mixing in my mouth with my hamburger. My mother ate her salad and traced a little design on the table with her finger.

After the table was cleared, I went upstairs to lie in bed. I would lie in the dark, sensing my body sprawled out before my head like a country I had seen only on maps. My thoughts formed a grid of checkered squares clicking off and on in an industrial pattern of light and dark. Once this grid was in place, what had happened at the dinner table became a tiny scene observed from far away, and I would turn on the light and get my book and read, eating from a bag of orange corn curls I kept under my bed.

In 1985 I dreamed that my entire life had to be lived in a school or some kind of academic institution. It was a beautiful complex of old buildings on expensively cared-for grounds. I was there to do a project of some kind involving writing or research. I went up into a tower to do it. But right away I was completely confused as to what I was actually meant to do. I tried to find someone who could help, but the floors were very strange; when I took a step, parts of the floor disappeared and parts remained in an irregular checkerboard pattern. There was a certain poetry to it; you could see through the empty spaces to floor after floor, shifting and changing as people walked, some of them sometimes falling through the empty spaces. An older woman next to me said she found this arrangement very disturbing but asked me not to tell anyone. Then she stepped into an elevator and the door closed, causing most of the floor before me to vanish. I stepped into the elevator very carefully and reached another floor without falling. The floor seemed to be more stable there.

When I was pretending to be someone else I had only two friends in school, really quasi-friends, because how could they be friends if I was almost completely hiding who I actually was? I do remember them physically; I especially remember the one named Patty, her large eyes and their tense, bewildered expression, the way she held her hands in her lap, her guarded body. Still, I could not feel any real attachment to either girl, and so I was surprised when many years later Patty wrote to me through my publisher. She had not read any of my books but she had seen a review of one of them in *People* magazine that made her want to write to me. She was divorced and living in a trailer park, raising two children alone. Her husband, who had abused her, had recently killed himself. I wrote back to her, but I don't remember what I said. I was moved and pained to read her letter and I wished I had more to say. I wondered if she also had hidden herself out of fear and that is why she remembered me well enough to write, that she had sensed the same thing in me. I wondered but I didn't know how to ask. I now so wish that I had. I wonder how many people live their entire lives that way, pretending that they are what they imagine other people to be, mimicking public surfaces out of fear that is so reflexive that they don't recognize it as fear. A few? A lot? How many people stop doing that in junior high out of self-respect as I did—but then can't figure out how else to be in a group? Words like "shy," "conforming," "insecure," and "individualist" seem inadequate to describe either way of being.

I open my eyes. I can't sleep. I wake after two hours and then spend the rest of the night pulled around by feelings and thoughts. I usually sleep again at dawn, then wake at 7:30.

When I wake, I'm mad at not sleeping, and that makes me mad at everything. My mind yells insults as my body walks itself around. Dream images rise up and crash down, huge, then gone, huge, gone. A little girl sinks down in the dark. Who is she? Gone.

I was raped when I was seventeen. The rapist hit me and threatened to kill me. He also talked at me a lot, sometimes ragefully, sometimes almost conversationally. The whole thing lasted maybe an hour; toward the end he fell asleep on me. (Years

later I read that this is not uncommon.) I referred
to the experience in an essay I wrote on the subject
of personal responsibility, which was, it's hard to
remember now, a belabored subject in the '90s. In a
section about emotional subjectivity, I said that I did
not feel traumatized by the rape and actually found it
relatively easy to recover from. I said:

> The terror was acute, but after it was over,
> it actually affected me less than many other
> mundane instances of emotional brutality I've
> suffered or seen other people suffer. Frankly,
> I've been scarred more by experiences I had
> on the playground in elementary school. I
> realize that may sound bizarre, but for me the
> rape was a clearly defined act, perpetrated on
> me by a crazy asshole whom I didn't know or
> trust; it had nothing to do with me or who I
> was, and so, when it was over, it was relatively
> easy to dismiss.

Decades later, when I did a radio interview,
the hostess was (still!) outraged by this statement,
which she seemed to understand as an expression of
pathological callousness and possible deep disregard
for the pain of other women. It did not occur to
her to ask me what happened on the playground in
elementary school.

But even if she had asked that question, I don't
know that the answer would've made sense to her.
What happened on the playground of my youth
happens every day and "nice" kids do it: they
humiliate, reject, and physically torment other kids

to the point that the other kids' humanity becomes distorted and worthless in their only social milieu. The little girl mocking Dr. King wasn't hurting her peers—strictly speaking she wasn't hurting anyone. She was celebrating a general ethos of hurting people, and, as young as she was, I don't believe she did not know what she was doing in the moment. I remember a feeling of horror as I watched her. The horror did not come specifically from what we might now call "anti-racism" but from a broader sense of terrible disjunction: the pretty, happy face of a "nice" girl with the blithe and grotesque grimace of cruelty meant to ridicule people who were already on the receiving end of great cruelty. Those two faces happened together and then separated almost as if before my eyes, and a chasm opened between them, a chasm in which, it seemed, anything might happen. It connected the juvenile cruelty of the playground to the adult world where people were dismembered and hanged from trees and nobody did anything to stop it and it was *normal*.

That sense of horror was deepened by another kind of experience, something that seems at first to be completely unrelated.

I was five when I was sexually molested by a family friend, a colleague of my father's. He lived down the street from us with his wife and young son. Because of my age, I don't remember a lot of details or how many times it happened. I do remember that it happened in a public park, that sometimes his son was present, and that at least once I could hear in the distance the light and happy sound of people's voices. What I remember far more clearly is how bewildered I was, how stunned. Remarkably I don't remember feeling fear. I was simply *stunned* and then mesmerized by the sensations roused in my body and even more by what I saw happening to his face. It was as if he turned into someone else, something else, a creature consumed by hunger and shame and pain that drove him to do what he did, to act itself out on my body, my mind, *everything* in me that might feel. And then it was over, and he turned back into himself and everything was *normal.*

I trust these memories because my mother confirmed that he sometimes took me to the park with his son who was roughly my age. She also confirmed that I told her what had happened at the time and that she did not believe me because she couldn't believe that a family man would do something like that. She didn't even tell my father because she didn't want him to be angry and "do something."

This experience was very different from watching children behave stupidly and cruelly on playgrounds or even having them behave that way to me. It is not comparable to thousands of people being brutalized and murdered because they were/are the "wrong" race. But the connection is this: the chasm between the normal face and the *other* face, the feeling that in that chasm *anything* might happen, right in front of people. Given this understanding, how could I be shocked at being raped much later in life? I was terrified, certainly. I don't doubt that the adrenal feeling of terror might've had a long-term effect on my nervous system—perhaps more than I realized when I wrote about it almost thirty years ago. But I wasn't traumatized in the way that people talk about. How could I be?

Then I was sitting in social studies, but instead of feeling the dread that I felt in class, I felt a sense of triumph. A popular song overlaid the class scene, not its sound but its evocation of friendship and the eventual moment when everyone drops their public pose and exposes the goodwill they've harbored all along. I sat erect in my seat, smiling at everyone. The song said,

> It's so groovy now
> That people are finally getting together.

I wobbled back awake. The room was covered with sleep fuzz. My father stood before my bed. I closed my eyes, imagining my innocent face as it appeared before him. He sat on the bed next to me. I peeked at him. I was surprised to see that he wasn't doing the nervous things he usually did when he came into my room at night; he didn't wipe his mouth or rub his fingers together, he just sat there exuding determined presence. I closed my eyes, feeling the tension and suspended contact. I remembered his nighttime kiss. There was a movement that seemed gracefully swooping and swanlike to me, even though I knew my father was pulling up his feet and awkwardly laying his body on my bed. My sense of anticipation, my feeling of intimacy, impending resolution, and fear, almost nauseated me. When he put his hand under the blankets, I was surprised and opened my eyes. He was waiting for me. His put his fingers on my lips and said, "Shhh." His eyes were bright and his forehead was lifted into friendly wrinkles. "I don't want to wake your mother," he whispered. "I just thought we could have a little talk." I nodded, feeling a sensation like warm tears trembling in my chest. It was as I thought: my father came into my room because he wanted to apologize. I felt so moved, I wanted to cuddle against his chest as I had done as a child, burying my nose in his warm, detergent-scented pajamas.

Reach out in the darkness!
Reach out in the darkness!

"I just wanted to let you know," he began, "that when you were born I thought you were the most beautiful little thing I ever saw. It wasn't just me either. Everybody in the hospital thought you were special. You had the intelligence, the sparkle, the beauty—you had it all."

I smiled spastically. My father touched the tip of my nose with his finger. "And still think so. Say, can I get under the covers? It's cold out here."

He kissed my face and neck as he had taken my hand during our walk: tenderly, the tenderness vibrant with inheld tension. He said how hurt he was when we "argued," when it seemed like I just didn't care about everything he'd fought for. I moved nearer to him to protest that I did care, and I smelled him, the deep smell produced by his particular combination of organs and glands and the food he ate. He pulled me against him, crushing my face into his chest hairs exposed by his open pajama top. I felt the power and insistence in his embrace, felt how tight were the muscles of his embracing arm, and for a second I was afraid. Then with his other hand he caressed my breasts and nipples through my light gown. My breath stopped. Arousal rose through my body and seized it. My excitement terrified me and made me feel ashamed because I knew it was wrong to be excited. But underneath the fear and shame, underneath the excitement, it seemed like what was happening now between my father and me was only the physical expression of what always happened between us, even when he verbally reviled me. Tears came to my eyes; it seemed that his cruel words had clothed these loving caresses all along. I put out my hands and clutched his pajamas in my fists. "Yes," he said, his voice crushed and strange. "Yes."

Now Ginger was not Ginger. She was starved hurting limbs. She was a dry, sore mouth and eyes. She was a straining heart. She was legs that stumbled as they were pulled forward by the mass of driven bodies. On one side was darkness, on the other a wall. The weight and smell were horrible. The stairs wound up and up. A long scream came searing down; a body fell from above into the pit, clawing the air with its limbs. Softer and nearer came a moan, not just a sound, but a voice. The person who used to be Ginger stirred inside, because she knew the voice. This stirring brought fear, but still she turned toward the voice. She looked at the creature beside her; she saw a face looking back at her with terrible stretched eyes, speaking eyes. Recognition came hurtling toward her.

My father died slowly and in delirious pain. He wanted to stay at home and so he did, he suffered in his own bed almost up until the end. There was only one hospice worker coming in a couple of times a day to give him care plus morphine, which wasn't strong enough and to which he became quickly accustomed. My sisters and I didn't realize until quite late that we needed to keep upping the dose; he couldn't speak by then, though he grimaced in rage and pain.

One of his few visitors during this horrible time was a minister named Amory Adamsen. He was a minister with some kind of half-assed training as a counselor. Before my parents separated, my mother requested that they try counseling. I think she requested it because she'd been going to AA meetings for years and had the lingo down cold; she probably thought she'd be seen as this reasonable person while he'd be seen as a mad, pawing bear, and she'd have official permission to dump him. But my father would agree only if it was a Christian counselor, even though he's not a Christian, and so Mother came up with this Adamsen person. All I knew about him was that (according to Mother) he considered my father the "least introspective person" he'd ever met and that he'd also quite avidly read my novel *Two Girls,*

Fat and Thin, which is about, among other things,
a girl being raped by her daddy. He even came to a
reading of that book I somewhat cluelessly performed
in Lexington (on Mother's Day!); he gave me his full
pious and slitty-eyed attention while my poor father
wandered the aisles. Now here he was at the house
with my father upstairs dying. Apparently, he and
my dad had kept up contact long after my parents'
separation, going to basketball games over the years.
Although the prick hadn't returned my father's last
call about a game, here he was, smiling at everyone,
hugging, dispensing comfort, looking around. He
told my father he was sorry about missing the game,
which I do not think my father gave a fuck about at
that point. He told him he'd sure enjoyed getting
to know him. Then he mingled with my uncle and
his wife, me and my sisters. He kept singling me out
with his eyes and finally asked if he could talk with
me privately, that he had something to ask. So we
went upstairs, shut the door, and he revealed that
what he wanted to know was: Did my father really
sexually abuse me? He said that he knew just how
rude and inappropriate it was to ask, and he added
that if I was offended, he was so sorry, he'd just drop
it. I said that whether I was offended depended on
why he was asking. If it was just curiosity, yes, I
was offended. But if it was a moral concern and had
something to do with what kind of prayer he wanted
to say, that was different. He allowed that he was
curious and that he knew it wasn't his business and
he was sorry. I maybe should've hit him and walked

out of the room, but just so he would know, I said my father never did anything like that, what I wrote was fiction. Amory said he knew it, he knew my father was very moral, he was no sex pervert. I said, "Well, actually he was, but only a little, no more than average, really." This confused the moron, but he got over that and said that even though he knew my dad was innocent, there was always this tiny question in his mind, and he was glad to finally put it to rest. He went on to declare, however, that even if I had said yes, my father raped me, it wouldn't have made a *bit of difference*, that he liked my dad a lot and would've made no judgment. We talked about how awful molestation is and how much of it there seems to be. He said my dad had worried about me. For example, he had always wondered why I didn't get married and was concerned that I might be a lesbian. I told him that I was in fact getting married. He seemed disappointed. He went into my dad's room to pray at him and I went downstairs to tell my sister Jane about this idiotic conversation. My sister said that although she had been planning to ask Amory to speak at the funeral, after hearing this, no way. We both decided not to tell our mother, who was easily upset about the subject of my writing just generally. Naturally Amory Adamsen wound up speaking at the funeral. I didn't stay for that event so at least I didn't have to listen to it.

•

I was forty-six years old when my father died. I was engaged to be married to a man I had met three years earlier. We had talked about having children. I thought I probably could; my sister had, without any medical intervention, given birth to healthy twins at the age of forty-five. But I wasn't sure I wanted it; we didn't have much money or even a consistent source of income. To create the necessary consistency, I would've had to give up writing, and I didn't want to.

When my father died, though, I became obsessed with the notion that if I got pregnant I could reincarnate him. It was a mild derangement; I believed that he could hear me and talk to me even in death, and I told him I would try to bring him back. And I did try, several times. But there was one time when I failed to keep my promise, and it was perhaps the time. It occurred during a particular intimate moment: I heard my father's voice in my head crying, *Now!* And right at the last minute, I disengaged. Because I heard my own voice louder. *No.* And so the idea died. I cried about it a little. But that idea was over.

VERONICA

I remember the time I said, "I don't think you love yourself. You need to learn to love yourself."

Veronica was silent for a long moment. Then she said, "I think love is overrated. My parents loved me. And it didn't do any good."

THE MARE

Ginger, on earth: I met her when I was forty-seven, but I felt still young. I looked young too. This is probably because I had not done many of the things most people that age have done; I'd had no children and no successful career. I married late after stumbling through a violent series of relationships and an intense half-life as an artist visible only in Lower Manhattan, the other half of my life being that of a drug addict.

I met my husband, Paul, in Narcotics Anonymous. It was six months before we even had coffee, but I immediately noticed his deep eyes, the animal eloquence of his hairy hands. We eventually moved to a small town upstate, the same town he'd come from, where he made a good living as a tenured professor at a small college.

When people asked me what I did I sometimes said, "I'm transitioning," and very occasionally, "I'm a painter." I was embarrassed to say the second thing even though it was true: I still painted, and it seemed like I was better than I was when I showed at a downtown gallery twenty years before. But I was embarrassed anyway because I knew I sounded foolish to people who had kids and jobs too, and who wouldn't understand my life before I came here. There were a few—women who painted at home too—whom I was able to talk about it with, to describe what art used to be to me and what I wanted to make it be again: a place more real than anything in "real" life. A place I remember now just dimly, a place of deep joy where, when I could get to it, was like tuning in to a radio frequency that was sacred to me. Regardless of anything else, nothing was more important than carrying that frequency on the dial of myself.

The problem was, other people created interference. It was hard for me to be close with them and to hear the signal at the same time. I realize that makes me sound strange. I am strange, more than the bare facts of my life would say. But I have slowly come to realize that so many people are strange that maybe the word is nearly meaningless when applied to human beings. Still, people interfered. And so I created ways to keep them at a distance, including an increasingly expensive drug habit. What I didn't see, or allow myself to see, was that drugs created even more interference than people; they were a sinister signal all their own, one that enhanced and blended with and then finally blotted out the original one. When that happened I got completely lost, and for many years didn't even know it.

When we finally moved out of the city, I began to feel the signal again, but differently. I felt it even when I was with Paul, which did not surprise me—he was not "other people." But I began to feel it with other people too, or rather through them, in the density of families living in homes, going back for generations in this town. I would see women with babies in strollers or with their little children in the grocery store, and I would feel their rootedness in the place around us and beyond— in the grass and earth, trees and sky.

To feel so much through something I was not part of was of course lonely. I began to wonder if it had been a mistake not to have children, to wonder what would've happened if I'd met Paul when I was younger. The third time we had sex he said, "I want to make you pregnant."

I must've had sex hundreds of times before, and men had said all kinds of things to me—but no one had ever said that. I never wanted anyone to say it; girlfriends would tell me a guy had said that and I would think I'd say, *How dare you, get off me!* But when Paul said it, I heard *I love you.* I felt the same; we made love and I pictured my belly swelling.

But I didn't get pregnant. Instead my sister Melinda died. I know the two things don't go together. But in my mind they do. My sister lived in Cleveland, Ohio. She had been sick a long time; she had so many things wrong with her that nobody wanted to think about her, including me. She was drunk and mean and crazy and would call saying fucked-up things in the middle of the night. I didn't want to talk to her, but I would, closing my eyes and forcing myself to listen. I would listen until I could remember the feeling of her and me as little girls, drawing pictures together, cuddled on the couch together, eating ice cream out of teacups. Sometimes I couldn't listen, couldn't remember; she'd talk and I'd check my email and wait for her to go away. And then she did.

She had a stroke while she was taking a shower. The water was still running on her when they found her a few days later. It was summer and her body was waterlogged and swollen. Still, I could identify her, even with her thin, tiny mouth nearly lost in her cheeks and chin and her brows pulled into an inhuman expression.

Paul went with me to clear out her apartment. I hadn't been to visit her for at least a decade—she always preferred to visit me or my mother and I could see why. Her apartment was filthy, full of old take-out containers, used paper plates and plastic utensils, boxes and bags crammed with the junk she'd been meaning to take out for years. Months of unopened mail lay on every surface. There was black mold on the walls. Paul and I stood there in the middle of it and thought, *Why didn't we help her?* The obvious answer was, we had helped her. We had sent her money; we had flown her out to visit on Christmas. I had talked to her, even when I didn't want to. But standing in her apartment, I knew it hadn't been enough. She'd known when I hadn't wanted to talk, which was most of the time. Given that, what good was the money?

When the shock was still wearing off, I would go for long walks through the small center of town, out onto country roads, then back into town again. I'd look at the women with their children; I'd look into the small, beautiful faces and think of Melinda when she was like that. I'd imagine my mother's warm arms, her unthinking, uncritical limbs that lifted and held us. There was this one time when our washing machine was broken and I had to go to the laundromat; I was there by myself, and this song came on the radio station that the management had on. It's a song that was popular in the '70s about a girl and a horse who both die. I was folding clothes when I recognized it. The singer's voice is thin and fake, but it's pretty, and somewhere in the fakery is the true sadness of smallness and failure and believing in beautiful things that aren't real because that's the only way to get through. Tears came to my eyes. When Melinda was little, she loved horses. For a while she even rode them. We couldn't afford lessons, so she worked in a stable to earn them. Once I went with my mother to pick Melinda up from there, and I saw her riding in the fenced area beside the stable. She looked so confident and happy I didn't recognize her; I wondered who that beautiful girl was. So did our mother. She said, "Look at her!" and then stopped short.

> They say she died one winter
> When there came a killin' frost
> And the pony she named Wildfire
> Busted down its stall
> In a blizzard he was lost.

It was a crap song. It didn't matter. It made me picture my sister before she was ruined, coming toward me on a beautiful golden horse.

> She's coming for me I know
> And on Wildfire we're both gonna go.

I cried quietly, still folding the clothes. No one was there to see me.

VERONICA

Someone is chasing me, and in order to reach safety, I have to run through my past and all the people in it. But the past is jumbled, not sequential, and all the people are mixed up. A nameless old woman who used to live next door is reaching out to me, her large brown eyes brimming with tenderness and tears— but my mother is lost in a crowd scene. My father is barely visible—I see him by himself in the shadows of the living room, dreamily eating a salted nut—while a loud, demented stranger pops right up in my face, yelling about what I must do to save myself now.

It's like the strangers are delivering messages for more important people, who for some reason can't talk to me. Or that the people who are important by the normal rules— family, close friends— are accidental attachments, and that the apparent strangers are the true loved ones, hidden by the grotesque disguises of human life.

THE MARE

Velvet, a girl on earth: That day I woke up from a dream the way I always woke up: pressed against my mom's back, my face against her and her turned away. She holding Dante and he holding her, his head in her breasts, wrapped around each other like they're falling down a hole. It was okay, I was an eleven-year-old girl and I didn't need to have my face in my mama's titty no more—that is, if I ever did. Dante, my little brother, was only six.

It was summer, the air conditioner was up too high, dripping dirty water on the floor, outside the pan I put there to catch it. Too loud too, but still I heard a shot from outside or maybe a shout from my dream; I was dreaming about my grandfather from DR, he was lost in a dark place, like a castle with a lot of rooms and rich White people doing scary things in all of them, and my grandfather was somewhere shouting my name. Or maybe it was a shot. I sat up and listened, but there wasn't anything.

That day we had to get on a bus and go stay with rich White people for two weeks. We signed up to do this at Puerto Rican Family Services in Williamsburg, even though we're Dominican and we just moved to East New York. The social worker walked around in little high heels squishing out of tight pants like she's a model, but with her face frowning like a mask on Halloween.

My mom talked to her about how our new neighborhood was all bad "negritas," no Spanish people. She told her how she had to work all day and sometimes at night, keeping a roof over our heads. She said it was going to be summer and I was too old for day care, and because I was stupid she couldn't trust me to stay inside and not go around the block talking to men. She laughed when she said this, like me talking to men was so stupid it was funny. But I don't go around talking to men, and I told the social worker that with my face.

"It sounds like Hell," whispered Dante, but Mask-Face didn't hear. We could swim and ride bicycles, she said. We could learn about animals. I took the booklet out of my mother's hands. It said something about love and having fun. There was a picture of a girl darker than me petting a sheep. There was a picture of a woman with big white legs sitting in a chair with a hat on and an orange plastic flower in her hand, looking like she was waiting for somebody to have fun with.

My mom doesn't write so I filled out the forms. Dante just sat there talking to himself, not caring about anything like always. I didn't want him to come with me, bothering me while I was trying to ride a bicycle or something, so when they asked how he gets along with people, I wrote, "He hits." They asked how he resolves conflict and I wrote, "He hits." It was true anyway. Then my mom asked if we could go to the same family so I could take care of Dante, and Mask-Face said, "No, it's against the rules." I was glad and then I felt sorry for saying something bad about Dante for nothing. My mom started to fight about it, and Mask-Face said again, "It's against the rules." The way she said it was another way of saying, *You're shit*, and the smell of that shit was starting to fill up the room. I could feel Dante get small inside. He said, "I don't want to go be with those people." He said it so soft you could barely hear him, but my mother said, "Shut up, you ungrateful boy! You're stupid!" The smell got stronger; it covered my mother's head, and she scratched herself like she was trying to brush it off.

But she couldn't, and so when we left, she hit Dante on the head and called him stupid some more. Going to this place with sheep and bicycles had been turned into a punishment.

But I still had hope that it would be fun. The lady I would stay with had called me to talk to me and she sounded nice. Her voice was little, like she was scared. She said we were going to ride a Ferris wheel at the county fair and swim at the lake and see horses. She didn't sound like the lady with the big legs, but that's how I pictured her, with a plastic flower. I thought of that picture and that voice and I got excited.

I got up and went out into the hall and got into the closet where our coats were. I dug into the back and found my things I keep in the old cotton ball box. I took them out through our living room into the kitchen, where it was heavy-warm from all the hot days so far. I poured orange juice in my favorite glass with purple flowers on it. I took the juice and my box to the open window and leaned out on the ledge. I took my things out of the box and laid them out on the ledge. They looked nice together: a silver bell I got from a prize machine, an orange plastic sun I tore off a get-well card somebody gave my mom, a blond keychain doll with only one leg wearing a checkered coat, a dried seahorse from DR that my grandfather sent me, and a blue shell my father gave me when I was a baby and he lived with us. My father gave me two shells, but I gave the brown-and-pink one to this girl Strawberry because her brother died.

I held the blue shell against my lip and felt its smoothness. I looked up and saw the sun had put a gold outline on the building across from us. I looked down and saw a ragged man stop against the wall, like he was trying to get the strength to breathe. Then he stretched up against the wall, his arms and hands spread out like he was crying. For a second everything was hard and clear and pounding beautiful.

I never met my grandfather, but he loved me. He talked to me on the phone, and when I sent him my picture he said I was beautiful. He told me stories about how bad my mother was when she was little, but in a way that made it funny. He sent the seahorse. He said one day my mom would bring me and Dante to visit and he would take us to the ocean. A month later, he died.

I put my things back in the box. I looked down in the street. The ragged man was gone. The gold outline on the building was gone too, spread out through the sky, making it shiny with invisible light. For some reason I thought of a TV commercial where a million butterflies burst out from some shampoo bottle or cereal box.

The night that Dante got poisoned my mother didn't talk to me. I helped her make dinner and we ate it. She hardly talked to me or looked at me. I cried and my tears ran in my mouth with my food. But when we got in bed, she didn't turn away from me. She lay on her back with her eyes open and said, "It's not your fault. You have bad blood from your father." I said, "Bendición, Mami." She didn't answer. "Mami?" I whispered. She sighed and blessed me, then turned her back and let me curl against her.

I thought of the big-legs lady in the booklet holding the fake orange flower, looking like she was hoping for someone to come have fun with her.

Imagine lying on top of Mother, melting into Mother, blending with her. It's as if our clitoris is the same, a swollen thumb of unified feeling, vibrating in silence like a tuning fork. I go deeper, into the muscles of Mother. I feel overwhelming emotion: love and pain and fear, anger like a single, striking snake. Go into the bones of Mother: pure will, mindless female will. With age, growing more diffuse, but still there. Go deeper and Mother dissolves. You are alone in darkness, heavy, salt-smelling darkness. A tiger walks through the darkness, patient and restless at the same time. Searching.

On earth Ginger says: I thought about the girl's voice on the phone, Velvet—she sounded so full and round, sweet and fresh. I wanted to give that voice sweet, fresh things, to gather up everything good and give it. The night before we had gone out and bought food for her: boxes of cereal and fruit to put on it, eggs in case she didn't want cereal, orange juice and bacon and white bread, sliced ham and cheese, chicken for barbecue, chocolate milk, carrots. "Did your daughter like carrots when she was little?" I asked Paul. "I don't remember," he said. "I think so." "All kids eat carrots," I said, and put them in the shopping cart. "Ginger, don't worry so much," he said. "Kids are simple. As long as you're nice to them and take care of them they'll like you. Okay?" And Velvet says: She didn't look like the lady in the booklet at all. She was wearing white pants and a white top with sparkles on it. She was smiling, but something else in her face was almost crying. It was okay, though, I don't know why. I smiled back. She smiled like she was seeing heaven. I got shy and looked down.

"Velveteen," she said, "that's a pretty name."

"Velvet," I said. "That's what people call me."

They said they were Ginger and Paul. They took me to their car. We drove past lots of houses with flowers and bushes in front of them. In the city when the sky is bright it makes everything harder on the edges; here everything was soft and shiny too, like a picture book of Easter eggs and rabbits I read in third grade when I was sick on the nurse's station cot. I loved that book so much I stole it from the nurse's station, and the next time I was sick I took it out and looked at it and it made me feel better, even though by then I was too old for it. I don't have it anymore; probably my mom cleaned it up when we moved.

The man turned around in the driver's seat and asked me if I liked school. I said yes. The lady turned around, smiling with no crying anywhere now. She said, "Really, you like school? I didn't think anybody actually liked school. I hated school!" She smiled like this lady in a movie I saw about a girl who everybody realizes is actually a princess. The girl gets discovered, and this lady with blond hair and blue eyes takes her into a room where all her jewels are waiting. The girl tries on her jewels while the lady smiles.

In the car it was just a little bit creepy because she was smiling like she knew me and she did not. But my face kept smiling back.

When my mother was ninety-three she had a strange, almost eerily compelling smile. It was not her normal smile, but it was there, in her. I saw it in the last year of her life. I was helping her at home; she was lying on the couch and I came to sit by her. I put my hand on her chest just to show affection. And she gave me the look, the smile that started in her eyes. It was a look of beckoning, a cross between a look you would give a young child and a look you would give a lover. It was literally a "come hither" look, but it was not about sex, not then anyway. It seemed to say, *I know what the best thing is, the most beautiful, delicious thing. I know it well because I have it right here inside me. Let me show you! We are almost there right now!* If she had been forty, no man could've resisted this look. If she was forty few could. Even if she had been fifty, a great many men would go to her on receiving this look. At sixty, at least a couple! And it was totally natural to her. It was not seduction, it was beckoning, and it was so subtle, yet so strong. It was perfectly, innately feminine.

And yet it did not help her at all. Combined with her longing it may actually have been a weakness, a wish to connect that was too ardent, too genuine, and too needy. Although in the moment with me it was not needy, only giving. But then I was her child.

I don't have the same kind of smile in me. But I do have the "almost eeriness." I have it, but I don't even know what it is. My family all believed that they—we—were somehow "different." For my father the difference was a curse that could be most simply explained by the word "sensitive." "We're all just so goddamned sensitive!" he would scream. For my mother and sisters, it was more mysterious, something to be protected, sometimes secretly giggled about yet treated with delicacy. When my mother was near death—near enough that her personality had become less ordered and less defended, but not so near that she couldn't speak coherently—I asked her what she meant when she said she was "different." The subject came up because she had told a hospice nurse that she was lonely; the nurse gaily responded that she, the nurse, could introduce my mother to lots of nice people and that they would "listen to your stories and tell you their stories." My mother shook her head. "I don't think I could talk to them," she said. "I'm just too different." The nurse made some kind of meaningless demurral. I waited until she left and asked my question. My mother gave it some thought. Finally, she said, "I don't know how to say it. Except that when I was a teenager, all the other girls were wearing these shoes, these brown-and-white shoes." "What kind of shoes were they?" I asked. "I don't remember what they were called," said my mother. "But everybody was wearing them. And I wouldn't wear them. We could afford them. But I didn't like them and I didn't wear them. Even if they made fun of me."

This answer frustrated me completely. And yet I was moved by it. Because it showed her utterly natural femininity. Perhaps it also showed her triviality—and her self-importance. How many people must believe themselves to be "different"? How many actually are? I think such people must be everywhere, in every class and culture. And yet I take my family's belief in their own weirdness (in modern parlance, their "self-identification") seriously. Because of their dysfunction and their hopeless struggle to, essentially, get around the block. And because of mine, even though my struggle has by most standards been more successful. I am thinking of a time in 2004, when I was in St. Petersburg for a literary conference. People from all over the world were there including a contingent from Kenya. I became friendly with one of the Kenyan women, and at the end of our two weeks together she said goodbye to me in a very striking way. She said that she would always remember me because she had never met anyone like me. I asked her what she meant. She said it was as if there were a glass separating me from everything, but I could make

myself heard through it. I did not know this woman
well. But I took her much more seriously than I
would take, for example, the lady down the street
because 1) she was from a culture very foreign to
mine, and foreign observers in any situation often see
more clearly than natives because they are looking
with fresh eyes, and 2) she was widely traveled and
had seen many different kinds of human specimens.
She did not speak with any unkindness or any
apparent wish to flatter. She made the observation
with the honest neutrality of a traveler. We hugged
and said goodbye.

Then Ginger was only Ginger and running down the
clean, well-lit stairway. At the bottom of the stairs was
a lit hall. Lizards the size of large dogs grew out of the
walls, but they were sleeping. The next room was made
of bathroom tiles and chunks of gold. Faucets and sinks
stuck out of the walls, also washing machines and dryers, televisions, cell phones, computers, refrigerators,
and microwave ovens—all the conveniences of the
world were here and all of them were running. The next
room was dark and full of glowing monitors embedded
in the darkness. Scenes of war and torture were playing
on all of them; Ginger saw bloody sights from the corner
of her eye but this time wisely did not stop to look.

Oh, but I stopped to look. I always stop to look.
And I often write what I see, or I try. Usually I fail

because my mind isn't big enough to understand
what I see or to contextualize it at all. But sometimes
I get a bit of it. You could describe it as an artistic
impulse or a prideful impulse. Or both.

Soon she came to a quiet, old-fashioned room. One of
its huge walls was made of bookcases full of books. In
another wall was an open window with flowing curtains;
it looked out on a starry night sky and, beyond the stars,
a universe of planets that was distant and vivid at the
same time. There was an enormous fireplace with a
pleasant fire in it. Before the fire was an armchair and in
it sat the Devil. He was reading a book. Except for his
red skin, horns, and tail, he looked like a regular man in
a peaceful mood. Ginger crept up and saw, behind the
chair, a bag of treasure. She grabbed it and ran.

What is in the bag behind the Devil's chair?
Knowledge of some kind? Surely something a little
girl did not know should be left alone. I've been
criticized—and sometimes admired—for what some
readers see as my affinity with cruelty, both in my
depictions of it and my supposed infliction of it on
characters. Maggie Nelson eloquently expressed
this point of view in her book of criticism *The Art
of Cruelty*, in which she remarked that my language
is "most definitely a tool used to penetrate, to
dismantle, to bore holes," not through "projections,
delusions, cant, or miscommunication" but through

the "self-esteem and dignity of [my] characters."
Nelson applied this description to my first collection
of stories, but it became the context for her analysis
of my later work—an analysis that seems based
on misunderstanding. Nelson describes me as
"captivated by cruelty, nastiness, and callousness";
that statement would be more accurate if the
word "captivated" were replaced by "stunned" or
"horrified." However horrifying cruelty is to you, if
you are exposed to enough of it, either as a witness
or as an object of it, it can become a mesmerizing
hugeness that you will strive to physically and
psychically accommodate, no matter how you must
distort yourself in the process, in order not to be
destroyed by it. I am stunned by the omnipresence
of cruelty, by the senselessness of its infliction, and
at the same time by its seeming inevitability, its
naturalness, its apparently primary place in our
human nature; its sometime connection to our
instinct to create or excel in some way, our vitality,
our love of beauty, of form, our need to feel that we
can affect another, to define ourselves, to survive. To
say this is beauty, this is not; this is good, this is not.

VERONICA

There is always a style suit, or suits. When I was young, I
used to think these suits were just what people were. When
styles changed dramatically— people going barefoot,
men with long hair, women without bras—I thought the
world had changed, that from then on everything would

be different. It's understandable that I thought that; TV and newsmagazines acted like the world had changed too. I was happy with it, but then five years later it changed again. Again, the TV announced, "Now we're this instead of that! Now we walk like this, not like that!" Like people were all runny and liquid, running over this surface and that, looking for a container to hold everything in place, trying one thing, then the next, incessantly looking for the right one. Except the containers were only big enough for one personality trait at a time; you had to grab on to one trait, bring it out for a while, then put it back and pull out another one. For a while, "we" were loving; then we were alienated and angry, then ironic, then depressed. Although we are at war with terror, fashion magazines say we are sunny now. We wear bright colors and choose moral clarity. While I was waiting to get a blood test last week, I read in a newsmagazine that terror must not change our sunny dispositions.

Of course, there is a lot of subtlety in all this, and complexity too. When John took those naked pictures, the most popular singer was a girl with a tiny stick body and a large deferential head, who sang in a delicious lilt of white lace and promises and longing to be close. When she shut herself up in her closet and starved herself to death, people were shocked. But starvation was in her voice all along. That was the poignancy of it. A sweet voice locked in a dark place, but focused entirely on the tiny strip of light coming under the door.

I drop the rag in the bucket and smoke some more, ashing into the sink. A tiny piece of movie from the naked time plays on my eyeball: a psychotic killer is blowing up amusement parks. At the head of the crowd clamoring to ride the roller coaster is a slim, lovely man with long blond hair and floppy clothes and big, beautiful eyes fixed on a tiny strip of light that only he can see.

Lift up the toilet lid—filthy again—and drop the cigarette in. Turn off the water and lift the bucket down. I set my teeth as pain tears a hole in my shoulder and I get sucked inside it. The roller coaster roars and everybody screams with joy; the blond man screams in terror as his car flies off into the sky and smashes on the ground. White froth gently disperses on the stirring bucket water as I set it down.

It's not an easy thing. If you can't find the right shape, it's hard for people to identify you. On the other hand, you need to be able to change shape fast; otherwise, you get stuck in one that used to make sense but that people can't understand anymore. This has been going on for a long time. My father used to make lists of his favorite popular songs, ranked in order of preference. These lists were very nuanced, and they changed every few years. He'd walk around with the list in his hand, explaining why Jo "G.I. Jo" Stafford was ranked just above Doris Day, why Charles Trenet topped Nat King Cole—but by a hair only. It was his way of showing people things about him that were too private to say directly. For a while, everybody had some idea what Doris Day versus Jo Stafford meant; to give a preference for one over the other signaled a mix of feelings that were secret and tender, and people could sense these feelings when they imagined the songs side by side.

"Stafford's voice is darker and sadder," he said. "But it's warmer too. She *holds* the song in her voice. Day's voice is sweet, but it's heartless—she doesn't hold it; she touches it and lets go—she doesn't mean it! Stafford is a lover; Day is a flirt—but what a cute flirt!"

"Um-hm," said my mother, and she gritted her teeth on her way out of the room.

But my father didn't see my mother's teeth. He was too charmed by Day singing "Bewitched."

He can laugh, but I love it.
Although the laugh's on me . . .

My father was right. If Jo Stafford sang that song, you would feel the pain of being laughed at by the one you love, and still you would love. When Doris Day sang it, the pain was as bright and sweet and harmless as her smiling voice.

I'll sing to him, each spring to him.
And long for the day when I cling to him . . .

My father smiled and imagined being the one she painlessly longed to cling to; then he went home—to Jo. She sang, *But I miss you most of all, my darling*, and hurt was evoked and tenderly held and healed, again and again, in waves.

But eventually those feelings got attached to other songs, and those singers didn't work as signals anymore. I remember being there once when he was playing the songs for some men he worked with, talking excitedly about the music. He didn't realize his signals could not be heard, that the men were looking at him strangely. Or maybe he did realize but didn't know what else to do but keep signaling. Eventually, he gave up, and there were few visitors. He was just by himself, trying to keep his secret and tender feelings alive through these same old songs.

I thought he was ridiculous. But I was only a kid. I didn't see that I was making the same mistake. He thought the songs were who he really was, and I thought the new style suit was who I really was. Because I was younger, I was even more naive: I thought everything had changed forever, that because people wore jeans and sandals everywhere and women went without bras, fashion didn't matter anymore, that now people could just be who they really were inside. Because I believed this, I was oblivious to fashion. I actually couldn't see it.

I wrote *Veronica* in 1992, or at least I wrote a draft of it then. It is hard for me to remember that time; the world was very different than it seems now, but of course the seeds of now were present then. Some people seemed to think the book was about the decade called "the '80s"; one critic said it described the "epic heartlessness" of that era. I still wonder at the statement. In the '80s we weren't officially torturing people. No one was suggesting that we sacrifice vulnerable or elderly people for the economy.

I met Veronica twenty-five years ago, when I was a temporary employee doing word processing for an ad agency in Manhattan. I was twenty-one. She was a plump thirty-seven-year-old with bleached-blond hair. She wore tailored suits in mannish plaids with matching bow ties, bright red lipstick, false red fingernails, and mascara that gathered in intense beads on the ends of her eyelashes. Her loud voice was sensual and rigid at once, like plastic baubles put together in rococo shapes. It was deep but could quickly become shrill. You could hear her from across the room, calling everyone, even people she hated, "hon": "Excuse me, hon, but I'm very well acquainted with Jimmy Joyce and the use of the semicolon." She proofread like a cop with a nightstick. She carried an "office kit," which contained a red plastic ruler, assorted colored pencils, Liquid Paper, Post-its, and a framed sign embroidered with the words STILL ANAL AFTER ALL THESE YEARS. She was, too. When I told her I had a weird tension that made my forehead feel like it was tightening and letting go over and over again, she said, "No, hon, that's your sphincter."

"The supervisor loves her because she's a total fucking fag hag," complained another proofreader. "That's why she's here all the time."

"I get a kick out of her myself," said a temping actress. "She's like Marlene Dietrich and Emil Jannings combined."

"My God, you're right," I said so loudly and suddenly that the others stared. "That's exactly what she's like."

When I say that the songs we listened to at the hostel had a feeling of sickness in them, that doesn't mean I don't like them. I did like them, and I still do. The sick feeling wasn't in all the songs either. But it was in many songs, and not just the ones for teenagers; you could go to the supermarket and hear it in the Muzak that roamed the aisles, swallowing everything in its soft mouth. It didn't feel like sickness. It felt like endless opening and expansion, and pleasure that would never end. The songs before that were mostly about pleasure too—having it, wanting it, not getting enough of it and being sad. But they were finite little boxes of pleasure, with the simple surfaces of personality and situation.

Then it was like somebody realized you could take the surface of a song, paint a door on it, open it, and walk through. The door didn't always lead to someplace light and sweet. Sometimes where it led was dark and heavy. That part wasn't new. A song my father especially loved by Jo Stafford was "I'll Be Seeing You." During World War II, it became a lullaby about absence and death for boys who were about to kill and die.

> I'll be looking at the moon,
> But I'll be seeing you.

In the moonlight of this song, the known things, the tender things, the carousel, the wishing well, appear outlined against the gentle twilight of familiarity and comfort. In the song, that twilight is a gauze veil of music, and Stafford's voice subtly deepens and gives off a slight shudder as she touches against it. The song does not go any further than this touch, because beyond the veil is killing and dying, and the song honors killing and dying. It also honors the little carousel. It knows the wishing well is a passageway to memory and feeling—maybe too much memory and feeling, ghosts and delusion. Jo Stafford's eyes on the album cover say that she knew that. She knew the dark was huge and she had humility before it.

•

Toward the end, Veronica's shoulder pads used to get loose sometimes and wander down her arms or her back without her knowing it. Once I was sitting with her in a good restaurant when a man next to us said, "Excuse me, there's something moving on your back." His tone was light and aggressive, like it was him versus the fashionable nitwits. "Oh," said Veronica, also light. "Excuse me. It's just my prosthesis."

Sometimes I loved how she would make cracks like that. Other times it was just embarrassing. Once we were leaving a movie theater after seeing a pretentious movie. As we walked past a line of people waiting to see the other movie, Veronica said loudly, "They don't want to see anything challenging. They'd rather see *Flashdance*. Now me, if it's bizarre, I'm interested." There was a little strut to her walk and her voice was like a huge feather in a hat. *She's not like that,* I'd wanted to say to the ticket holders. *If you knew her, you'd see.*

But she *was* like that. She could be unbelievably obnoxious. In the locker room of the gym we both went to, she was always snapping at somebody for getting too close to her or brushing against her. "If you want me to move, just tell me, but please stop poking me in the bottom," she'd say to some open-mouthed Suzy in a leotard. "Fist fucking went out years ago. Didn't you know that?"

The new songs had no humility. They pushed past the veil and opened a window into the darkness and climbed through it with a knife in their teeth. The songs could be about rape and murder, killing your dad and fucking your mom, and then sailing off on a crystal ship to a thousand girls and thrills, or going for a moonlight drive. They were beautiful songs, full of places and textures—flesh, velvet, concrete, city towers, desert sand, snakes, violence, wet glands, childhood, the pure wings of night insects. Anything you could think of was there, and you could move through it as if it were an endless series of rooms and passages full of visions and adventures. And even if it was about killing and dying—that was just another place to go.

Of course, Veronica had a lot of smart cracks stored up. She needed them. When she didn't have them, she was naked and everybody saw. Once when we were in a coffee shop, she tried to speak seriously to me. Her skin was gray with seriousness. Her whole eyeball looked stretched and tight; the white underpart was actually showing. She said, "I've just got to get off my fat ass and stop feeling sorry for myself." Her tough words didn't go with the look on her face. The waitress, a middle-aged Black lady, gave her a sharp, quick glance that softened as she turned away. She could tell something by looking at Veronica, and I wondered what it was.

The endless beautiful rooms inside the songs—wander through them long enough and their beauty and endlessness become horrible. There is so much, you always want more, so you keep moving, traveling ever more quickly, until you can't stop. Ten years ago, I used to see these kids running around in white makeup, sleeping in phony coffins, and paying dentists to give them vampire fangs. It was stupid, but it made sense too. You want the endlessness to end; you want to go home, but there is no home. You despise the tender attachments of the liver and the body, but you also crave them; you bite other people in an attempt to find them, and when that doesn't work you bite yourself.

Ginger tried to retrace her route back home, but she took a wrong turn and suddenly realized that she didn't have the bag of treasure. Where had it gone? She had not dropped it! She was about to go back and look for it when she saw a naked old woman walking toward her, carrying something horrible and glowing. Ginger didn't know why something that glowed should seem horrible, only that it did. As if the old woman could hear her, she said, "I carry love wrapped in pain. That is my treasure and soon it will be yours."

"Thank you," said Ginger politely, "but I don't want that. I want the treasure I found. Can you tell me where it is?"

But the old woman continued as if she hadn't heard. "Sometimes it is heavy in my arms, sometimes it is weightless," she said. "Sometimes I don't know anymore if it really is love. I have been carrying it for so long."

Veronica sat in a doctor's office, singing, *We've got the horse right here; his name's Retrovir,* to the tune of a big *Guys and Dolls* number. The receptionist smiled. I didn't.

Veronica burst into laughter. "You're like a Persian cat, hon." She made primly crossed paws of her hands and ecstatic blanks of her eyes; she let her tongue peep from her mouth. She laughed again.

The rain is out again, hammering the puddles full of holes, pocking the black-and-silver world with shining darkness. Rain soaks each leaf and blade of grass, bloating the lawns until they seem to roll and swell. Houses recede. The wind rises. The eyes and ears of God come down the walk.

I should go home. I'm tired and weak. Should take the bus. Should call my father. He is alone in an apartment with junk mail and old newspapers spread all around. Looking here and there in bafflement while dry heat pours out on him from a vent in the ceiling. His radio with a bent antenna on the dining table is tuned to a sports channel. People on magazine covers smile up from the floor and tabletops—a flat field of smiles blurred with slanted light from the cockeyed lamp. My father doesn't listen to his old songs anymore. They finally went dead for him. Instead, he has these people in magazines and on TV: actors, singers, celebrities. He knows they are vessels for a nation of secret, tender feeling, and he respects them. I think he tries to cleave to them. But I don't think he can.

Above me, the treetops wave back and forth, full of shapes, like the ocean. Wild hair, great sopping fists, a rippling field, a huge wet plant with thousands of tiny flowers that open and close with the wind. Form recedes. All the smiling television faces blend to make a shimmering suit that might hold you.

•

At the end of the '80s I moved from New York City to a canyon in Marin County, California. I lived in a renovated garage/cottage with a floor like plywood covered by thin carpet; in this one particular spot, I could peel up a loose edge of carpet and see the ground (once even a bug!) under the wood. I remember thinking I should be disgusted by this, but I was not. It was my first actual house that I didn't share with anyone else, and in it I had my first full complement of furniture including a couch, which felt luxurious to me. The canyon around me was luxurious too, lush and dense, full of colors and shapes that I had never seen before; in the winter chartreuse moss was so thick on the trees that it grew away from trunks in rough, hairy phalanges. I walked in this place for hours sometimes, absorbing the feeling of the moss and everything else: the floor of dirt and crumbling leaves; the quick, shining skin of a creek; fallen trees with dried bark crumbling off them; slender, humorously twisted trunks of ocher-colored madrones.

This natural abundance was amplified by what seemed an almost unnatural social and economic abundance: all around me were enormous, elaborate homes built up steep hills and surrounded by gardens, the air of which was daintily dotted by wind chimes—except when these dainty dots were blotted out by the tireless hammers and drills of home improvement, which was often. It seemed as if

the beautiful homes were constantly being improved.
The people who lived in them also had countless
opportunities for improvement; everywhere were
advertisements for healing, therapy, meditation, and
personal evolution. Even at the grocery store and the
fruit stand, flawless, free-range food was on display,
and the rows of shining produce seemed to strive
to be something more than mere food, something
impossibly ideal.

I had never owned a television before; I had not
paid much attention at all to "culture." I had been
too busy trying to pay my rent and to negotiate the
world immediately around me. Now, in this strange,
abundant place, I turned on the TV and listened to
the radio; I opened magazines of all kinds. I took
very seriously what I saw there, absurdly and naively
so. I read the endless, hectoring opinions telling us
who "we" were and what "we" were doing with great,
baffled interest. But what stood out most loudly and
violently were images of beauty so intense they were
almost warped; some of these images were human.
The fashion model seemed suddenly at the center of
the cultural world, inextricably wound in with music,
art, and cinema. These human images snagged in my
imagination, which twisted and turned reactively,
picking and chewing over them, foolishly trying to get
nourishment from them—for I wanted to be part of
this vibrant and powerful world. I wanted beauty too,
not merely physical beauty, but the heightened pitch
of existence the magazines hinted at. I think I believed
in some murky way in what I was being shown, that

ideal experience could be found in a particular, *correct* example of human identity and form, form that appeared in a variety of magazine personae that were subliminally linked to higher ideals.

My mind, of course, knew better. My mind did not like my psyche's vulnerability to this chimera and sounded the alarm with imagistic assertions of its own: I remember seeing *Pet Sematary* (Stephen King's horror story of burial and reanimation) during this time and being pierced by the image of a grotesquely reanimated person digging with his hands in somebody's yard, looking for bones to chew on, bewildered and ashamed but unable to stop—unable too to get any nourishment from the bones he dug up. To me it was an image of compulsion that represented, with blunt, poetic accuracy, my psyche's stimulated wish to have the "beauty" being fed it, along with a great collective psyche's stimulated wish. This understanding protected me from more fully absorbing such poisonous wishes because of the truth I intuited in the image, the seed of deprivation hidden in a fevered dream of perfection. Indeed, part of the reason I think this "dream" was so compelling to me from the start was my stricken feeling for the underlying wound of deprivation.

I remember the first time I was made to see beauty according to fashion. It was the first time I met a fashion model. Strangely, it was also one of the first times I saw someone for who she really was inside.

I was sixteen when this happened. I had run away from home, partly because I was unhappy there and partly because running away was what a lot of people did then—it was part of the new style. This style was expressed in articles and books and TV shows about beautiful teenagers who ran away even when their parents were nice; the parents just had to cry and struggle to understand. The first time I left, I was fifteen. My parents had fought and refused to speak to each other for three days; I slipped out through the silence and hitchhiked to a concert in upstate New York. United by my disappearance, my parents called the police, who picked me up in a shopping mall a week after I'd returned of my own accord. Daphne said that while I was gone, our mother acted like somebody on one of the TV specials about runaways—always on the phone talking to her friends about it. "I think she enjoyed it," said Daphne.

But our mother said she did not enjoy it. "We won't let you put us through that again," she said. "If you leave now, you're on your own. We won't be calling the police."

So a year later, I left again. I packed right in front of them. I said I would just be gone for the summer, but they assumed I was lying. "Don't call here asking for money!" shouted my father. "If you walk out that door, you are cut off!"

"I would never ask you for money!" I shouted back.

"She thinks she won't need it," said my mother from the couch. "She thinks being pretty will make her way." Her voice was angry and jealous, which made me think that leaving must be something great.

"She thinks she's going to make her way in the world," she said. But this time her jealousy was touched with wistfulness. She could've been talking about a girl in a fairy tale, walking down a path with her bundle on a stick.

I lived from apartment to apartment, sometimes with friends, sometimes strangers. I got a ride to San Francisco and stayed in a European-style hostel, where you could stay a limited number of nights for a fixed fee. It was a large, dilapidated building with high ceilings and sweet, moldy drains. The kitchen cabinets were full of stale cereal, the kind with frosting or colored sweet bits made to look like animals or stars. You had to chip in for food staples. You weren't supposed to bring in drugs; people did, but they were moderate and they shared. The man who ran it, a college student with a soft stomach and a big ball of hair on his head, even kept a record player in one of the common rooms, and we gathered there at night to share pot and listen to playful elfin songs about freedom and love. These songs had the light beauty of a summer night full of wonderful smells and fireflies. They also had a feeling of sickness hidden in them, but we didn't hear that then.

For the first few days, I was one of two girls, the other being a little fifteen-year-old with suspicious eyes and a sexuality that was sharp and raw as her elbows. But she was with a boyfriend in his thirties, the kind of guy who put on airs about his clothes and manners even though he looked like shit. I tried to be friends with her, but she acted like I was beneath her, maybe because she had an older boyfriend who bought her dresses. The only time she was friendly with me was when she let me see her dresses, pulling them out of a canvas bag and laying them across her arm, smoothing them with her free hand and telling me where and how Don had gotten each of them for her.

Otherwise, when we were in the kitchen with the others, she'd roll her eyes when I talked. The boys were nice to me, though; it was a treat for them to have a single girl around. Even the older boyfriend was secretly nice to me. He told me I'd be beautiful in ten years if I "cleaned up." *But in ten years*, I thought, *I'll just be old.*

Then a German woman came to the hostel. She was already old; she was thirty-one. But the boys were stunned by her. Even before they said so, I could tell. When she came in the room, they looked alert and dazed at the same time, like the beautiful night world of the music had appeared before them and begun swirling around their heads. When she left, they all said, "She is so beautiful!"

I didn't understand; she just looked like a girl to me, only old. Then someone said, "She used to be a model," like that explained everything. "She was very famous ten years ago," he added.

The feeling of dazzlement increased. The next time she appeared, conversation stopped, and people were self-conscious about starting it again. The fifteen-year-old girl didn't even try. She just sat there smoking and staring, not even suspicious anymore, like finally here was something that was exactly what it was supposed to be. She didn't even care that her boyfriend was staring at this woman like he was in love with her. She looked at the model as if she were a glimmering set of dresses, like she'd drape her over her arm and stroke her if she could.

Every day, the German woman would walk into this reaction, eating her cereal, taking her turn at the toilet, sometimes joining in a smoke around the stereo. If she walked into the kitchen carrying a book: What was she reading? Oh really! And what did she think of it? The German woman answered thoughtfully and pleasantly, but also stiffly, like she was trying to pass a test.

I still didn't understand. I didn't think she was beautiful and I didn't care that she had been a model. This is probably hard to believe. It is hard for me to believe. Now everybody knows models are important; everybody knows exactly what beauty is. It is hard to imagine that a young girl would fail to recognize a former model with full, perfectly shaped features as beautiful. It wasn't that I didn't care about beauty; I liked beauty as much as anyone. But I had my own ideas about what it was. This woman didn't look like anything to me. Now I would be staring at her like everybody else. But back then, I was the only person in the hostel who did not react to her appearance. The few times we were alone in the kitchen together, we made small talk, and I didn't think she was paying me any more attention than I paid her.

I left the hostel after a week. I moved into a rooming house with an older boyfriend who made a living handing out flyers on the street. One day in the fall, I was walking down the street, doing nothing, when suddenly the German woman was there— so suddenly, it felt like she'd leapt out from around a corner.

"Oh!" she exclaimed. "It's so great to see you! How are you doing? I was wondering what happened to you!"

Under her friendliness, her face was wild, like something inside her was crashing together and breaking, then crashing together again. Her voice was pleasant, but she did not look pleasant, or thoughtful, or like she gave a fuck about passing a test.

I told her about my boyfriend, with whom I now lived. "That sounds wonderful!" she said. "I have my own place just a few blocks away from here. Would you like to come visit?" Then, seeing my expression, she added, "Or maybe just go for a coffee now?" I stood there, nervous and speechless. She frowned, peering at me slightly, maybe noticing finally that I was just a kid. "Or—or . . . an ice cream! Would you like an ice cream?"

"Yeah," I said. "But I don't have any money."

"It's all right," she said, already leading me away without checking to see if I was following. "It's my treat." From the side, her eye was glassy and hard. Gingerly, I fell in with her.

We must have looked strange together. I was tall, but she was taller, and her high heels made her taller yet. Her burgundy dress was silken and plain, and it flattered the cutting, angular quality of her body. She wore sparkling earrings and nail polish. It was hot and she was slightly wet under the armpits, but still she gave an impression of dryness and gleaming. I wore sneakers, jeans, and a T-shirt with no bra underneath. My hair was unkempt and I wore no makeup. I didn't wear deodorant or bathe often; I might actually have smelled. She did not seem to notice any of this.

She took me to a very stylish and expensive place with little white tables covered by green-and-white-striped umbrellas. A year later, I would know enough to be uncomfortable sitting in this place looking like I did then. But at that time, I only felt bewildered; we didn't need to go there to get ice cream. I stared at the menu, dimly aware of the crudeness of my person for the first time. We ordered our ice cream. She looked at hers dully and began to eat as if she couldn't taste.

As we ate, a man in a suit came to our table and spoke to her in a foreign language. His voice was soft and he spoke briefly, but what he said enraged her. She did not act enraged, but I could see it, first in the muscles of her jaw and neck, then in her eyes. Rage was leaping from her eyes, but she answered him with a politeness so bitter, it seemed a kind of despair.

"What did he say to you?" I asked, thinking it must have been very obscene.

She literally clenched her teeth and said, "'You are very beautiful.'" Hatred illuminated her face like a bright flare and then went out. She returned to her ice cream.

I was even more bewildered; I had known many girls who, when men flirted with them, would pretend to be offended and disgusted, but it was clear that this woman was not pretending. I looked at her, really curious now why people thought she was beautiful and why it made her angry that they did.

But I didn't ask her what I wanted to know. We talked awkwardly for about half an hour and then got up to go. When we returned to the street, she said we should get together again—tomorrow. Did I want to come to her apartment and listen to records? Another flare lighted her face; it was need, not hate, but it was as strong as the hate had been. I was very uncomfortable now and felt that she was too. But her need flared unabated, like a pounding drum that pulls you along to its beat and overrules your own emotions. I said yes, I would drop by her apartment at eight o'clock the next evening.

But I didn't. When I talked to my boyfriend about her, I said she was weird. "Then don't go," he said. "I have to," I replied. "It would be mean not to." But I sat there in the kitchen with my boyfriend, eating cheesecake from a tin and watching his huge black-and-white TV until I sank into a torpor. From there, the German woman's loud drum was hard to hear. I pictured sitting with her on a nice pillow in front of her stereo. Lots of records would be scattered about—she would have a huge selection. She would go through them with her long, manicured hands and then put one on and listen to it dully, like she couldn't hear. Just picturing it made me feel heavy and tired. The gray figures running around on the TV screen made me feel heavy and tired too, but in a comforting way. Eight o'clock came and I thought I'd sit in my heavy comfort just ten minutes more and then go. At 8:30, I pictured her sitting alone, going through her records, need and hate surging under her stiff face. She would still be waiting for me to arrive. By nine o'clock, I realized I wouldn't go. I felt bad—I felt like I was deserting a person who was sick or starving. But I still didn't go.

About six months later, I saw her on the street again. I was dressed better then; I'd streaked my blond hair platinum and wore platform shoes. Maybe that's why the German woman didn't recognize me, or maybe she pretended not to see me, or maybe she didn't see me. She didn't seem to see anything. She was walking alone, her arms wrapped around her torso. Her clothes were ill-kempt and didn't fit her right because she had lost a lot of weight. Her eyes were hollow and she stared fixedly before her, as if she were walking down an empty corridor. I wanted to stop her, but I didn't know what to say.

I had seen loneliness before that and had felt it too. But I had never seen or felt it so raw. Thirty years later, I still remember it. Only now I am not bewildered. Now I understand that a person can be wild with loneliness. I understand that she wanted so badly to talk to me exactly because she sensed I was the only person in the hostel who was indifferent to her appearance. But it didn't work because she didn't know how. She had put on the suit of "model" many years before and now she couldn't take it off, and it hurt and confined her.

What's funny about this story is that a year after I met her, I became a model.

We were stupid for disrespecting the limits placed before us. For tearing up the fabric of songs wise enough to acknowledge limits. For making songs of rape and death and then disappearing inside them. For trying to go everywhere and know everything. We were stupid, spoiled, and arrogant. But we were right too. We were right to do it even so.

One night on the street, a small man wearing a red suit bought a yellow rose from me. I remember the color of the rose because I looked down at his feet and saw he had yellow socks on. The rose matched his socks! He said he ran a modeling agency and that I could be a model. He handed me a card with gold lettering on it. I took it, but I kept staring at his eyes; his expression was like somebody giving his hand to an animal so it could sniff and holding back the other. He said, "Very nice." He put the flower back in my basket and walked away like he was tossing and catching a coin, like the pimp bouncing his ball, except he didn't have anything to bounce. The card said CARSON MODELS, GREGORY CARSON.

Carson Models was up a staircase between store windows full of cheap, sassy clothes and glaring sun. I noticed a bag of shocking pink fur with a smooth gold clasp and then ran up the cool stairway. Gregory Carson was waiting for me with a photographer who had a large head and the eyes of a person looking from far away at terrible, beautiful things. He took my hand and looked at me. His name was John. He was the only other person there because it was Saturday; Gregory Carson had wanted me to come on a weekend so that he could give me his full attention.

Gregory Carson said the same thing about my boobs as the fat man, but not right away. First, we drank wine while John set up his camera. Gregory paced, as if he could barely contain his excitement. He talked about how important a model's personality was. He talked about sending me to Paris. When I asked what Paris was like, he cried, "You're going to find out!" and leapt straight up and did a jig, like a chipmunk scrambling in the air. I glanced at John. He looked like a cardboard display of a friendly person. Gregory went into a corner and flicked a switch; music came on. It was a popular song with a hot liquid voice. *Ossifier*, it sang. *Love's desire. High and higher.*

I didn't know how to pose, but it didn't matter; the music was like a big red flower you could disappear into. The sweetness of it was a complicated burst of little tastes, but under that was a big broad muscle of sound. It was like the deep feeling of dick inside and the tiny sparkling feelings outside on the clit. Except it was also like when you're in love and not thinking the words "dick" or "clit." Gregory Carson watched ecstatically, a tiny, complicated thing looking for a big, broad thing to hold him. "Doesn't she remind you of Brandy G.?" he cried. "Do you remember her, John?" John said yes, he did, and Gregory leapt up and scrambled again. I pictured him tiny, scrambling on a giant clit. I giggled, and Gregory said, "That's right! Have fun!" So I did. It was like the first time I made a sex noise, and instead of being embarrassing, it was great. It was like being with people I didn't know and making them stop so I could go in a store and buy chocolate milk, instead of worrying they would think I was a baby or a pig—and it tasted great. It was like eating pudding forever, or driving in your car forever, or feeling the dick you love forever, right before he sticks it in. Far away, my dad was playing songs for men who thought he was crazy. I was going to be a model and make money walking around inside songs everybody knew.

Then Gregory said he had to see me naked. "We aren't taking any more pictures," he said. "No one ever shoots you nude. I have to look at you because I'm the agent." He went to turn the music off, and suddenly John was in the room. He looked at me so hard, it was like a meaty head zoomed out of his cardboard body. His eyes were different: there was no BS about beautiful and terrible things. He was saying something—what was it? The music shut off. "All righty!" said Gregory. John's head got pulled back into the cardboard. He smiled and said he hoped he'd see me again. Gregory walked him to the door. When he came back, I was naked. The stereo was still making an electrical buzz. The big, broad thing had sucked the music back inside it.

Gregory looked at me. "You're five pounds overweight," he said gently. "And your breasts aren't that good." He touched my cheek with the back of his hand. "But right now, that doesn't matter." Ossifier's bright red voice sang in my head: *Don't hesitate 'cause the world seems cold.* "Alison," said Gregory Carson, "I'd like you to tell me about the first grade." He said "first grade" like it was something wonderful to eat, something he hadn't had for a long time. He looked like he might jump up and dance on the clit again. I looked down and felt my face frown. In the first grade, Miss Field was my teacher. She taught me how to write in big black letters. Ossifier stopped singing. Miss Field sat at her desk and folded her hands. A terrible feeling came over me. I felt like she was there, getting sucked into the electrical buzz. I didn't want her to be there. I didn't want her to be eaten.

Gregory reached out and took a tear out of my eye right as it fell. He put it in his mouth. He was tasting the terrible feeling and his eyes were full of pity. He had come to the deep liver place, where I was still a child attached to my family. He recognized it and he respected it, a little. "It's okay," he said. "You don't have to say." He reached down and held me between the legs. Here it was. Ossifier. Miss Field floated in a bright, distant oval. He watched my face as he rubbed me with his hand. He didn't care if he was a pig or a baby. The chocolate milk was delicious. His face came close and his one eye grew giant. Miss Field's bright oval winked shut and she was gone. Gregory Carson's eye said, *After you, baby!* and then we got sucked into the electrical buzz together.

•

One night at work, Veronica asked me how I got into modeling, and I said, "By fucking a nobody catalog agent who grabbed my crotch." I said it with disdain, like I didn't have to be embarrassed or make up something nice, because Veronica was nobody— like why should I care if an ant could see up my dress? Except I didn't notice my disdain; it was habitual by then. She noticed it, though. The arched eyebrows shot up and the lined, prissy face zinged out an expression sharp and hard as a bee sting. This ugly little woman had a sting! I would've stung back, but I was suddenly abashed by her buzzing ugliness. But then her expression became many expressions, and when she talked, her voice was kind.

"Every pretty girl has a story like that, hon," she said. "I had that prettiness too. I have those stories."

The old woman kept walking and Ginger fell in with her. She did this because while the old woman seemed weird, she did not seem bad, and also because Ginger thought she might be able to help find the treasure.

My parents went with me to the agency in Manhattan. They were not going to put me on a plane to a foreign country just because I'd won some contest. They were going to ask questions and get the truth. They put on their good clothes and the three of us took Amtrak into the city to a building of gold and glass. In the elevator, we stared silently at the numbers above the automatic door as they lighted up and dimmed in a quick sideways motion. For the first time in years, I could feel my parents subtly unite.

The agency person was a woman with a pulled-back, noisy face. Her suit looked like an artistic vase she'd been placed in up to her neck. When she smiled at me, it was like a buzzer going off. I could tell right away that my parents didn't know what to do.

"Can you assure me that our daughter will be taken care of?" asked my mother.

"Absolutely!" said Mrs. Agency. She spoke of roommates, vigilant concierges who monitored the doors, benevolent chaperones, former models themselves.

"Aren't there a lot of homosexuals in the fashion industry?" asked my father.

Mrs. Agency emitted a joyless laugh. "Yes, there are. That's another reason your daughter will be as safe as a kitten."

My father frowned. I felt forces vying in the room. He sighed and sat back. "I just wish you didn't have to interrupt your school," he said. And then I was on another plane, humping through a gray tunnel of bumps. I stared into the sky and remembered Daphne at the airport, closing her face to me. She hugged me, but there was no feeling in it, and when she pulled away, I saw her closed face. Sara didn't hug me, but when she turned to walk away, she looked back at me, the sparkle of love in her eye like a kiss. Droning, we rose above the clouds and into the brilliant blue.

When the plane landed, it was morning. Invisible speakers filled the airport with huge voices I couldn't understand. I walked with a great mass of people through a cloud of voices, aiming for the baggage claim. I was distracted by a man in a suit coming toward me with a bouquet of roses and a white bag that looked like a miniature pillowcase half full of sugar. His body was slim and his head was big. Deep furrows in his lower face pulled his small lips into a fleshy beak. His lips made me think of a spider drinking blood with pure blank bliss. Suddenly, he saw me. He stopped, and his beak burst into a beautiful broad smile that transformed him from a spider into a gentleman. "I am René," he said. "You are for Céleste Agency, no?" Yes, I was. He took one of my bags and handed me his roses. He took my other bag, put it on the floor, and kissed my hand. In a flash, I understood: seeing me had made him a gentleman and he loved me for it. I liked him too. "It is Andrea, yes?" "No," I said. "Alison."

His car was sleek and white and had doors that opened upward, like wings on a flying horse. We got inside it. He opened the bag (which was silk) and scooped the cocaine out of it with his car key. He placed the key under one winged nostril and briskly inhaled. I thought of the time my father was insulted by a car salesman who said, "All you want is something to get around in!" For a week after, my father walked around saying, "What do you do with it, you son of a bitch? Screw with it?" We passed the key back and forth for some moments. Finally, he licked it and put it in the ignition. He said, "Alison, you are a beautiful girl. And now you are in a country that understands beauty. Enjoy it." He started the car. The drug hit my heart. Its hard pounding spread through my body in long, dark ripples and for a second I was afraid. Then I stepped inside the electrical current and let it knock me out. We pulled out of the lot and into the Parisian traffic.

I had read about Paris in school. It was a place where ladies wore jewels and branches of flowers, even live birds in tiny cages woven into their huge wigs. The whipping boy sometimes played chess with the prince. The Marquis de Sade painted asylum inmates with liquid gold and made them recite poetry until they died. Charlotte Corday stabbed Marat butt-naked in the tub. I looked at the car speeding next to us; a plain girl with glasses on the end of her nose frowned and hunched forward. She cut us off and René muttered a soft curse. American pop music came out of her car in a blur. *Ossifier. Love's desire.* Huge office complexes sat silent in fields brimming with bright green desire. The queen knelt before a guillotine. Blood shot from her neck in a hot stream. The next day, her blood stained the street and people walked on it; now her head was gone, and she could be part of life. René asked what I wanted to do. I told him I wanted to write poetry. Cancan girls laughed and kicked. In paintings, their eyes are squiggles of pleasure, their mouths loose-shaped holes. On the street, people waiting for the light to change frowned and glanced at their watches.

René waited for me in the car while I went into the agency.

It was a medium-sized building with a shiny door on a cobbled street. The doorman had mad blue eyes and beautiful white gloves. The halls were carpeted in aqua. Voices and laughter came from behind a door. It opened and there was a woman with one kind eye and one cruel eye. Behind her was a man looking at me from inside an office. His look held me like a powerful hand. A girl's small white face peeped around the corner of the same office. The hand let go of me. The girl blinked and withdrew. "Where is your luggage?" asked the double-eyed woman. "With René, outside," I replied. "*René?*" She rolled her eyes back in her head. When they came forward again, they were both cruel. "Very well. Here." She handed me a piece of paper. "This is a list of go-sees for tomorrow and Wednesday. I suggest you use a taxi to get to them. Now tell René that Madame Sokolov says he must take you straight to rue de l'Estrapade."

"Ah," said René. "Madame Sokolov is not always aware." He tapped his head with two fingers and drove us to a dark door squeezed between a tobacco shop and a shoe store. The concierge was an old woman with a brace on her leg. She led me slowly up the dingy stairs, with René following, bags in hand. We moved slowly to respect the brace. Each short flight of steps came to a small landing with ticking light switches that shut off too soon. "*Merde,*" muttered the old lady. The light had turned off while she was looking for the key to my room. In the dark, I felt René's hot breath on my ear. "Take a nap this afternoon, eh? I'll be by at eight." He bit me on the ear. I started and he disappeared down the stairs. The old lady pushed open the door; there was a weak burst of light and television noise and a high, cunty voice: "But don't you see, I want you here *now*. Two days from now will be too late!" My roommate, in bra and underpants, sat cross-legged on the sagging couch, the phone to her sulky face. She acknowledged me with a look, then rose and walked into a back room, trailing the phone cord. She carried her slim butt like a raised tail and her shoulders like pointy ears. When the old lady left, I sat on the couch and picked at a bowl of potato chips on the side table. Out a window, enamel roof-tops with slim metal chimneys were bright against the white sky; a shadow weather vane twirled on a shadow roof. I watched it until my roommate got off the phone and I could call my family. When René came, I told him I wanted to go someplace that had pie. He laughed and said, "You will have French pie!" We went to a patisserie with cakes that looked like jewelry boxes made of cream. I ate them, but I didn't like them. They had too many tastes, and I wanted the plain chemical taste of grocery store pie. But the tables were made of polished wood and the people sitting at them were drinking coffee from tiny white cups. A woman next to us took a cigarette out of a case and lit it with a silver lighter. And because René asked him to, the waiter sang to me. The song was about little boys peeing on butterflies.

Papillon, pee, pee, pee.
Papillon, non, non, non.

The waiter bent down to the table and sang softly. His pocked face hung in bristly jowls and I saw he was missing teeth. But his voice opened the song like a picture book with feelings and smells in it. Blue flowers bobbed on the wind and butterflies dodged the piss of laughing boys. Mothers called; the boys buttoned their flies and ran home. I had awakened in New Jersey with my parents and I was going to sleep tonight with my French lover.

And so we lay naked on his rumpled bed. I was dimly aware that my body was exhausted and bewildered, but that didn't matter. I was in an upper chamber, far above those feelings, eating sugar with both hands. The silky sheets were scattered with white powder, mixed with granules and little hairs that were pleasant to feel. A brown moth flapped around a rose-colored lampshade. Cold air from an open window stirred the papers on the night table. René held me in his hairy arms and sang the pee-pee song. He said, "You fuck humpty-hump, like a little witch riding her broom!" I smiled and he stroked my hair. "That's right, is good. I love my little witch! Riding humpty-hump in the night!"

Then he jumped up and said he wanted to go to a nightclub. But I had go-sees the next day! He laughed and said, "Don't think like a shopgirl! Think like a poet!"

The nightclub was dark and had hot laser lights speeding through it. The music was like something bursting and breaking. People's faces looked like masks with snouts and beaks. But I knew they were beautiful. If the German ex-model I'd met in San Francisco had walked in, I'd have known she was beautiful too. But I didn't remember her. My eyes and ears were so glutted I had no room for memory. I didn't sleep, but René was right: it didn't show on my face. I got a job for an Italian magazine and left for Rome the day after. Little witch riding humpty-hump in the night.

Ginger and the old woman had turned a corner and entered a corridor with black walls out of which protruded hundreds of human heads. They were male, female, young, old, beautiful, ugly. Ginger was afraid, but not as afraid as you would think. "Can you tell me where my treasure is?" she asked the old woman again.

The woman turned and stared at her as if she were very stupid. "Don't you know?" she said. "It's in you. You'll never get rid of it now."

Riding still, out of the roaring night into a pallid day of sidewalks and beggars with the past rising through their eyes. Shadows of night sound solemnly glimmer in rain puddles; inverted worlds of rippling silver glide past with lumps of mud and green weeds poking through. The past coming through the present; it happens. On my deathbed, I might turn toward my night table and see René's rose-colored lampshade with the brown moth flapping inside it. My sisters could be blubbering at my side, but if Alana walked in and stuck her tongue out at me, she'd be the one I'd see.

In Paris, things happened fast. Two weeks after my first job, I met the head of Céleste. His name was Alain Black; he was a South African with a French mother. He was the man I had glimpsed on my first day there. He was lean and pale, nearly hairless. His eyes had thick, heavy lids. They were green, gold, and hazel, so mixed that they gave an impression of something bright swarming through his irises. Mostly, the swarming was just emotions and thoughts happening quickly. But there was also something else, moving too fast for you to see what it was. He asked if I had a boyfriend yet. When I said, "René," he laughed and said, "Oh, René!" Then he said I needed a haircut. Called a hairdresser, told him what to do, and sent me to the salon in a taxi. The salon was full of wrinkled women staring fixedly at models in magazines. When I walked in, they frowned and glared. But the girl at the desk smiled and led me through rows of gleaming dryers, each with a woman under it, dreaming angrily in the heat. The hairdresser didn't even need to talk to me. He talked to someone else while I stared at myself in the mirror. When it was done, I made the taxi take me back to the agency. It was closed, but the doorman with mad eyes knew to let me in. He knew where I was going and he knew who else would be there. Alain looked up and smiled. "Do you like it?" I asked. He stood and said of course he liked it, it had been his idea. Then he jumped on me.

I say "jumped" because he was quick, but he wasn't rough. He was strong and excessive, like certain sweet tastes—like grocery pie. But he was also precise. It was so good that when it was over, I felt torn open. Being torn open felt like love to me; I thought it must have felt the same to him. I knew he had a girlfriend and that he lived with her. But I was still shocked when he kissed me and sent me home. At "home," I wrapped myself in a blanket and looked out the window at the darkening mass of slanted roofs. René came by. I wouldn't see him. Darkness gradually filled the room. The phone rang; it was my mother—her tiny voice curled up in a tiny wire surrounded by darkness. I talked to her through clenched teeth. I told her she was a house-wife who didn't understand anything about the real world. She told me I didn't know what I was talking about, but I could hear she was hurt. After I hung up, I could feel it too. Her hurt was soft and dark and it had arms to hold me as if I were an infant. I sank into her soft dark arms, into a story of a wicked little girl who stepped on a loaf and fell into a world of demons and deformed creatures. She is covered with snakes and slime and surrounded by the hate of every creature trapped with her. She is starving, but she can't eat the bread still stuck to her feet. She is so hungry, she feels hollow, like she's been feeding on herself. In the world above, her mother cries for her. Her tears splash scalding hot on her daughter's face. Even though they are tears cried for love, they do not bring healing; they burn and make the pain worse. My mother's tears scalded me and I hated her for it.

When Alain locked me out and stole my money, I went back home. Eventually, I moved to New York; eventually, I returned to modeling. Eventually, I lived in a big apartment too. I remember returning home to my big apartment alone and drunk. Moving through rooms, turning on the lights. The buzz of my own electricity loud and terrible in my head. Someday to be cut off. That doesn't happen when I go home to my place on the canal. I am glad to be there. I always turn on the space heater first thing, a wonderful humming box filled with orange bands of dry heat. Take off my wet shoes, sit in the chair, warming my wet feet. Look out the window, look at the wall. Travel slowly through the wall. My millions of cells meeting all its millions of cells. We swarm together like ants touching feelers. Now I know you. Good, yes, I know you. I have some coffee. Listen to the radio. This afternoon maybe I'll call my father.

But not yet; I won't go home yet. I'll take the bus and go someplace beautiful and I'll walk until I'm so tired that

I won't be able to stay awake tonight. So tired that my sleep will not be pestered by dreams or fairy tales.

When I returned home to New Jersey, everybody met me at the airport. My mother had a fake smile on her face, meant to shield me from her tears. Daphne did not smile. She looked at me calmly, except that her brow was knitted up so high, her eyes were almost popped. My father's face had the awful tact of a witness to an accident with bloody people sprawled out naked. Sara was the only one who seemed the same. She glanced at me to be sure I was still there, then went back into herself.

I sat in the back seat with my sisters as if we were children again. For a second, they held apart from me, and then we were joined together in the old membrane. My mother had come back to my father just weeks earlier, and the membrane was active and vibrating with recent vigor.

"Do you want anything special to eat?" My father raised his eyes in the rearview mirror but did not look at me.

"I've made spaghetti," said my mother.

"Spaghetti would be good," I replied.

We drove past low-built gray stores set back in lots half full of cars and hunks of dirty snow. Their lights were starting to come on. The Dress Barn, RadioShack, the 99-Cent Store. My mother began to cry; her tears scalded my face.

I enrolled in the community college. Daphne was already there. Sara had dropped out of school and taken a job at an old people's home a few blocks over. She didn't yell anymore. There were no boys to slap her ass. She came home from work and went down into the basement. It was winter and we could hear her hacking cough rise all the way up to the second floor. It was winter and my mother's skin dried and her face grew thin and shrunken. I might look at her in her rubber boots and her wool cap pulled down over her forehead, the wool darkening with sweat as she worked to scrape ice off the chugging car, and I would think, *No sexy pantsuit now. Nobody wants you now!* And with that thought, my heart contracted and the world shrank around me so fast that I thought it would crush me. Every morning, my father got up looking like he felt the same way. The expression on his face said that the world shrank around him every day, so close in that it was hard to move. The expression on his face said that he pressed against the hard case of the shrunken world and pushed it back with every step. It was an expression I knew without knowing. I put my forehead down and I helped him push.

Our father dropped Daphne and me off at the college before he went to his job. He let us off at the end of the parking lot and we walked a long concrete path caked with blue-and-gray ice that gleamed on sunny days. The school was small and dingy. The people inside it stared at me like I was a stuck-up bitch. To get away from their stares, I climbed further up my stick. But I didn't feel stuck-up. I felt scared. I felt like I had to prove I was smart enough to go to college. I worked hard. I wrote poems. The poetry teacher was a little man with sparse hair on his dry head and spotted, trembling hands. But I loved him because he wrote "very good" on my poems. At the end of the day, Daphne and I would sit in the student union eating sweetened yogurt and dime doughnuts. Night students came and stood in the cafeteria line. At six o'clock, we walked back down the concrete to meet the car.

If we got home and our mother wasn't there, our dad danced around the house, pretending he was an ape. He did it to relieve tension. He'd run into the living room swinging his arms and going, "Ooooh! Oooh! Eeee eee eee!" He'd jump up on a chair, scratching his armpit and his head. Daphne and I did it too; we ran around after him. It was like dancing on the green chairs, only it wasn't a song everybody knew. It came from the deep flesh place, except it was quick and alive and full of joy. Not that I thought of it that way. I just knew I loved it. If it had gone on longer, it would've been better than any song. But it lasted only a minute. Our dad would always call it; he'd suddenly go back to normal and climb down off the chair, his smile disappearing back into his face. "Whew!" he'd say. "I feel a whole lot better now!" Except once between ape and normal, he took my shoulders and hugged me sideways. "I'm proud of you," he whispered, and kissed my ear.

I was proud too; I knew I was doing something hard. Sometimes I was even happy. But another world was still with me, glowing and rippling like a dream of heaven deeper than the ocean. I could be studying or watching TV or unloading clothes from the washing machine, when a memory would come like a heavy wave of dream rolling into life and threatening to break it open. During the day, life stood stolid, gray and oblivious. But at night, heaven came in the cracks. I would want Alain, and want his cruelty too. I would long for those cabinets of rich food and plates of drugs, for nights of sitting alone in the dark, eating marzipan until I was sick. For bitches who yanked at me and yelled at me for sweating. For nightclubs like cheap boxed Hell, full of smoke and giant faces with endlessly talking lips and eyes and snouts swelling and bulbous with beauty. For my own swollen hugeness, spread across the sky. It didn't matter that I had been unhappy in the sky or that I had been cheated and used. I cried for what had hurt me and felt contempt for those who loved me; if Daphne had put her arm around me then, I would've clenched my teeth with contempt. Then, lying next to her warm body was like lying in a hole with a dog and looking up to see gods rippling in the air of their hot-colored heaven. I wanted her to know that she was a dog, ugly and poor. I wanted all of them to know. I wanted my father to know that he would always be crushed, no matter how hard he pushed.

"You're different now," said Sara. "You walk through the house like you're alone on a beach. Like nobody's there but you."

On the last night I saw Alain, he took a bunch of us to a sadomasochist sex club. It was a dump guarded by a fat tattooed man who smacked his blubbery lips at us. Inside the cave, there was a bar and a handsome young man pouring drinks behind it. Cheerful music played. Two middle-aged women with deep, sour faces sat at the bar wearing corsets and garter belts. Some people were dressed in costume like them; other people were dressed normally. One man was naked. He was skinny as a corpse—you could see his ribs and the bones of his ass. He had long matted gray hair and thick yellow nails like a dog's. He crawled on the floor, moaning and licking it with his tongue. The hair on the back of my neck stood up. Nobody even looked at him. He crawled to the women at the bar and got up on his knees. He moaned and pawed the air like he longed to touch them but didn't dare. Without looking, one of them took the riding crop from her lap and lightly struck him across the shoulders. "Va, va!" she scolded gently. He reached down and yanked at his limp penis. He yanked it hard and fast but also daintily. She returned the crop to her lap and he scuttled away, balls swinging between his withered thighs. She saw me staring and made a face, as if I had broken a rule. I looked for Alain and saw him disappearing into a crowded back room with his arm around a dimly familiar girl. "Don't worry." Jean-Paul was suddenly beside me. "It is harmless here." He winked at me. "Just a show, mostly. Unless you want to join." But I pushed through the crowd.

Sometimes the spell would break: I would look away from the terrible heaven and see my sister lying next to me, her neat, graceful form and her even breath beautiful and inviolate. If I put my hand on her warm shoulder, my thoughts might quiet; heaven would vanish and the ceiling would be there again, protecting us from the sky. I could lie against her and feel her breath forgive me. The day would come. My night thoughts would pale. My sister and I would go to school.

But sometimes I would barely sleep, then get up with heaven still burning my eyes. I would be full of hate and pain because I could not get back to it. On one of those mornings, I told Daphne the story of the sex club. We were moving around the room quickly, getting out of our warm gowns and into our cold clothes. I told her about the crawling man and the women at the bar. I could tell she didn't want to hear. But I kept talking, faster and faster. I pushed through the crowd. A hand reached out of it and grabbed my wrist. I took its little finger and bent it back. It let go. I threw my gown on the bed and walked across the room naked. Daphne turned her back, bent, and showed me the gentle humps of her spine. With dignity, she put on her pants.

In a reeking back room, I found Alain with Lisa from Naxos. Her sensitive little lips were tense and strange. They were watching a middle-aged woman climb onto a metal contraption so that a man could whip her. Daphne yanked open a drawer and slammed it shut. I brushed my hair with rapid strokes. Alain smiled at me. I told him I wanted to go home, now. "Then go home," he said. Lisa was not looking at me on purpose. Daphne pared her nails. She was not looking at me either. The man with the whip was waiting for the woman to get settled into the proper knee and hand grooves. He seemed nervous; twice he moved his arm, like he was anxious to assist her, then moved it back. "I want to go home!" I nearly screamed. Both the man with the whip and the climbing woman turned to look at me; she brushed a piece of hair from her quizzical eye. The people watching them looked too. There was a crash; "Shit!" hissed Daphne. She had knocked a water glass off the bed table, splashing the mattress. Without looking at me, Alain took an ice cube out of his drink and threw it at my face. The woman settled her face into the metal headrest. I kicked Alain's shin and ran.

"That's poetry," I said. "Life and sex and cruelty. Not something you learn in community college. Not something you write in a notebook." Daphne slammed the glass back on the table so hard, I thought she'd break it. She went out of the room and down the stairs. She knew what I'd said was stupid, but she half believed it too.

When I saw Jean-Paul next, I tried to ask him more about Alain's father. We were at a party, some kind of function. It was dark and crowded. Big plates of food soaked up the smoke in the air. Jean-Paul frowned and blearily leaned into me, trying to hear. The beauty of his eyes was marred by deep stupor. Rum-soaked spongy crumbs fell down his rumpled shirtfront. One hand drunkenly cleaned the shirt; the other loaded the wet mouth with more tumbling crumbs. An ass paraded by in orange silk. Half the crumbs went down the shirt. He did not know who I meant. His tongue came out and licked. "Alain's father," I repeated. "How did he know that man who crawls on the floor of that place?" Recognition lit his stupor and made it flash like a sign. "You believed that?" he cried. "Ha ha ha ha ha!" He threw his head back into the darkness of the room, rubbed with the red and purple of muddled sex and appetite, drunken faces smeared into it and grinning out of it. His handsome face was a wreck before my eyes. The smell of wreckage came out of his open jacket as he leaned over to cram more food in his mouth. Ha ha ha!

Then the protruding heads started talking. Some spoke in foreign languages, others spoke English. This was the funny thing: Ginger could understand them all, regardless of their language. But even so, what they said made no sense to her. She stopped before the head of a man with black hair that was talking to the head of a woman with yellow hair. Their faces were rigid like death, but tears poured freely from their eyes. Ginger knew they were talking to each other, but although they were speaking the same language, neither was able to understand the other's words, probably because they were both talking at the same time. And they could not stop.

Ginger looked for the old woman, hoping she would explain. But she had kept walking while Ginger had stopped and was already gone in the darkness of the corridor. And then things got harder to understand.

When I first moved here, I lived in this town. I didn't live in the canyon, but I'd come to walk in it. I'd come especially when I felt afraid, knowing I had hepatitis but not feeling sick yet. I'd look at the big trees and the mountain and I'd think that no matter how big any human sickness might be, they were bigger. Now I'm not so sure. How much sickness can even a huge heart take before it gets sick itself? The canyon is full of dead and dying oaks. Scientists don't know why. It's hard to believe we didn't kill them.

The wind rises. The rain dashes sideways. Slowly, the trees throw their great hair. Their trunks creak and mull. My fever makes a wall in my brain. A door appears in the wall. It opens and another dream comes out. Is it from last night, or the night before, or every night? In it, a man and woman are on a high-speed train that never stops. Music is playing, a mechanical xylophone rippling manically up a high four-note scale again and again. *Bing bing bing bing!* It is the sound of a giant nervous system. The man and woman are built into this system and they cannot leave it. They are crying. Looking out the window, they see people hunting animals on game preserves. There are almost no animals left, so they have to be recycled— brought back to life after they've been killed and hunted again. Mobs of people chase a bear trying to run on artificial legs. It screams with fear and rage. The man and woman cry. They are part of it. They can do nothing. *Bing bing bing bing!*

My forehead breaks into a sweat. I unfasten a button and loosen my scarf. The air cools my skin; the fever recoils, then sends hot tadpoles wiggling against the cold. Drive the animal before you and never stop. Starve it, cut it, stuff silicone in it. Feed it until it's too fat to think or feel. Then cut it open and suck the fat out. Sew it up and give it medication for pain. Make it run on the treadmill, faster, faster. Examine it for flaws. Not just the body but the mind too. Keep going over the symptoms. It's not a character defect; it's an illness. Give it medication for pain. Dazzle its eyes with visions of beauty. Dazzle its ears with music that never stops playing. Send it to graze in vast aisles of food so huge and flawless that it seems to be straining to become something more than food. Dazzle its mind with visions of terror. Set it chasing a hot, rippling heaven from which illness and pain have been removed forever. Set it fleeing the silent darkness that is always at its heels. Suck it out. Sew it up. Run. When the dark comes, pray: *I love my ass.*

I button my coat and let myself sweat. I try to think of something else. I think of an interview I heard with a religious person who had two kinds of cancer. The radio host asked her if she'd prayed for God to heal her. She said that she had and that it hadn't worked. When she realized she was going to die, she asked God why He hadn't healed her, and He answered. She actually heard His voice. He said, "But I am."

I am not religious, but when I heard that, I said yes inside. I say it now. I don't know why. There's a reason, but it's outside my vision.

The mouth of the canyon opens to swallow the road. I walk down its slippery, muddy throat. Old trees slowly tip into the ravine, gripping the crumbling pavement on one side, seizing fists of wet earth on the other. Their root systems come out of the soaked embankment like facial bones, clenched in unseeable expressions. At the bottom, their children—oak and madrone—stand close together and hold open their shining arms. They are covered to the waist with wet chartreuse moss; it grows away from the trunks in long green hairs that stand in the air like prehensile sense organs. I take off a glove and stroke the cold fur, then sniff my rank, wormy palm. I put my hand on the tree again to see my white skin against the green. When I was a kid, chartreuse was my favorite color. But I didn't think it was real. The city was so big and bright that for a moment my terrible heaven paled, then went invisible. I thought it was gone, but what I couldn't see, I felt walking next to me in streets full of vying people. I felt it in their fixed outthrust faces, their busy rigid backs, their jiggling jewelry, their creeping and swagger.

I felt it in the office workers who perched in flocks on the concrete flower boxes of giant corporate banks, eating their lunches over crossed legs and rumpled laps, the wind blowing their hair in their chewing mouths and waves of scabby pigeons surging at their feet, eating the bits that fell on the pavement. I felt it in the rough, sensate hands of subway musicians playing on drums and guitars while the singer collected money with his cup, still singing like he was talking to himself in a carelessly beautiful voice while riders streamed down concrete stairs like drab birds made fantastic in flight. I felt monstrous wants and gorgeous terrors that found form in radio songs, movie screens, billboards, layers of posters on decayed walls, public dreams bleeding into one another on cheap paper like they might bleed from person to person. I took it in and fed on it, and for a while, that was enough.

It was as if I were seventeen again and longing to live inside a world described by music—a world that was sad at being turned into a machine, but ecstatic too, singing on the surface of its human heart as the machine spread through its tissues and silenced the flow of its blood. In this world, there were no deep things, no vulgar goodwill, only rigorous form and beauty, and even songs about mass death could be sung on the light and playful surface of the heart.

It's raining again. I am deep in the unfolding. All around me living green opens and closes, undulating in ripples and great waves. The creek flashes, eager for the piercing rain, its hard, concentrated pouring. A slim tree naked of bark, ocher, smooth, comes out of the ground in a sinuous twist. A piece of fungus grows in a neat half wheel around a twig, like a hat on a lady with a long neck. I think of Veronica.

"Well, hon, if I were you I'd try again. This is New York, not Paris." She lit another cigarette. "But this time don't let some nobody grab your crotch." She smiled again.

I come to a clearing filled with little sticks poking out of the ground. Whatever they had been, somebody had chopped them off. Hard people, real hearts. So many of Veronica's stories were coarse and sentimental. Another time, she told me about being raped by a man who broke into her apartment. He said he was going to kill her, but she talked him out of it. "I told him, 'If you kill me, you won't be killing just one person. You'll be killing my parents. They're old and it would kill them to know their daughter died like that.'" She shrugged and held out her hands like a Borscht Belt comedian. "And he didn't!" She smoked luxuriously and leaned back in her chair, into the sky with red writ across it. "He was very tender." Her voice deepened; it became fulsome, indulgent, almost smug. "My rapist was very tender."

Smart people would say she spoke that way about that story because she was trying to take control over it, because she wanted to deny the pain of it, even make herself superior to it. This is probably true. Smart people would also say that sentimentality always indicates a lack of feeling. Maybe this is true too. But I'm sure she truly thought the rapist was tender. If he'd had a flash of tenderness anywhere in him—a memory of his mother, of himself as a baby, of a toy—she would've felt it because she was desperate for it. Even though it had nothing to do with her, she would've sought it, reaching for it as it sank away in a deep pool.

I'll be looking at the moon,
But I'll be seeing—

I see myself, home for Christmas. There I am in the warm kitchen, seasonal music coming from the living room in great swollen chords. I see the red mixing bowl on the counter. I see the mixer, mashed potatoes stuck to its dull blades. My mother opens the oven; there is a golden turkey sweating juice. My father sits in his living room chair, his eyes like deep holes full of layered visions invisible to us. Good King Wenceslas looks down at pictures flashing on the mute TV. A local family is turned out of their apartment; alone and defiant, the mother leads her children down the hall, her eyes flaring into the camera. My mother stirs hunks of butter into the peas; she lays the pecan pies out on tattered pot holders. The local family finds shelter with a church group that has pledged to help them. Daphne decorates the tree with nimble, loving gestures. The children accept stuffed toys from strangers; their mother smiles and rapidly blinks. I light the red candles and put them on the dining room table. Rows and rows of wonderful cars are for sale. Santa takes aspirin for a headache. *So bring him incense, gold, and myrrh*; the music is deep and rich, with sparkling colors flashing in its depths. The TV station's logo opens and closes like an eye. A mute reporter talks into a microphone; rows of hands pull up rows of pant legs to show rows of lesions. "This is outrageous!" cries my father. "Showing this tonight!" Mute doctors talk and speculate. "Everyone knows they're diseased," says my father. "We don't need it shoved in our faces."

The rooms roll by. In them there are plates heaped with apples and oranges, bowls filled with nuts in complex, perfect shells. There are stockings our grandmother made for us before she died, our names spelled in felt letters. There is a crystal dish of cranberry sauce, marked around its shiny middle with the circular impress of its tin. There is a feeling of fear. It connects and holds and flavors everything else like aspic. My father gets up and turns off the TV. It is not really fear of homosexuals. That is just something to say. The real fear is of things that can't be said. The fear shows through the purposeful expression in my mother's eyes as she carries the turkey to the table. It gathers in every corner of the house and pools in the basement, where Sara hides in her room, splay-legged before the TV, eating painkillers and hard candy by the handful. My father searches, but his brother has gone too far away to find in any song; when my father looks, he reaches into darkness and grasps nothing.

Against this darkness, our stockings were filled with candy canes and little toys; the table was laden and the tree—a real one my father held upright while my mother and Daphne struggled with the screws in the metal stand—was decorated with ropes of lights and tinsel and dear, strange ornaments: striped balls and snowmen and a silver peacock with its face worn away. How sad and weak these talismans seemed to me, like the music my father played for men who turned away from him. How weak against the fear and the terrible unsaid things. At night, when the others had gone to sleep, Daphne and I went out and walked in the neighborhood. Street- and starlight made the shoveled walks gray corridors of soft white mass and softer black shadow, and the *crunch-crunch-crunch* of our boots played up and down them in the ringing dark. Across the billowing snow, gaunt trees signed in shadow language. Modest houses hung their squares and rectangles with lights the blunt sweet colors of happiness—secret delight hidden in the cold body of winter. Felt but unseen except for now, the deity's birthday, when people climb wobbling ladders to string symbolic lights on trees and around windows. *Crunch-crunch.* We used to run across these yards, shouting. There was a birdbath and a strawberry patch behind that house hidden in pine bushes, under a sloping roof swollen twice its size with snow. There was a little girl named Sheila Simmons, who sat on the sidewalk and played with a red rubber ball and a handful of shiny jacks. *Crunch-crunch-crunch.* In some glossy folded place, they were still there, unseen but felt. And so, unseen but felt, were the unsaid things.

When we got back, the house was warm and dark except for the Christmas tree, its burning lights making glowing caves in its branches, jeweled with soft colors and the lit intensity of tiny needles. The blood tingled in our legs as we stamped our feet on the front mat; dangling tinsel stirred with our motion, ghost light alive in each strand. It was beautiful and brimmed with love. Yet the unsaid things remained mute and obdurate. As we went upstairs to bed, they stood like invisible stone tablets, unreadable and indifferent to our words. When we lay down, Daphne slept, but I turned back and forth between sleep and wakefulness. It was there again, clanging between dream and thought—the mental sensation that in the next room our parents were screaming curses and attacking each other like animals. I turned on the light and remembered them as I had seen them earlier that day at the grocery store: an overweight man and a tall, pear-shaped woman with their glasses on the ends of their noses, staring about them in mild confusion, their cart full of bargain eggnog and candy canes. I remembered the tree downstairs, the lights outside, and the sky.

Yes, we were stupid for disrespecting the limits placed before us, for trying to go everywhere and know everything. Stupid, spoiled, and arrogant. But we were right too. *I* was right. How could I do otherwise when the violence of the unsaid things became so great that it kept me awake at night? When I saw my father sitting in a chair, desperate to express what was inside him, making a code out of outdated symbols even his contemporaries could no longer recognize? When I saw him smile because my mother fell on her face and then put the smile away like it was a piece of paper? When I heard him rail against dying men because otherwise he had no form to give his hates and fears? All the meat of truth was hidden under a dry surface, and so we tore off the surface with a shout. We wanted to have everything revealed and made articulate, everything, even our greatest embarrassments and lusts.

And then things got harder to understand. Because instead of words, pictures poured from the talking mouths, blurred and run-together pictures, like there was a giant movie going on in the air in front of her, but it was too mixed up to see what it was.

But we were not satisfied with revealing and articulating; we came to insist that our embarrassments and lusts were actually beautiful. And sometimes they were—or at least could be made to look it. The first high-end job I had in New York was with two other girls, one of whom was an unstable lesbian with dark, dramatic looks and a known hard-on for the other, a bland blonde from Norway who didn't speak English. The photographer had us pose at night against the chain-link fence of a deserted ball field. He put me and Ava, the Nordic girl, on one side of the fence and Pia, the dyke, on the other. He photographed Pia alone. He photographed Ava and me together, me slightly behind her to indicate my sidekick status. He photographed Ava and me holding hands while Pia pressed up against the fence. At the end, he had Pia strip down to her underwear and hurl herself onto the fence, like she was "trying to get to Ava," grabbing it with her hands and bare feet. Most models of Pia's stature would never have done that. But he knew she would. She was half out of her mind with lovelessness and rage, and she wanted people to see it—she wanted it revealed and articulated. She threw herself at the fence again and again, until her hands and feet were bleeding. That shot ran at the end of a three-page spread and it was a great picture: Pia's nakedness was blurred by the fence and by her motion, but her face and flying hair came at you like demon beauty bursting out of darkness to devour human beauty. Ava and I huddled together in our pale spring lace, two maids lost in a postmodern wood, she moving forward, me half turning toward the demon who silently howled at us with her great gold eyes, her genital mouth and long, flawless claws with just a hint of anguish in their swollen knuckles. Of course, you didn't see any blood.

You didn't see human pain on the demon's face—or rather, you saw it as a shadow, a slight darkness that foregrounded the beauty of the picture and gave it a sort of luscious depth.

The wind is strong now. I'm afraid it will pick me up and throw me off the ridge. I picture falling, breaking on tree branches, and cracking my head on the rocks below. I picture a tree branch falling on me and pinning me. How long would I lie there before someone found me? Night would come. The softness and greenness and moving stillness would make an immense fist and it would close around me. Bugs would come. I would die. Animals would come. Bugs and animals would eat me. I would rot and disperse. The dispersed flesh would travel down into the ground in tiny pieces, burrowing in the dirt, deeper and deeper. I would cease to be an I and become an it. It would get eaten by bugs, come out their assholes, and keep going. It would come to the center of the earth. The heat and light would be like Hell for a human. But it would not be human. It would go on in.

Two entwined trees with roots that break the ground form a lumpy cradle half on the path and half hanging out over the ridge. I squat between them, umbrella over my head. I drink big mouthfuls of water. I look down into the canyon at the treetops, vast and textured, twisting and moving like seagrass under an ocean of air and mist, full of creatures I can't see. Veronica raises her wand; it bursts into flame.

Finally one scene stood still. It was an image of a beautiful young man. He had pale blond hair and full, pale lips and hazel eyes that were full of movement. He was like a song playing in a locked room, a song you could not quite hear but that you strained to hear, because something in it promised that it was beautiful, more beautiful than any other song, more beautiful than anything of any kind.

Ginger heard herself say in a voice she did not recognize as hers, "I love him."

I imagine being in a hospital bed, holding my dying, unfaithful lover in my arms. I imagine feeling the beat of his heart, thumping with dumb animal purity. Once, when I was working in Spain, I went to a bullfight, where I saw a gored horse run with its intestines spilling out behind it. It was trying to outrun death by doing what it always did, what always gave it joy, safety, and pride. Not understanding that what had always been good was now futile and worthless, and humiliated by its inability to understand. That's how I imagine Duncan's heart. Beating like it always had, working as hard as it could. Not understanding why it was no good. This was why Veronica got into the bed—to comfort this debased heart. To say to it, *But you are good. I see. I know. You are good.* Even if it doesn't work.

The rain has dissipated into a silent drizzling mist. The air feels like wet silk. Veronica lowers her wand. I get up out of my squat; in the canyon below I see dozens of ocher-colored trees swathed in mist. I think, *They are so beautiful.* I think, *The disease is spreading.*

I took the train to see my family almost every month; I brought them magazines with my picture in them. In Paris, I had sometimes torn pages out and sent them across the rumpled sea, but I'd never seen a reaction to them. My mother looked at my image as if she were looking at a wicked little girl come to scornfully show herself to her poor mother. There was love in her look, but with such jealousy mixed in that the feelings became quickly slurred. It was what my mother gave me, so I took it and I gave it back; I reveled in her jealousy as she reveled in my vanity. Reveling and rageful, we went between sleep and dreams right there in the dining room. Silent and still, we attacked each other like animals.

When I was a young child, my mother told me that love is what makes the flowers grow. I pictured love inside the flowers, opening their petals and guiding their roots down to suck the earth. When I was a child, I prayed, and when I prayed, I sometimes would picture people not as flowers but as grass— plain and uniform, but also vast and vibrant, each blade with its tiny beloved root. By the time I moved to New York, I had not prayed for many years. But there was a soft, dark place where prayer had been and sometimes my mind wandered into it. Sometimes this place was restful and kind. Sometimes it was not. Sometimes when I went into it, I felt like a little piece of flesh chewed by giant teeth. I felt that everyone was being chewed. To ease my terror, I pictured beautiful cows with liquid eyes eating acres of grass with their great loose jaws. I said to myself, *Don't be afraid. Everything is meant to be chewed and also to keep making more flesh to be chewed. All prayer is prayer to the giant teeth. Maybe sometimes there is pity for the chewed thing, and that is what we pray to. Maybe sometimes there is love.*

Now the young man was in a delightful room where people wearing beautiful clothes were smiling and talking like they were outside in the sun and playing the most wonderful, complicated game—except that they weren't, they were only talking. In this room the song that you could not quite hear was one of mysterious, powerful joy translated as social beauty, personality, and bodily love, and because the young man had so much of it, he was surrounded by girls who loved him. Ginger could not see herself, but she felt that she too was there.

She whispered it again: "I love him."

"Yes," said a voice. "He is your love. You see him now as he will live in the world."

On the street, everything was rushing and corporeal, and the sky was soft blue, with small salmon-colored clouds. We went into a deli and wandered giddily among the rows of cans and bottles, wrapped pastel sponges, and a flashing orange cat. Tiny pictures that had smiled at us as children smiled at us as adults: a tuna wearing sunglasses, a laughing green man wearing leaves. We got potato chips and juices and went back out under the soft, glowing sky. A taxi shuddered to a halt and took us into its creaking dimness with a slam. A song came out of the radio, bouncing like balls of colored candy on a conveyor belt. *One more shot!*

Bounce bounce! *'Cause I love you!* The city rolled along, breaking against our driver's stalwart hairy neck.

"I have something for you," said Patrick. Smiling, he held out his bunched fist. "Hmm?"

He smiled and opened his hand. I saw my wadded underpants. I blinked. The world opened its mouth and laughed like it was a baby being tickled. I'd forgotten to put them on when we were leaving the bathroom; he'd seen them come out my pant leg and fall on the deli floor. The cat flashed past; the green man laughed. We laughed, rolling around in the taxi, kissing. The city rolled along beyond the clouded bulletproof plastic that protected the driver with its hinged pocket for the wadded fare. It was stickered with advertisements for clubs and bands, and the stickers were doodled on with ballpoints and the radio drew its doodles on everything. Oh, Miss Big Bitch, even you are overlaid with doodles and radio songs.

"I love you," I said.

He held me close and kissed me, and his body said, *Yes, and here we go.*

She wore a red jacket that had been fashionable five years earlier, a lacquered hide with gold buckles, shoulder pads, and trick pockets. She wore it defiantly. She wore it as if to say yes, it was ugly, yes, it was tasteless, but right now only the forceful character of ugliness and taste-lessness could help her shake her booty one last time. She danced the same driven way she moved in aerobics class—leaping and kicking with manic propriety. As if to show a disbelieving someone, once and for all, what she could really do. But with each repetitive movement, she seemed to wind more deeply into a place where she didn't have to show anybody anything, a place where there was no propriety. I looked up; on crude stages, fat men in wigs haughtily, expertly danced. Hot colored lights crashed down around them in waves. Sirens went off and clown horns honked as they danced in the face of death and in the face of life. The music blared gigantically, as if it were propelling a baby into the outrageous world and bellowing with shock at what it saw. The queens danced and Veronica danced, and their dancing said, *World, kiss my fat middle-aged butt.*

I don't know what I said when I danced. Probably nothing. Probably *I'm a pretty girl, I'm a pretty girl, I'm*— I sighed. "Look," I said. "I know it's shit. But you've got to decide if you want to live or not. Because if you do, you're going to have to start fighting for your life."

"Yes, I know, hon. I'm just not sure it's worth it."

"Okay. Maybe it's not. Probably it's not. You've got insane parents and your sister is useless to you. You're lonely and you have a crummy job. And you're not going to beat the disease whatever you do."

Veronica stared like I'd slapped her out of a crying jag.

At least I'd refrained from telling her she looked like shit. "But even if you live only five more years, even if you live only two more years or one year, if you use that time to really . . . to really . . ." I fumbled, embarrassed.

She looked at me, sorry for me.

"To really find out who you are and care for yourself and . . . and forgive yourself—I mean—I don't mean—"

"I'll let that pass," she said softly.

"I *don't* mean forgive yourself for getting sick." My words were wooden and trite. I had gotten them out of articles in health-food magazines. I did not know what they meant any more than she did. Still I said them: "I mean loving yourself."

"I understand what you're saying, Alison." Veronica spoke gently. "I think it's lovely. But it's just that it's . . . it's not my personality."

"Okay. But then there's the physical stuff. If you don't like that doctor, there's others. There's herbs, there's acupuncture, there's yoga. There's GMHC, there's Shanti, there's support groups—women's groups too. Medicine won't cure you, but it'll ease the pain. It'll let your body know you're caring for it, loving it. I know it's corny, but—"

"I don't have insurance."

I stared. "But I thought you got insurance a while ago."

"I did, but it lapsed. It was lousy insurance anyway."

I was speechless.

"I tried an acupuncturist a year ago. I can't say it did much for me, though he was awfully nice. He talked about the organs and how they relate to different emotions. Lungs are sadness; liver is anger. He said my main weakness was my small intestine. Would you like to guess what emotion that's related to? Deep unrequited love. The small intestine! Who knew?"

That night, I dreamed I was in Paris, posing for a magazine cover. The studio was filled with people—René, Alana, Simone, Cunt-Face, every drunk bitch and bastard from rue du Temple. And sliding among them, bending and flattening his body like a snake, Alain showed his white flattened face. There was no movement in his eyes now. They were still and empty as a waiting grave. The photographer was furious, but there was nothing he could do. Alain smiled and disappeared. The crowd milled. The photographer cursed and pinched me.

So I left my body and went to a place emptier than a desert, a place that seemed to stretch into forever. In it shimmered thousands of veils and masks and personalities, each as still as a statue and waiting for someone to step inside it and make it live. Quickly and lightly, I stepped from one to the next. Pleasure zipped across my surface like a water bug.

But under the surface, something heavy pulled and twisted. It pulled and twisted because it did not want to take these shapes. It pulled me back into my body and twisted my face off my head. But it was okay. No one noticed; the camera flashed. I smiled and woke up thrashing, like I was trying to throw off a great blanket of darkness.

I went home and took a hot bath. My mind talked and talked. I got into bed. The darkness of the room grew over me. Just before I curled into it, I started awake and thought, *Where am I?* Then I sank back to sleep as if slipping into black water. Under the water, I saw two naked little boys tightly bound and hung upside down. One of them was dead. His rectum had been torn open and gouged so deep that I could see into his belly. Something white moved inside him. The living child sobbed with terror. "He has

AIDS and now I have it," he sobbed. "I'm going to die." I put my arms around him and tried to hold him upright, but he was too heavy. I said, "I'm sorry you have AIDS," and the insipid words were loathsome, even to me. In a fury, he bit me; I dropped him and ran, terrified he would give me the disease. Veronica rode past in a cab; I was in the cab telling her about the boys. "And then he bit me," I said. Her eyes grew wild and she bit me with razor teeth. I jumped out of the car and ran. I woke up and a voice inside me said, *You will go to Hell.*

Ginger could not look away from the young man to see who spoke to her, but the voice made her feel such fear she could hardly stay on her feet.

"Here he is in the world. Now feel him as he will be with you."

And Ginger was knocked on her back. She could still hear the sound and speech of the delightful room, but she could not see it because it was dark and someone was on top of her. His tongue was in her mouth and her tongue was in his. At the same time her tongue was up his bottom and his was in her brains. Their tongues were poison and both of them knew it, but still she sucked on his like she'd tear it from him. All around them people spoke lightly and laughingly, as if they did not know or were pretending not to know. She felt terror. Still she sucked and grabbed and so did the man, and she was gnawed by pain until she stopped being able to see or feel anything else.

I arrived back in L.A. at night. John picked me up and took me to dinner at an all-hours place with a boiling dark air. He looked angry. He kept telling me I had to learn to drive if I expected L.A. to work out for me. I drank too much and took him back to my place. Maybe I felt I owed him. Maybe I liked him. Maybe the demon whispered, *Do it with him!* In any case, it didn't work out. He kissed me too hard and touched me with violent shyness. We rolled awkwardly on my sectional couch; it came apart and almost dumped us on the floor.

"You're so beautiful," he blurted.

"I'm not beautiful," I blurted back. "I'm ugly."

He reared away, frowning. He was taking it as an insult, and with reason. But it would not be taken back. "You're beautiful," he said angrily.

"No, I'm not. I'm ugly."

He slapped me. I fell off the couch. He sat on the edge of it and held my shoulders. I could see in his eyes that his heart was pounding. "Stop saying that!" he said intensely.

"No! I'm ugly, ugly!" My voice *was* ugly.

He slapped me again. I tried to stop him. He held my wrists. Now we were really in it. The room was buzzing with the energy of it. "Tell me you're beautiful!" he said, coldly now. I wouldn't. "You're beautiful," he said, and slapped me again.

"John, please stop."

"Say you're beautiful."

But I couldn't get the words out. He slapped me until my ears sang. Finally, to stop the hitting, I said what he wanted to hear. He let go of me and sat back as if deflated.

"Don't you see?" My voice broke. I was nearly crying. "Don't you see how ugly I am?"

"No," he said quietly. "I don't." He crossed his legs and looked away.

I asked if he wanted a drink. He said no, that was okay. He said he was going to go but that he could tuck me in if I wanted. I said no, that was okay. I saw him to the door; we kissed quickly, on the lips.

We didn't see each other for a few weeks. Then I called him and asked him to drive me to a job, and things went back to normal. Except I didn't see anger in his eyes for a long time. I saw sadness.

I sit on the wet ground. My cruelty had been pointless. My kindness had been pointless. I remember rubbing the small bones in the center of Veronica's chest. I remember her surprise at being touched that way, the slight shift in her facial expression, as if feelings of love and friendship had been wakened by the intimate touch. The subtle muscles between her chest bones seemed to open a little. Then I left.

I never should've touched her like that and then turned around and left, leaving her chest opened and defenseless against the feelings that might come into it—feelings of love and friendship left unrequited once more. I put my head on my knees. I fantasize giving Veronica a full-body massage, with oil, with warm blankets wrapped around the resting limbs. Drops of sweat would've rolled from my arms to melt on her skin. When I finished, I would've held her in my arms. Except she never would have allowed any of that. She responded to the chest touch only because I took her by surprise.

My mind distends from me, groping the air in long fingers, looking for Veronica. The air is cold and bloated with moisture; Veronica is not here. I draw back inside myself. Again, I try to imagine. This time, I can. I imagine Veronica lying on her couch, descending slowly into darkness, the electronic ribbon of television sound breaking into particles of codified appetites, the varied contexts of which must have been impossible to remember. I wonder if, at certain moments, a peal of music or an urgent scream had leapt in tandem with the movement of the darkness and, if so, what it had felt like. I wonder if Veronica's spirit had tried to cling to the ersatz warmth of the TV noise; I think of a motherless baby animal clinging to a wire "mother" placed in its cage by curious scientists. I imagine Veronica drawing away from everything she had become on earth, withdrawing the spirit blood from what had been her self, allowing its limbs to blacken and fall off. I imagine Veronica's spirit stripped to its skeleton, then stripped of all but its shocked, staring eyes, yet clinging to life in a fierce, contracted posture that came from intense, habitual pain. I imagine the desiccated spirit as a tiny ash in enormous darkness. I imagine the dark penetrated by something Veronica at first could not see but could sense, something substantive and complete beyond any human definition of those words. In my mind's eye, it unfurled itself before Veronica. Without words it said, *I am Love*. And Veronica, hearing, came out of her contraction with brittle, stunted motions. In her eyes was recognition and disbelief, as if she were seeing what she had sought all her life and was terrified to believe in, lest it prove to be a hoax. *No*, it said to Veronica. *I am real. You have only to come.* And Veronica, drawing on the dregs of her strength and her trust, leapt into its embrace and was gone.

I stare at the clay dirt before me. I think of the great teeth, the lion cub torn to pieces in the adult's embrace. I imagine the methodical grind of digestion and blood. I imagine a moving black coil with white shapes inside it disintegrating in a grind of dirt, roots, and bones. I look up. Before me is a small tree with delicate orangey skin, its limbs, with dull sparse clusters of leaves and buds, arrayed like static flame. It plants its roots in the bones and the dirt and it drinks. I think of my sister's bit of flesh, red with triumph, and my mother's joyous head. I think of Veronica leaping into complete embrace, her love requited now forever.

After the memorial, I visited my family. While my mother and Sara were out, I asked my father to play *Rigoletto* for me. I told him I had a friend who loved a particular aria and that I'd like to hear it. "It's a love song," I explained. My father was happy to play it for me. I rarely spent time alone with him, and I even more rarely showed any interest in the things he loved. I wasn't really showing interest now. I didn't want to hear his *Rigoletto*. I wanted to hear Veronica's *Rigoletto*, and it didn't seem possible to hear both. If my father had met Veronica, he would've liked her. But he would not have wanted to meet her. She had loved a bisexual and thus had done wrong. It wouldn't matter to him that she'd loved the music he loved, that she might've understood his sentimental passions in ways that I could not.

With self-righteousness and also a wish that he might know me, I talked to my father about Veronica. I could tell immediately that he didn't want to hear what I said but that, because he respected death, he would suffer it. This made me all the more determined to make him hear me. I told him of Veronica's loneliness, her idiosyncrasy, her love of order. I told him how kind she had been to Sara. I told him that Veronica too had despised the way people used words like "choices." "It's terrible for anybody to get a disease like AIDS," I said. "But it seemed even worse for her. Because she tried so hard to be proper and dignified. She didn't want to be phony; she didn't want pity. She wound up being and getting what she didn't want. But at least she fought."

My father's face had the retracted look of a threatened animal—tense around the jaw, ready to bite. But he nodded to let me know he was listening.

I told him about sitting in the café with Veronica, listening to the aria from *Rigoletto*. "The sad thing is, I think she was telling me the truth. I think there probably was love between her and Duncan. But it got put together with a lot of other horrible stuff that both of them couldn't stop doing to themselves. So the love didn't help them. That's sadder to me than if they didn't love each other."

He didn't answer. Loud voices leapt up in declarative oblongs, then divided into fine, vibrant strands of delicacy and strife; father and daughter sang against each other. But my father didn't answer me. He didn't look at me. He said, "Now Rigoletto is talking to Gilda, his daughter. He's warning her not to leave the house. He says, 'It would be a good joke to dishonor the daughter of a jester.'"

He said this last phrase with relish, as if the idea of a daughter's honor was like a precious jewel to him, a jewel the world no longer valued (not even his own daughter!), and now here it was, celebrated and jealously guarded in *Rigoletto*. The *idea* of a daughter's honor, I thought bitterly, not the reality. In reality, he didn't honor me enough to answer what I'd said to him. I thought of telling him more, of forcing him to respond. But how could I insist that he face what I had failed to face?

"Now here's the love duet," he said. "The Duke has come to woo Gilda, only she doesn't know who he is."

I listened to see if this was the music I had heard in the café. I didn't recognize it. I imagined a vessel of fluted glass falling through the air, landing, and shattering. I had just said that there was love between Veronica and Duncan. But how could I believe Duncan had loved her, when he had been so careless with her life and his? How could I believe she even knew what love was? My thoughts faltered and will-lessly followed the music. No. People who loved each other would never treat each other, or allow themselves to be treated, with such indifference and cruelty. But even as I thought this, I felt, rising from under thought, the stubborn assertion of love living inside their disregard like a ghost, unable to make itself manifest, yet still felt, like emotion from a dream.

"Now Rigoletto's back," said my father. "And Gilda's gone! He cries out, 'Gilda! Gilda!'"

The words cracked his voice as they burst from his lips, more fierce and dramatic than the voice of the singer. The music rose in a great fist. He said it again, more quietly this time. "'Gilda! Gilda!'" I stared at him, shocked.

His voice was full of emotion, but his face was rigid, his eyes glassy.

When *Two Girls* was published, a reporter from the *Lexington Herald-Leader* in Kentucky called my father and asked him about his feelings regarding what I'd written, specifically what I'd written about the father who raped his daughter. Was he, my father, worried about what people would think? My father asked the reporter, "Do you know who Edgar Rice Burroughs is?" The reporter answered, "Wasn't he the one who wrote the Tarzan books?" "Yes," said my father. "That's right. Do you think Edgar Rice Burroughs was raised by apes?" I am not surprised that this wonderful exchange did not make it into the paper; it was too wonderful for the paper. It still makes me smile to think about it. The wonderfulness of it may've been made possible by the fact that my father never read *Two Girls*; he never read anything I wrote except maybe one or two stories. But still, the attitude is wonderful.

Some years ago I got an email from a former roommate from my college years. She said she had loved *Veronica*, particularly the way I wrote about my father. In truth the father in *Veronica* isn't my father, nor is the mother my mother. They share some of the same DNA, but they are not representatives of the actual people, any more than the parents in *Two Girls* are actual representations; I told my friend that. After that exchange, she apparently read more of my

work, because she wrote me another email shortly
after the first one, this time ironically very angry to
have recognized that I'd based a character in a story
on her. (And in this case, the character *was* based
more closely on her than the characters in *Veronica*
or *Two Girls* had been based on my parents.) I'm sure
it did not matter to her when I said that I did not
mean the portrait to be an unflattering one, and that
in fact many people found the character touching.
I'm sure it mattered less when I explained that, while
my memory of her had been the clay that built the
image of that character, in my mind the image was
not literally an image of her, the real person. I'm
guessing that sounded like fanciness to her. But I
was sincere. I have had characters based on me too,
and I didn't like it. So I understood. If I had known
where to find my former roommate when I wrote the
story, it's possible I would've shared it with her first.
But I hadn't seen or heard from her in decades; she
had found me through the website of a university
at which I had taught, but I would not have known
where to find her, especially since she had legally
changed her name. She had been important to me;
the story was important to me too. And in my mind
the story and the woman were very separate.

I sank down into darkness and lived among the demons
for a long, long time. I almost became one of them. But
I was not saved by an innocent girl or an angel crying in
Heaven. I was saved by another demon, who looked on

me with pity and so became human again. And because I pitied her in turn, I was allowed to become human too.

This comes at the very end of *Veronica*. The words are so simple and literal, but for me they evoke moral chaos and the difficulty of seeing clearly, the ferocity of conflicting impulses that might feel demonic or even be it. But the words also evoke pity and commonality, the painful touch of mutual woundedness that can, sometimes, reveal and transform. You can't say this to a person in real life about whom it might be true. Or more accurately you *wouldn't* say it. It would never occur to you. But you can write it in a story. Sometimes you have to write it.

Veronica is also based in part on a real person, someone I knew and did not know well. Someone who, at the time, I was not equipped to know well, and yet for whom I felt love. After her death I was sad to realize that I hadn't begun to comprehend the depth of what she had suffered, not only in her illness but in her life before that, the seemingly adverse forces that had formed her and to which she had reacted with courage and humor. It was not entirely my fault that I didn't comprehend—maybe it wasn't my fault at all. She was not easy to know or to get close to and neither was I. Still we found friendship and happiness in each other. Perhaps it sounds pathetic. But so many people live like this, finding each other only briefly; small people in every class and culture struggling to live and grow and find a shape for themselves in a monstrous, grinding world of social gaming, power, and florid illusion, while the million-headed hydra of mass culture screams, "We are this! We are that!" and explodes with pictures that promise to hold us forever, deathless and lifeless too.

Veronica is dense with similes and metaphors to the point of nearly choking. Even I find it hard to read in places. But similes and metaphors make secret connections to the essence shared by seemingly unrelated things, and it was through these connections that I tried to feel my way into the pith of this story about the mystery of feeling and identity, about the strange faces and forms we assume, sometimes randomly defined as beautiful or not; the social clothing with which we dress our raw, unknowable selves, searching for a form that will be recognized and understood by others, that can move in the world, love and be loved. Some people are very skilled at this, some are not at all. But how peculiar that it is so important; how terrible the loneliness and suffering that comes from simply getting the outfit wrong.

When I was working on *Veronica*, I had a frightening dream that I did not, at first, realize was related to the work. In the dream a woman had been murdered and disfigured, and somehow her body had been stolen. There was a police search and fear all around. With inarguable dream logic, I realized that the murdered woman was the Black Dahlia, the victim of an infamous torture-murder in L.A. in the 1940s. I picked up the phone to call the police, but there was already someone on the other end of the line, a spiteful accusing voice telling me that the body was buried in my backyard. I was afraid, but I decided that I had to dig the body up and rebury it. I don't remember exactly why I wanted to do this, if I were afraid of being caught with it or for some other reason. But I was determined to do it, even though I was also afraid to see the body. I went to my yard (which really looked like my yard, with its little vegetable garden) and began to dig. I was almost there when a literary critic who had disliked my first book intensely appeared and said, "You know you aren't supposed to be doing this, don't you?" And I stopped, confused. Because on one hand he was right, what I was doing looked very wrong and might even *be* wrong. But at the same time, I felt I was right, that it must be done, and I didn't know how to tell him this.

It was the presence of the literary critic that made me realize the dream was about the book I was writing. Once I made the connection it was obvious: the book was about a woman "murdered" by a virus that seemed malign in its attack on people who were trying to find passionate connection, a woman who was, in a figurative sense, murdered by lovelessness, in some way disfigured by it, then disfigured further by her misdirected attempts to find something better, searching, like the Black Dahlia, for glamor and beauty up until the moment of her terrible end, and then improperly buried by people who possibly understood her less than I did. I don't say "improperly buried" in a literal sense; she was cremated according to her wishes. But I attended her memorial, and I came away feeling that she was buried unknown, with sorrow but not enough honor.

This dream made me wonder if I was doing something wrong in writing the book, exploiting my friend's suffering or inappropriately, *foolishly*, defining that suffering in a way that she almost certainly would not have—not because she would've found what I wrote so objectionable, but because it could not feasibly have been completely true to who she was. It's an ancient idea that to take someone's picture is to take something of their soul, ancient but troubling; it's essentially about the power to trap someone in a representation. But fiction is to literal representation what painting is to photography; it's not claiming to be "real" in the same way. Even so, some unease about the subject was being expressed in my dream, and I took it seriously. But I also took seriously another way of seeing it. If someone has been wrongfully buried, it is not wrong to disinter and rebury them. On the contrary, it is actually proper.

I wasn't trying to be proper when I wrote the book. But I wanted to treat my friend with honor. I wanted to show her strange beauty and, by extension, the beauty of those who might be in any way like her. I wanted to show how I gradually felt, through the clumsy artifice and habitual hardness of the shape she had built for herself, something that was warm, alive, humorous, and deeply kind; something I can only call goodness. It strikes me that it was perhaps the awkward nature of her persona that made it easier to feel the real woman beneath it, the lush soul flowing through the cracks in the weird social mask. But this is also true: I came to feel the connection between that warm, live inner character and the outer "mask" that gave it expression in the world; I came to feel the private delightfulness of that connection. I wanted—*needed*—other people to feel it too.

I also wanted to honor the world I saw when I walked out into the canyon I lived in. After years of city living it astonished me, the depth, complexity, and aliveness of it. It made me aware that my body, every human body, was part of this naturally occurring amazement; indeed everything human that we might consider opposed to "nature" struck me instead as perverse—that is, a twisted and elaborately torqued aspect of nature. The living world seemed so powerful and yet so vulnerable under the structures imposed by humanity, not just physical structures but sociological structures, hierarchies, and things like fashion, that strange mask that believes itself ultimately and exclusively beautiful.

It wasn't that I thought fashion was bad. I was seduced and fascinated by it. But I suddenly saw it as strange, which was the way I had originally seen it. Like Alison, when I was young I didn't see what people were talking about when they referred to certain movie stars or models as "beautiful." I loved beauty, but when it came to how people looked my tastes were completely connected to how I felt about a person, how their personality got expressed by their body and face, the way they moved. In comparison, models and stars looked rigid and frightening, over-shaped by insistent hands wielding implements like tweezers and curling irons. But when I was writing *Veronica* (between the ages of thirty-eight and fifty-one!), I was perhaps finally becoming socially mature, for I was beginning to see the relationship of the "warm, live inner character" to the mask that gave it social shape. At the same time there was still fear. Because I was also seeing how the power of the mask, the social structure, could dominate to the point of killing the live, raw thing that had actually made it possible. This fear is described in Alison's dream of the man and the woman on a high-speed train, watching as a mob "hunts" a recycled bear trying to run on artificial legs while terrible music plays. *Bing bing bing bing!*

The last time I visited the beautiful canyon it was parched and brown and the trees were diseased. It is hard to remember it as it once was, so lush I could disappear into it, as if between curtains of heavy gray rain: on one side of me the structured world of beautiful homes, on the other side the world of trees and grasses, fungus and mashed leaves, silently disintegrating and re-forming, each thing there also wanting to find its shape. As I walked, these worlds blended with each other, came apart, and grew up again. The natural world held the social world with equanimity, even as the social world blithely devoured it; I believed I could sense every nuance of personality, impulse, emotion, expression, or artifice voicelessly alive, devouring, growing, and dying all around me. It was not about words; it was too big for words and did not care about words. But because I am a person I needed words; I needed form.

LOST CAT

Last year I lost my cat Gattino. He was very young, at seven months barely an adolescent. He is probably dead but I don't know for certain. For two weeks after he disappeared people claimed to have seen him; I trusted two of the claims because Gattino was blind in one eye, and both people told me that when they'd caught him in their headlights, only one eye shone back. One guy, who said he saw my cat trying to scavenge from a garbage can, said that he'd "looked really thin, like the runt of the litter." The pathetic words struck my heart. But I heard something besides the words, something in the coarse, vibrant tone of the man's voice, that immediately made another emotional picture of the cat: back arched, face afraid but excited, brimming and ready before he jumped and ran, tail defiant, tensile and crooked. Afraid but ready, startled by a large male—that's how he would've been. Even if he was weak with hunger. He had guts, this cat.

Gattino disappeared two and a half months after we moved. Our new house was on the outskirts of a college campus near a wildlife preserve. There are wooded areas in all directions, and many homes with decrepit outbuildings sit heavily, darkly low behind trees, in thick foliage. I spent hours at a time wandering around calling for Gattino. I put food out. I put a trap out. I put hundreds of flyers up. I walked around knocking on doors, asking people if I could look in their shed or under their porch. I contacted all the vets in the area. Every few days, someone would call and say they had seen a cat in a parking lot or behind their dorm. I would go and sometimes glimpse a grizzled adult melting away into the woods or behind a building or under a parked car.

After two weeks there were no more sightings. I caught three feral cats in my trap and let them go. It began to snow. Still searching, I would sometimes see little cat tracks in the snow; near dumpsters full of garbage, I also saw prints made by bobcats or coyotes. When the temperature went below freezing, there was icy rain. I kept looking. A year later I still had not stopped.

Six months after Gattino disappeared my husband and I were sitting in a restaurant having dinner with some people he had recently met, including an intellectual writer we both admired. The writer had considered renting the house we were living in and he wanted to know how we liked it. I said it was nice but it had been partly spoiled for me by the loss of our cat. I told him the story and he said, "Oh, that was your trauma, was it?"

I said yes. Yes, it was a trauma.

You could say he was unkind. You could say I was silly. You could say he was priggish. You could say I was weak.

•

A few weeks earlier, I had an email exchange with my sister Martha on the subject of trauma, or rather tragedy. Our other sister, Jane, had just decided not to euthanize her dying cat because she thought her little girls could not bear it; she didn't think she could bear it. Jane lives in chronic pain so great that sometimes she cannot move normally. She is under great financial stress and is often responsible for the care of her mother-in-law as well as the orphaned children of her sister-in-law who died of cancer. But it was her cat's approaching death that made her cry so that her children were frightened. "This is awful," said Martha. "It is not helping that cat to keep him alive, it's just prolonging his suffering. It's selfish."

Martha is in a lot of pain too, most of it related to diabetes and fibromyalgia. Her feet hurt so badly she can't walk longer than five minutes. She just lost her job and is applying for disability, which, because it's become almost impossible to get, she may not get and which, if she does get, will not be enough to live on, and we will have to help her. We already have to help her because her COBRA payments are so high that her unemployment isn't enough to cover them. This is painful for her too; she doesn't want to be the one everybody has to help. And so she tries to help us. She has had cats for years and so knows a lot about them; she wanted to help Jane by giving her advice, and she sent me several emails wondering about the best way to do it. Finally she forwarded me the message she had sent to Jane, in which she urged her to put the cat down. When she didn't hear from Jane, she emailed me some more, agonizing over whether Jane was angry at her and wondering what decision Jane would make regarding the cat. She said, "I'm afraid this is going to turn into an avoidable tragedy."

Impatient by then, I told her that she should trust Jane to make the right decision. I said, "This is sad, not tragic. Tragedy is thousands of people dying slowly of war and disease, injury and malnutrition. It's Hurricane Katrina, it's the war in Iraq, it's the earthquake in China. It's not one creature dying of old age."

After I sent the email, I looked up the word "tragic." According to *Webster's College Dictionary*, I was wrong; its second definition of the word is "extremely mournful, melancholy, or pathetic." I emailed Martha and admitted I'd been wrong, at least technically. I added that I still thought she was being hysterical. She didn't answer me.

I found Gattino in Italy. I was in Tuscany at a place called Santa Maddalena run by a woman named Beatrice von Rezzori who, in honor of her deceased husband, a writer, has made her estate into a small retreat for writers. When Beatrice learned that I love cats, she told me that down the road from her, two old women were feeding a yard full of semi-wild cats, including a litter of kittens who were very sick and going blind. Maybe, she said, I could help them out. No, I said, I wasn't in Italy to do that, and anyway, having done it before, I know it isn't an easy thing to trap and tame a feral kitten.

The next week one of her assistants, who was driving me into the village, asked if I wanted to see some kittens. Sure, I said, not making the connection. We stopped by an old farmhouse. A gnarled woman sitting in a wheelchair covered with towels and a thin blanket greeted the assistant without looking at me. Scrawny cats with long legs and narrow ferret hips stalked or lay about in the buggy, overgrown yard. Two kittens, their eyes gummed up with yellow fluid and flies swarming around their asses, were obviously sick but still lively; when I bent to touch them, they ran away. But a third kitten, smaller and bonier than the other two, tottered up to me mewing weakly, his eyes almost glued shut. He was a tabby, soft gray with strong black stripes. He had a long jaw and a big nose shaped like an eraser you'd stick on the end of a pencil. His big-nosed head was goblin-ish on his emaciated, potbellied body, his long legs almost grotesque. His asshole seemed disproportionately big on his starved rear. Dazedly he let me stroke his bony back—tentatively, he lifted his pitiful tail. I asked the assistant if she would help me take the kittens to a veterinarian and she agreed; this had no doubt been the idea all along.

The healthier kittens scampered away as we approached and hid in a collapsing barn; we were only able to collect the tabby. When we put him in the carrier, he forced open his eyes with a mighty effort, took a good look at us, hissed, tried to arch his back, and fell over. But he let the vets handle him. When they tipped him forward and lifted his tail to check his sex, he had a delicate, nearly human look of puzzled dignity in his one half-good eye, while his blunt muzzle expressed stoic animality. It was a comical and touching face.

They kept him for three days. When I came to pick him up, they told me he would need weeks of care involving eye ointment, ear drops, and nose drops. The baroness suggested I bring him home to America. No, I said, not possible. My husband was coming to meet me in a month and we were going to travel for two weeks; we couldn't take him with us. I would care for him, and by the time I left, he should be well enough to go back to the yard with a fighting chance.

So I called him "Chance." I liked Chance as I like all kittens; he liked me as a food dispenser. He looked at me neutrally, as if I were one more creature in the world, albeit a useful one. I had to worm him, de-flea him, and wash encrusted shit off his tail. He squirmed when I put the medicine in his eyes and ears, but he never tried to scratch me—I think because he wasn't absolutely certain of how I might react if he did. He tolerated my petting him, but seemed to find it a novel sensation rather than a pleasure.

Then one day he looked at me differently. I don't know exactly when it happened—I may not have noticed the first time. But he began to raise his head when I came into the room, to look at me intently. I can't say for certain what the look meant; I don't know how animals think or feel. But it seemed that he was looking at me with love. He followed me around my apartment. He sat in my lap when I worked at my desk. He came into my bed and slept with me; he lulled himself to sleep by gnawing softly on my fingers. When I petted him, his body would rise into my hand. If my face were close to him, he would reach out with his paw and stroke my cheek.

Sometimes I would walk on the dusty roads surrounding Santa Maddalena and think about my father, talking to him in my mind. My father had landed in Italy during World War II; he was part of the Anzio invasion. After the war he returned as a visitor with my mother, to Naples and to Rome. There is a picture of him standing against an ancient wall wearing a suit and a beret; he looks elegant, formidable, and at the same time tentative, nearly shy. On my walks I carried a large, beautiful marble that had belonged to my father; sometimes I took it out of my pocket and held it up in the sun as if it might function as a conduit for his soul.

My husband did not like the name Chance and I wasn't sure I did either; he suggested McFate, and so I tried it out. McFate grew stronger, grew a certain one-eyed rakishness, an engaged forward quality to his ears and the attitude of his neck that was gallant in his fragile body. He put on weight, and his long legs and tail became soigné, not grotesque. He had strong necklace markings on his throat; when he rolled on his back for me to pet him, his belly was beige and spotted like an ocelot. In a confident mood, he was like a little gangster in a zoot suit. Pensive, he was still delicate; his heart seemed closer to the surface than normal, and when I held him against me, it beat very fast and light. McFate was too big and heartless a name for such a small, fleet-hearted creature. "Mio Gattino," I whispered, in a language I don't speak to a creature who didn't understand words. "Mio dolce piccolo gatto."

•

One night when he was lying on his back in my lap, purring, I saw something flash across the floor; it was a small sky-blue marble rolling out from under the dresser. It stopped in the middle of the floor. It was beautiful, bright, and something not visible to me had set it in motion. It seemed a magical and forgiving omen, like the presence of this loving little cat. I put it on the windowsill next to my father's marble.

I spoke to my husband about taking Gattino home with us. I said I had fallen in love with the cat, and that I was afraid that by exposing him to human love I had awakened in him a need that was unnatural, that if I left him he would suffer from the lack of human attention that he never would have known had I not appeared in his yard. My husband said, "Oh no . . ." but in a bemused tone.

I would understand if he'd said it in a harsher tone. Many people would consider my feelings neurotic, a projection onto an animal of my own need. Many people would consider it almost offensive for me to lavish such love on an animal when I have by some standards failed to love my fellow beings—for example, orphaned children who suffer every day, not one of whom I have adopted. But I have loved people; I have loved children. And it seems that what happened between me and the children I chose to love was a version of what I was afraid would happen to the kitten. Human love is grossly flawed, and even when it isn't, people routinely misunderstand it, reject it, use it, or manipulate it. It is hard to protect a person you love from pain because people often choose pain; I am a person who often chooses pain. An animal will never choose pain; an animal can receive love far more easily than even a very young human. And so I thought it should be possible to shelter a kitten with love.

I made arrangements with the vet to get me a cat passport; Gattino endured the injection of an identifying microchip into his slim shoulder. Beatrice said she could not keep him in her house, and so I made arrangements for the vet to board him for the two weeks Peter and I traveled.

Peter arrived; Gattino looked at him and hid under the dresser. Peter crouched down and talked to him softly. Then he and I lay on the bed and held each other. In a flash, Gattino grasped the situation: the male had come. He was friendly. We could all be together now. He came onto the bed, sat on Peter's chest, and purred thunderously. He stayed on Peter's chest all night.

We took him to the veterinarian the next day. Their kennel was not the quiet, cat-only quarters one finds at upscale American animal hospitals. It was a common area that smelled of disinfectant and fear. The vet put Gattino in a cage near that of a huge, enraged dog that barked and growled, lunging against the door of its kennel. Gattino looked at me and began to cry. I cried too. The dog raged. There was a little bed in Gattino's cage and he hid behind it, then defiantly lifted his head to face the gigantic growling; that is when I first saw that terrified but ready expression, that willingness to meet whatever was coming, regardless of its size or its ferocity.

When we left the vet I was crying absurdly hard. But I was not crying exclusively about the kitten, any more than my sister Jane was crying exclusively about euthanizing her old cat. At the time I didn't realize it, but I was, among other things, crying about the children I once thought of as mine.

Caesar and his sister, Natalia, are now twelve and sixteen, respectively. When we met them they were six and ten. We met him first. We met him through the Fresh Air Fund, an organization that brings poor urban children (nearly all of whom are Black or Hispanic) up by bus to stay with country families (nearly all of whom are White). The Fresh Air Fund is an organization with an aura of uplift and hope about it, but its project is a difficult one that frankly reeks of pain. In addition to Caesar, we hosted another little boy, a seven-year-old named Ezekial. Imagine that you are six or seven years old and that you are taken to a huge city bus terminal, herded onto buses with dozens of other kids, all of you with big name tags hung around your neck, driven for three hours to a completely foreign place, and presented to total strangers with whom you are going to live for two weeks. Add that these total strangers, even if they are not rich, have materially more than you could ever dream of; that they are much bigger than you and, since you are staying in their house, you are supposed to obey them. Add that they are white as sheets. Realize that even very young children "of color" have often learned that White people are essentially the enemy. Wonder: Who in God's name thought this was a good idea?

We were aware of the race-class thing. But we thought we could override it. Because we wanted to love these children. I fantasized about serving them meals, reading to them at night, tucking them in. Peter fantasized about sports on the lawn, riding bikes together. You could say we were idealistic. You could say we were stupid. I don't know what we were.

We were actually only supposed to have one, and that one was Ezekial. We got Caesar because the FAF called from the bus as it was on its way up full of kids and told us that his host family had pulled out at the last minute due to a death in the family, so could we take him? We said yes because we were worried about how we were going to entertain a single child with no available playmates; I made the FAF representative promise that if it didn't work out, she would find a backup plan. Of course it didn't work out. Of course there was no backup plan. The kids hated each other, or, more precisely, Ezekial hated Caesar. Caesar was younger and more vulnerable in every way: less confident, less verbal, possessed of no athletic skills. Ezekial was lithe, with muscular limbs and an ungiving facial symmetry that sometimes made his naturally expressive face cold and masklike. Caesar was big and plump, with deep eyes and soft features that were so generous they seemed nearly smudged at the edges. Ezekial was a clever bully, merciless in his teasing, and Caesar could only respond by ineptly blustering "Ima fuck you up!"

"Look," I said, "you guys don't have to like each other, but you have to get along. Deep down, don't you want to get along?"

"No!" they screamed.

"He's ugly!" added Ezekial.

"Oh, dry up, Ezekial," I said, "we're all ugly, okay?"

"Yeah," said Caesar, liking this idea very much, "we're all ugly!"

"No," said Ezekial, his voice dripping with malice, "you're ugly."

"Try again," I said. "Can you get along?"

"Okay," said Caesar. "I'll get along with you, Ezekial." And you could hear his gentle, generous nature in his voice. You could hear it, actually, even when he said "Ima fuck you up!" Gentleness sometimes expresses itself with the violence of pain or fear and so looks like aggression. Sometimes cruelty has a very charming smile.

"No," said Ezekial, smiling. "I hate you."

Caesar dropped his eyes.

We were in Florence for a week. It was beautiful, but crowded and hot, and I was too full of sadness and confusion to enjoy myself. Nearly every day I pestered the vet, calling to see how Gattino was. "He's fine," they said. "The dog isn't there anymore. Your cat is playing." I wasn't assuaged. I had nightmares; I had a nightmare that I had put my kitten into a burning oven and then watched him hopelessly try to protect himself by curling into a ball; I cried to see it, but could not undo my action.

Peter preferred the clever, athletic Ezekial and Caesar knew it. I much preferred Caesar, but we had made our original commitment to Ezekial and to his mother, whom we had spoken with on the phone. So I called the FAF representative and asked her if she could find another host family for Caesar. "Oh great," she snapped. But she did come up with a place. It sounded good: a single woman, a former schoolteacher, and an experienced host of a boy she described as responsible and kind, not a bully. "But don't tell him he's going anywhere else," she said. "I'll just pick him up and tell him he's going to a pizza party. You can bring his stuff over later."

I said, "Okay," but the idea didn't sit right with me. So I took Caesar out to a park to tell him. Or rather I tried. I said, "You don't like Ezekial, do you?" and he said, "No, I hate him." I asked if he would like to go stay at a house with another boy who would be nice to him where they would have a pool and—"No," he said. "I want to stay with you and Peter." I couldn't believe it—I did not realize how attached he had become. But he was adamant. We had the conversation three times, and none of those times did I have the courage to tell him he had no choice. I pushed him on the swing set and he cried, "Mary! Mary! Mary!" And then I took him home and told Peter I had not been able to do it.

Peter told Ezekial to go into the other room and we sat Caesar down and told him he was leaving. "No," he said. "Send the other boy away." Ezekial came into the room. "Send him away!" cried Caesar. "Ha ha," said Ezekial, "you go away!" The FAF woman arrived. I told her what was happening. She sighed. "Oh, God. Why don't you just let me handle this?" And she did. She said, "Okay, Caesar, it's like this. You were supposed to go stay with another family but then somebody in that family *died* and you couldn't go there."

"Somebody *died*?" asked Caesar.

"Yes, and Peter and Mary were *kind* enough to let you come stay with them for a little while, and now it's time to—"

"I want to stay here!" Caesar screamed, and clung to the mattress.

"Caesar," said the FAF woman. "I talked to your mother. *She* wants you to go."

Caesar lifted his face and looked at her for a searching moment. "Lady," he said calmly, "you a liar." And she was. I'm sure of it. Caesar's mother was almost impossible to get on the phone and she spoke no English.

This is probably why the FAF woman screamed, actually screamed: "How dare you call me a liar! Don't you ever call an adult a liar!"

Caesar sobbed and crawled across the bed and clutched at the corner of the mattress; I crawled after him and tried to hold him. He cried, "You a liar too, Mary!" and I fell back in shame.

The FAF lady then made a noble and transparently insincere offer: "Caesar," she said, "if you want, you can come stay with me and my family. We have a big farm and dogs and—"

He screamed, "I would never stay with you, lady! You're gross! Your whole family is gross!"

I smiled with pure admiration for the child.

The woman cried, "Oh, I'm gross, am I?"

And he was taken down the stairs screaming, "They always send me away!"

Then Ezekial did something extraordinary. He threw his body across the stairs, grabbing the bannister with both hands to block the exit. He began to whisper at Caesar, and I leaned in close thinking, *If he is saying something to comfort, I am going to stop this thing cold.* But even as his body plainly said, *Please don't do this,* his mouth spitefully whispered, "Ha ha! You go away! Ha ha!"

I stepped back and said to Caesar, "This is not your fault!" He cried, "Then send the other boy away!" Peter pried Ezekial off the bannister and Caesar was carried out. I walked outside and watched as Peter put the sobbing little boy into the woman's giant SUV. Behind me Ezekial was dancing behind the screen door, incoherently taunting me as he sobbed too, breathless with rage and remorse.

If gentleness can be brutish, cruelty can sometimes be so closely wound in with sensitivity and gentleness that it is hard to know which is what. Animals are not capable of this. That is why it is so much easier to love an animal. Ezekial loved animals; he was never cruel with them. Every time he entered the house, he greeted each of our cats with a special touch. Even the shy one, Tina, liked him and let him touch her. Caesar, on the other hand, was rough and disrespectful—and yet he wanted the cats to like him. One of the things he and Ezekial fought about was which of them Peter's cat Bitey liked more. On the third day in Florence I called Martha—the sister I later scolded for being hysterical about a cat—and asked for help. She said she would psychically communicate with Gattino. She said I needed to do it too. "He needs reassurance," she said. "You need to tell him every day that you're coming back."

I know how foolish this sounds. I know how foolish it is. But I needed to reach for something with a loving touch. I needed to reach even if nothing was physically there within my grasp. I needed to reach even if I touched darkness and sorrow. And so I did it. I asked Peter to do it too. We would go to churches and kneel on pews and pray for Gattino, for Caesar, for Natalia, for Martha and Jane. We were not alone; the pews were always full of people, old, young, rich and poor, of every nationality, all of them reaching, even if nothing was physically there. "Please comfort him, please help him," I asked. "He's just a little thing." Because that was what touched me: not the big idea of tragedy, but the smallness and tenderness of this bright, lively creature. From Santissima Annunziata, Santa Croce, and Santa Maria Novella, we sent messages to and for our cat.

I went into the house to try to comfort Ezekial, who was sobbing that his mother didn't love him. I said that wasn't true, that she did love him, that I could hear it in her voice—and I meant it, I had heard it. But he said, "No, no, she hates me. That's why she sent me here." I told him he was lovable and in a helpless way I meant that too. Ezekial was a little boy in an impossible situation he had no desire to be in and who could only make it bearable by manipulating and trying to hurt anyone around him. He was also a little boy used to rough treatment, and my attempts at caring only made me a sucker in his eyes. As soon as I said "lovable" he stopped crying on a dime and starting trying to get things out of me, most of which I mistakenly gave him.

Caesar was used to rough treatment too—but he was still looking for good treatment. When I went to visit him at his new host house, I expected him to be angry at me. He was in the pool when I came, and as soon as he saw me, he began splashing toward me, shouting my name. I had bought him a life jacket so he would be safer in the pool and he was thrilled by it; kind treatment did not make me a sucker in his eyes. He had too strong a heart for that.

But he got kicked out of the new host's home anyway. Apparently he called her a bitch and threatened to cut her. I could see why she wouldn't like that. I could also see why Caesar would have to let his anger out on somebody if he didn't let it out on me.

Ezekial was with me when I got the call about Caesar's being sent home. The FAF woman who told me said that Caesar had asked her if he was going back to his "real home, with Peter and Mary." I must've looked pretty sick when I hung the phone up, because Ezekial asked, "What's wrong?" I told him, "Caesar got sent home and I feel really sad." He said, "Oh." There was a moment of feeling between us—a moment that could scarcely have felt good to him—which meant that he had to throw a violent tantrum an hour later in order to destroy that moment.

After Ezekial left I wrote a letter to Caesar's mother. I told her that her son was a good boy, that it wasn't his fault that he'd gotten sent home. I had someone translate it into Spanish for me, and then I copied it onto a card and sent it with some pictures I had taken of Caesar swimming. It came back, MOVED, ADDRESS UNKNOWN. Peter told me that I should take the hint and stop trying to have any further contact. Other people thought so too. They thought I was acting out of guilt and I was. But I was acting out of something else too. I missed the little boy. I missed his deep eyes, his clumsiness, his generosity, his sweetness. I called the Fresh Air Fund. The first person I talked to wouldn't give me any information. The next person gave me an address in East New York; she gave me a phone number too. I sent the letter again. I prayed the same way I did later for Gattino: "Spare him. Comfort him. Have mercy on this little person." And Caesar heard me—he did. When I called his house nearly two months after he'd been sent back home, he didn't seem surprised at all. He asked about Bitey; he asked about his life jacket. We talked about those things for a while. Then I told him that I was sad when he left. He said, "Did you cry?" And I said, "Yes. I cried." He was silent; I could feel his presence so intensely, like you feel a person next to you in the dark. I asked to talk to his mother; I had someone with me who could speak to her in Spanish, to ask her for permission to have contact with her son. I also spoke to his sister, Natalia. Even before I met her, I could hear her beauty in her voice—curious, vibrant, expansive in its warmth and longing.

I sent them books and toys when Caesar's birthday came. I talked more to Natalia than to her brother; he was too young to talk for long on the phone. She reached out to me with her voice as if with her hand, and I held it. We talked about her trouble at school, her fears of the new neighborhood, and movies she liked, which were mostly about girls becoming princesses. When Caesar talked to me, it was half-coherent stuff about cartoons and fantasies. But he could be suddenly very mature. "I want to tell you something," he said once. "I feel something but I don't know what it is."

I wanted to meet their mother; I very much wanted to see Caesar and meet his sister. Peter was reluctant because he considered the relationship inappropriate, but he was willing to do it for me. We went to East New York with a Spanish-speaking friend. We brought board games and cookies. Their mother kissed us on both cheeks and gave us candles. She said they could come to visit for Holy Week—Easter. Natalia said, "I'm so excited." I said, "I am too."

And I was. I was so excited I was nearly afraid. When Peter and I went into Manhattan to meet them at Penn Station, it seemed a miracle to see them there. As soon as we got to our house Caesar threw a tantrum on the stairs—the scene of his humiliation. But this time I could keep him, calm him, and comfort him. I could make it okay, better than okay. Most of the visit was lovely. We have pictures in our photo album of the kids riding their bikes down the street on a beautiful spring day and painting Easter eggs; we have a picture of Natalia getting ready to mount a horse with an expression of mortal challenge on her face; we have another picture of her sitting atop the horse in a posture of utter triumph.

On the way back to New York on the train, Caesar asked, "Do you like me?" I said, "Caesar, I not only like you, I love you." He looked at me levelly and said, "Why?" I thought a long moment. "I don't know why yet," I said. "Sometimes you don't know why you love people, you just do. One day I'll know why and then I'll tell you."

When we introduced Gattino to the other cats we expected drama and hissing. There wasn't much. He was tactful.

He was gentle with the timid cats, Zuni and Tina, slowly approaching to touch noses or following at a respectful distance, sometimes sitting near Tina and gazing at her calmly. He teased and bedeviled only the tough young one, Biscuit, and it's true that she didn't love him. But she accepted him.

Then things began to go wrong—little things at first. I discovered I'd lost my passport; Peter lost a necklace I'd given him; I lost the blue marble from Santa Maddalena. For the sixth summer in a row, Caesar came to visit us, and it went badly. My sister Martha was told she was going to be laid off. We moved to a new house and discovered that the landlord had left old junk all over the house, the stove was broken and filled with nests of mice, one of the toilets was falling through the floor, and the windowpanes were broken.

But the cats loved it. Especially Gattino. The yard was spectacularly beautiful and wild, and when he turned six months old, we began letting him out for twenty minutes at a time, always with one of us in the yard with him. We wanted to make sure he was cautious and he was: he was afraid of cars; he showed no desire to go into the street or really even out of the yard, which was large. We let him go out longer. Everything was fine. The house got cleaned up; we got a new stove. Somebody found Peter's necklace and gave it back. Then late one afternoon I had to go out for a couple of hours. Peter wasn't home. Gattino was in the yard with the other cats; I thought, *He'll be okay.* When I came back he was gone.

Because he had never gone near the road I didn't think he would cross the street—and I thought if he had, he would be able to see his way back, since across the street was a level, low-cut field. So I looked behind our house, where there was a dorm in a wooded area, and to both sides of us. Because we had just moved in, I didn't know the terrain, and so it was hard to look in the dark—I could only see a jumble of foliage and buildings, houses, a nursery school, and what I later realized was a deserted barn. I started to be afraid. Maybe that is why I thought I heard him speak to me, in the form of a very simple thought that entered my head, plaintively, as if from outside. It said, *I'm scared.*

I wish I had thought back, *Don't worry. Stay where you are. I will find you.* Instead I thought, *I'm scared too. I don't know where you are.* It is crazy to think that the course of events might've been changed if different sentences had appeared in my mind. But I think it anyway.

The second day we made posters and began putting them up in all the dorms, houses, and campus buildings. We alerted campus security, who put out a mass email to everyone who had anything to do with the college.

The third night, just before I went to sleep, I thought I heard him again. *I'm lonely,* he said.

The fifth night we got the call from a security guard saying that he saw a small, thin, one-eyed cat trying to forage in a garbage can outside a dorm. The call came at two in the morning and we didn't hear it because the phone was turned down. The dorm was very close by; it was located across the street from us, on the other side of the field.

•

Something I wonder: Who decides which relationships are appropriate and which are not? Which deaths are tragic and which are not? Who decides what is big and what is little? Is it a matter of numbers or physical mass or intelligence? If you are a little creature or a little person dying alone and in pain, you may not remember or know that you are little. If you are in enough pain you may not remember who or what you are; you may know only your suffering, which is immense. Who decides? What decides—common sense? Can common sense dictate such things? Common sense is an excellent guide to social structures, but does it ever have anything to do with who or what moves you?

Then Ginger was alone and standing, though reeling, before a huge, saturating image of the beautiful young man. She nearly fell and the voice said, "Stay on your feet, we're not done yet."

She looked to see who was speaking. It was a demon. It looked like a man, but she knew it was a demon. Its eyes were lit by inhuman strength, and its gaze ate her from the inside. She nearly fell again; she felt its will like a cold iron hand that held her steady.

"Now see him as he is with himself."

Both my sisters and I sat with my father when he was dying; we all took care of him with the help of a hospice worker who stopped by every day. But Martha was alone with him when he died. She said that she had felt death come into the room. She said that death felt very gentle.

Later she told us that she felt and even saw terrible things before he died. But she seemed at peace about witnessing his death.

When Martha returned home she had to go right back to work. She was not close to the people she worked with and they were not ideal confidants. But she needed to talk to someone and so she did. When she described my father's life to a coworker, he found it absurd that Martha seemed to place as much emphasis on the death of my father's dog as she did on the death of his parents, and he spoke to her coolly. "I love dogs," he said. "I'm sad when a dog dies. But no dog should ever be compared to family."

When I was out looking for the cat, so late that no one else was around, I remembered this story, and I wished I had been with my sister when her coworker spoke to her that way. I would have said, *Imagine you are a nine-year-old boy and you have lost your mother. You are in shock, and because you are in shock you are reduced to a little animal who knows its survival is in danger. So you say to yourself,* Okay, I don't have a mom. I can deal with that. *And then the next year your father dies. You think,* A'ight. I don't have a dad either. I can deal with that too. *Then your dog dies. And you think,* Not even a dog? I can't even have a dog? I would've said, *Of course the dog didn't mean as much to him as his parents did, you moron. His parents meant so much to him he could not afford to feel their loss. The dog he could feel, and through the door of that feeling came everything else.*

When my father was alive, he and Martha were distant, uncomprehending, nearly hostile. He was cold to her, and she felt rejected by him. As he became more and more unhappy with age and was eventually rejected by my mother, he tried to reach out to Martha. But the pattern was too set. During one of our last Christmas visits to him, I saw my father and Martha act out a scene that looked like a strange imitation of a cruel game between a girl who is madly in love with an indifferent boy and the boy himself. She kept asking him over and over again, did he like the present she had gotten him? Did he really, really like it? Would he use it? Did he want to try it out now? And he responded stiffly, irritably, with increasing distance. She behaved as if she wanted to win his love, but she was playing the loser so aggressively that it was almost impossible for him to respond with love, or to respond at all. What was the real feeling here? What was the dream or the self-deceit? Something real was happening, and it was terrible to see. But it was so disguised that it is hard to say what it actually was. Still, as he lay dying, she was the one who knew to hold his hand, to sing to him.

My sister offered my father love in a form he could not accept, just as he, with increasing desperation, offered my mother love she could not accept or even recognize. In each offering purity and perversity made a strange pattern; each rejection made the pattern more complete. If he had acted differently toward Martha, it is possible that he could've broken this pattern. Because he was the parent, it's possible that the burden was on him to do so. But I don't think he could. He wasn't sophisticated when it came to his emotions. His emotions were too raw for sophistication.

Before I met Gattino, before I went to Italy, I talked with Caesar on the phone, and during that conversation he asked why I sent his mother money. I should have said, *Because I love you and I want to help her take care of you.* Instead I said, "Because when I first met your mother and she told me she made $6.40 an hour, I felt ashamed as an American. I felt like she deserved more support for coming here and trying to get a better life."

He said, "What you're saying is really fucked up."

I said, "Why?"

He said, "I don't know, it just is."

I said, "Put words on it. Try."

He said, "I can't."

I said, "Yes, you can. Why is what I'm saying fucked up?"

He said, "Because it's good enough that she came here to get a better life."

I said, "I agree. But she should be acknowledged. I have a hard job and sometimes I hate it, but I get acknowledged and she should too. And somebody besides me should do it, but nobody is, so I am."

He said, "People are acknowledging her. She makes more money now."

I said, "That's good. But it still should be more."

He said, "You act like you feel sorry for her."

I said, "I do, so what? Sometimes I feel sorry for Peter, sometimes I feel sorry for myself. There's no shame in that."

He said, "But you talk about my mom like she's some kind of freak."

I said, "I don't think that."

He said, "You talk about her like you think you're better than her."

And for a moment I was silent. Because I do think that—rather, I feel it. Before God, as souls, I don't feel it. But socially, as creatures of this earth, I do. I'm wrong to feel it. But I do feel it. I feel it partly because of things Caesar and Natalia have told me.

He heard my hesitation and he began to cry. And so I lied to him. Of course he knew I lied.

He said, "For the first time I feel ashamed of my family."

I said I was sorry; I tried to reassure him. He asked me if I would take money from someone who thought they were better than me, and I said, "Frankly, yes. If I needed the money I would take as much as I could, and I would say to myself, *Fuck you for thinking you're better than me.*"

Passionately, he said he would never, ever do that.

I snapped, "Don't be so sure about that. You don't know yet."

He stopped crying.

I said, "Caesar, this is really hard. Do you think we can get through it?"

He said, "I don't know." Then, "Yes."

I asked him if he remembered the time on the train when he was only seven, when he asked me why I loved him and I said I didn't know yet. "Now I know why," I said. "This is why. You're not somebody who just wants to hear nice bullshit. You care. You want to know what's real. I love you for that."

This was the truth. But sometimes even loving truth isn't enough. He said he was sorry he'd bothered me and that he was tired. I asked him if he still felt mad at me. He hesitated and then said, "No. Inside, I am not mad at you, Mary."

•

For months after Gattino disappeared, I still dreamed of him at least once a week. I would dream that I was standing in the yard calling him, like I had before he'd disappeared, and he'd come to me the way he had come in reality: running with his tail up, leaping slightly in his eagerness, leaping finally into my lap. Often in the dream he didn't look like himself; often I blended him with other cats I have had in the past. In one dream I blended him with Caesar. In this dream, Caesar and I were having an argument, and I got so angry I opened my mouth, threatening to bite him. He opened his mouth too, in counter-threat. And when he did that, I saw that he had the small, sharp teeth of a kitten.

"Please," Ginger cried, "it hurts!"

The demon laughed. "Of course it hurts! You're in Hell, girl! And you came here deliberately! You came to steal!"

THE MARE

On earth, Velvet's mother prays: *Remember, gracious Virgin Mary, that never was it known that anybody who fled to thy protection, implored thy help, or sought thine intercession was left unaided. Confident in this, I fly to you, Virgin of virgins, my mother; to you I come, before you I stand, sinful and sorrowful.*

My daughter hangs on my back, my son to my breast. In my dreams a woman cried that her baby had been cut from her heart before it could reach her womb. A nightmare story like the story my mother used to tell, only more horrible. Why was the baby in her chest? My daughter stirs, like she feels the nightmare through my back.

And Ginger says: It was a year later that I started talking about adoption. At first Paul said, "We can't." Although he didn't say it, I think he was hurt that I hadn't really tried to have his child, but now wanted some random one. Also, his daughter from his first marriage, Edie, didn't want to go to school where he teaches and he'd promised to pay her tuition at Brown after his ex-wife had thrown a fit about it. Even if money weren't an issue, he didn't think we would have the physical energy for a baby. "What about an older child?" I asked. "Like a seven-year-old?" But we wouldn't know anything about the kid, he said. It would come fully formed in ways that would be problematic and invisible to us until it was too late.

We went back and forth on the subject, not intensely, but persistently, in bed at night and at breakfast. Months went by; spring came and the dry, frigid winter air went raw and wet, then grew full and soft. Paul's eyes began to be soft when we talked too. One of his friends told him about an organization that brought poor inner-city kids up to stay with country families for a few weeks. The friend suggested it as a way to "test the waters," to see what it might be like to have somebody else's fully formed kid around.

We called the organization and it sent us information, including a brochure of White kids and Black kids holding flowers and smiling, of White adults hugging Black kids and a slender Black girl touching a woolly white sheep. It was sentimental and flattering to White vanity and manipulative as hell. It was also irresistible. It made you think the beautiful sentiments you pretend to believe in really *might* be true. "Yes," I said. "Let's do it. It's only two weeks. We could find out what it's like. We could give a kid a nice summer, anyway."

She prays: *God help us. Mother of God, do not despise us but hear and have mercy on us, me and my children, and on the terrible woman in my dreams. Please. Despise us not but with mercy hear and answer.*

Ginger thinks: She was so beautiful, so solid in her body, but so shy in the way she took things. I felt excited and scared about how to act—I couldn't even respond properly to my own family, so how could I take care of a needy child from another culture? It was a cliché to think that way, but I could feel her difference. At the same time, I could feel her child's goodness, her willingness to help us, and that was more compelling. We gave her privacy to talk to her mother, and when we got downstairs, I whispered to Paul, "What do you think?"

"She's a sweetheart," he said. "It's going to be fine."

She came downstairs almost immediately. Her face was sad, and the shift of emotion was profound—for a moment I thought something terrible had happened. But she just said her mom wasn't home. I got her to eat some cookies and asked her what she wanted to do. I said we could go to see the town or to the lake or the bowling alley or for a walk around the neighborhood. Or we could walk over and visit the horses in the stables across the road from us. "The horses," she said, some cookie in her mouth. "We could see the horses?"

Velvet says: I said we could go to the horses, but I didn't really care. I just said that because I knew they were close—I *did* want to see horses, but I didn't feel like it right then. Because my mom was gone when I called and I felt alone, like she was *really* gone, and I was stuck here with a devil on the wall and nice people who didn't have anything to do with me.

But I went with the lady, Ginger. She talked about something, I don't know what. I was trying to count the hours in the days I had left and trying to subtract how much time I'd been there, starting from the bus. We passed through a gate with a sign and a picture of a horse on it; suddenly there was too much space around us—green and green and green with some little fences and, in the distance, a big building with a giant hole for a door. I wanted to reach for Ginger's hand, and that made me mad at myself because I was too old for that. Then she said, "They give riding lessons for kids here. That's something we could do if you want to."

I didn't say anything.

And then we came to the building with the giant door.

"Here's the stable," said Ginger.

It looked scary from a distance, but inside it was not. It was dark and warm. It was all wooden. The smell of it was deep. You could feel it, like it was breathing all around you, but it wasn't scary, it was the opposite. And there was a horse, looking at me from an opening in his cage. A sign over him said GRAYLIE, and there were pictures and a dirty red teddy bear next to his face. And then there was another one and another one: DIAMOND CHIP JIM (he had a purple fish toy and a bunch of fake flowers), BLUE BOY (he had a bunch of plastic bottles), BABY (she had a doll), OFFICER MURPHY (he had a bunch of stuff written on some papers and a blue ribbon), LITTLE TINA (she didn't have nothin'). There were some people too, walking around, but I didn't notice them. The horses were all looking at me and Ginger, and some of them were saying things: *Who are you? Come over here! Have you got something for me? I'm lonely. Don't bother me!* And then there was a gold-brown horse kicking and *biting* the hell out of her cage. Her eyes were rolling in her head and you could see the whites around them. But she was the best one so far, not the most beautiful, the *best*. There were no ribbons or toys or even a name on her cage, just a sign that read DO NOT TOUCH. I came close to her and she looked at me. That's when I saw the scars on her face, straight deep scars around her nose and eyes. She turned her head all the way to one side and then the other. I thought, *Your scars are like the thorns on Jesus's heart.* She stopped biting and kicking. I could see her think in the dark part of her eye. The white part got softer. The wonderful horse came up to me. I put my hand out to her. She touched it with her mouth.

•

Ginger: When she asked me why I didn't have kids I told her it was because I was an artist. I told her that if I'd had kids I didn't think I could do art. I thought art was what I did best, and I should try to do it even if I never made any money.

She was quiet a long time after I said this. I felt her puzzlement and then her acceptance.

Velvet: I had woken up pressed against my mother and little brother, and now I was alone in a bed with a pink cover and this blond lady sitting there, her face full of niceness with pain around the edges. Why was this even happening? I missed my mom next to me. Instead Ginger was next to me, reading with her eyes down, her voice like white dream horses running across the sky: A little girl playing hide-and-seek goes into the closet to hide and comes out in a snowy country. She meets a man with hairy goat legs (like Paul!). Hairy-Leg says a beautiful witch has come to the land and made it winter all the time. Ginger looked at me with her blue, blue eyes and then away. Hairy-Leg says the little girl has been sent to help, that only she can help.

Ginger: That night Paul and I went to bed feeling close, our arms wrapped around each other. When I woke up in the middle of the night, scared and sad from a dream I couldn't remember, I reached for him, pressing myself against his back. But instead of his name I heard myself say, "M'lindie!" Which is what I called Melinda when I was five. Then I was awake enough to know it was Paul's big male back I was holding—but still I whispered, "Melinda." And then I fell back to sleep.

Which maybe isn't as weird as it sounds. Melinda and I slept together until I was ten and she was twelve.

Velvet: I woke up feeling sad without knowing why. Then I realized why. I was remembering a time a long time ago when I thought my mom was a witch and I wouldn't eat what she made me. I wouldn't eat, and at first she yelled at me and then she was worried I was sick. She stroked my hair and asked if my stomach hurt and tried to give me tea with ginger. I was too afraid to drink it, but because she was talking so nice I told her why. I said, "Mami, I'm afraid a witch might be living in your body." And then the witch came out. Her eyes got red flames inside them and she left the room angrily; Dante laughed and pointed at me, because I would be whipped, not him. But when she came back with the belt, he shut up and put his hands over his pee-pee. I tried to run, but she grabbed my hair and pulled up my shirt and she beat me until I bled, until Dante was screaming louder than me. Then she sat and dropped the belt, put her hands over her face, and cried. I heard Manuel; he was looking at me out his cracked-open door. I pulled my shirt down.

Ginger: I stood to the side and watched Velvet secure the horse in the middle of the barn and begin to groom it. The way she moved was very different from the way she moved around the house; there was no deference or absentmindedness in her, just purpose. She looked bigger, stronger, and completely comfortable with the huge animal. "She's a natural," said Pat. "It takes most kids twice as long to get where she got today."

Velvet: When I saw Ginger there I felt the same as when I first got in the car with her and Paul, that she was a strange nice lady with a mixed face who didn't have anything to do with me. I liked her taking my picture; I liked it that I was going to have some pictures to take back home with me. But it was strange.

And then it wasn't. I can't explain it. Just all of a sudden, it made sense, her being there, my being with her. I still don't know why. But I got it. It was like I was looking at puzzle pieces all over the floor that magically got snapped into place and I went, "Oh, okay." I still couldn't say what the picture was. But it made sense.

Ginger: It was like we were both living a dream we had known from television and advertisements and children's books, a dream that neither of us had believed in, yet both of us had longed for without knowing it. A dream in which love and happiness were the norm.

Velvet: That night they both sat on the bed and read to me like always. The witch had hypnotized this boy by giving him too much candy, and it made him bad so that he went over to the witch's side against his family. They took turns reading and their voices made me think about my mom, singing at night:

The little chicks say "pio pio pio"
When they are hungry, when they are too cold to sleep.
The mother looks for corn and wheat,
She gives them food to eat.

"What's wrong with satisfying a mutual need?"

"Nothing, if you're talking about people in an equal position. But you aren't. She's a disadvantaged child. She has needs you can't satisfy. It's unfair to act like you can. And—"

"I can get her horse-riding lessons."

"—you have needs *she* can't satisfy."

I dreamed that I woke up and it was day, but only for me; that it was light for me and dark for Paul and Ginger and they were sleeping. I got up and walked through their house, looking at everything: the fruit in the bowls, the colored curtains, the paintings and tiny giraffe toys on the windowsill. I went out into their yard and looked at Paul's garden; in the plants and flowers I saw a trapdoor, and I knew that it was the door to Hell. I was scared, but then I realized that my grandfather was there, in the backyard. "Don't be afraid," he said. "The Devil isn't paying attention—now is your chance. I'll guard the door."

"Grandfather," I said, "why are you telling me to go to Hell?"

"Because someone you love is there and she is in danger of being lost."

"Who is it?"

"I can't tell you."

"Is she evil?"

"No. But she is close to evil. You can help her because you call to the good in her. You have to hurry, she is getting more lost every second."

Ginger: Velvet's mother was short, thick, powerful looking. She was much older than I imagined, I thought at least forty, maybe close to fifty. Her heavy jaw and low brow had none of her daughter's lush softness. She was very light-skinned and her features were small, hard, and fine. Even if she lacked her daughter's dark beauty, she had obviously been pretty once. It took me a minute to realize that the power in her body didn't come from her musculature or size, but from her character; she sat in her body like it was a tank. When I walked in with Velvet, she looked at me first; it was an intensely focused look, rapid and bright, going instinctively from assessment to approval in seconds. She greeted her daughter, but her eyes dimmed at the sight of the child, no longer approving but acknowledging only. Docile, Velvet sat on the couch next to her. I sat in a chair to the side. In front of us were two erect, alert, smiling women from the Fresh Air Fund, one of whom was Carmen, the sweet-voiced Latina who had translated for me on the phone. But Mrs. Vargas sat there like she was alone in her tank, bored like a fighter is bored when there is no fight.

In the coffee shop, though, her demeanor changed. She sat across from me, next to Velvet, touching the girl with a proprietary air. When she looked at me, her face was open. I couldn't understand what she said, but she was out of the tank; I could *feel* her. I couldn't say exactly what she felt like, except that she was substantial. I liked her. I liked her even though she had made that nasty face when I'd told her Velvet was beautiful. First I didn't understand why and then I knew: it was the way she met my eyes. When I need to know who someone is and if I can trust them, I sometimes look too probingly into their eyes. I don't do it on purpose, but sometimes I can feel it happening and that it makes people uncomfortable—most people just look away, some get pissed off. Some look back, but like they're scared. So I don't do it on purpose, but if I need to know, I can't help it, I look. I looked at Velvet's mother in the diner. And she looked back. She looked in exactly the same way I was looking, like she wanted to know who I was and if she could trust me. It was like, for that moment, we were speaking the same language. I could not remember the last time I'd had that experience.

Paul, thinking: But there was something unnerving about the way Ginger was toward Velvet, something fevered, with a whiff of addiction. I knew it had to do with Melinda and with maternity, but in relation to the latter, it seemed distorted, mistaken, a version of reverse imprinting, like baby ducklings who will take the first creature they see to be their mother and follow the thing, no matter how hopelessly.

.

Dante says: "Those people weird. That ugly man and that lady like a cat food and sugar sandwich."

Velvet: I went to bed that night not even wanting to touch my mom because she threw my horseshoe out the window and started screaming when Ginger called. But I fell asleep and then I woke up and she wasn't there and I was scared. Instead of her, Dante was holding a pillow put sideways, like somebody took my mom and put the pillow there to fool him. I hoped she was just in the bathroom, but I knew she wasn't and I was right. I got out of bed and went to look for her. When I got to the kitchen I thought she'd gone away and left us. I opened the window, I don't know why, maybe to call for help—but I looked down and saw she was standing on the sidewalk with her hoodie on over her nightgown. It didn't make sense; she was afraid of this place. She turned her head sideways so I saw her nose and forehead from above; that made her look small, like a kid who was lost. I went downstairs and opened the door. I put my head out and said, "Mami, what are you doing?" When she turned around, her face was quiet and far away. She didn't answer, but I saw she had my horseshoe in her hand. I came out and I said, "Mami, I'm sorry I was bad." We stood together. The air was smelling like fall already. I saw that her legs were bare, but she had her sneakers on untied. "Peaceful," she said. "It's peaceful."

Ginger: Then we fought. He repeated the things he'd said about my needs, her needs, expectations I would not be able to meet. He said we had nothing in common. Then he started about race. He said things like "White benefactor" and "she's too different from you" and "what are you going to do when she gets pregnant?" Which made me yell, "And you think *I'm* racist?" before I left the house and slammed the door.

Of course, from a certain point of view, Ginger *is* racist, and Paul is racist too; Ginger and Paul are two racist White people bitching at each other over who is most racist. Their racism isn't vicious or extreme; it's what I think of as low-level garden-variety racism that isn't much aware of itself. For some people, from a certain point of view, the whole book is racist in this way, because it was written by a White person trying to speak from the point of view of a Latinx girl.

I was once politely confronted on this subject at a bookstore reading, though not about this book. I wasn't even reading from this book, I was reading from *Lost Cat*, the essay about the experience I had with Natalia and Caesar, an experience that was very different from what I wrote in *The Mare* but had inspired it. Still, it was basically the accusation that Paul makes against Ginger and in nearly the same language. A young Black man raised his hand and asked why I wanted to be so involved with these children. I don't remember most of what I said; I believe I listed various traits that the kids had and how lovable they were to me. Then he asked if I was trying to be a "White savior." Again, I don't remember my exact words, but I think I said that if anyone was saved by the experience it would've been me, that I benefited at least as much from it as the kids, but that no, I wasn't out to save anyone. I don't think I was persuasive to him; I recall that he looked quite skeptical, and I guess I don't blame him. He might've been less skeptical if I'd said something more real. Which would've been this: *You seem like a nice guy. You plainly care about what's right and what isn't. If you saw children, of any race, who were poor and in need of material and emotional care, who only had one parent of limited resources, children who were looking for nurture, and you were in a position to give them at least some of that—wouldn't you do it? And then what if you discovered that you really liked these children? What if in some impossible to articulate way you felt commonality with them, regardless of everything and everyone who was telling you that you couldn't possibly have anything in common with them? What if you felt more connected with them than your own family? The term "White savior" is a cliché, however it's a cliché that exists for a reason. But you don't know me. You don't know anything about me. If you did you would realize that the idea of me saving anybody of any race or color is ridiculous. I can't save my own family. I've sometimes tried to help them—not save, help—and I've accomplished very little. I've handed out Band-Aids, basically. I don't think I did harm to my family by trying to help them. I just wasn't able to help enough. As for myself, well . . .*

•

How stupid to think I could break this pattern when I could not break my own. During the decades before I got married, I can't offhand say how many times I've asked for or demanded some sort of relationship with someone who shut the door in my face, then opened it again and peeked out. I would, metaphorically, pound on the door and follow the person through endless rooms. At least a few times the door opened and I fell in love—before losing interest completely. I thought then that my feelings were false and had been all along, but the pain that came from rejecting or being rejected was real and deep. It did not help when I realized that I was as much to blame for the result as the people I pursued, that I often "played the loser" so aggressively that I scarce gave the person opposite me much choice in their response.

When I talk about my relationship with the children and how frustrating it is, some people say, "But you're showing them another way." Am I? Deeper than my encouraging, ideal words is my experience of the closed door and the desperate insistence that it open—emotional absence, followed by a compulsive reaction that becomes its own kind of absence. Even if they don't identify it, I'm sure the children feel it.

I'm also sure that they feel the true, live thing trapped somehow inside the false game—if in fact "game" is the right word for what I have described. A game is something conscious, with clear rules and goals that everyone agrees to. What I experienced too often, inside myself or with another, was a half-conscious, fast-moving blur of real and false, playfulness and anguish, ardent affection and its utter lack. More than a game, it was as if I were stumbling, with another person or alone, through a labyrinth of conflicting impulses and complex, overlaid patterns, trying to find a way to meet, or to avoid meeting, both at the same time. In spite of everything, sometimes I did meet with people, and lovingly. I met my husband in that way almost by accident. And sometimes, after ten years, he and I nonetheless find ourselves wandering apart and alone.

Now Ginger watched as the young man walked alone on a gray path, so gray and vague that she could not make out if it was a paved street or a natural landscape or a moonscape. Neither could he; she could tell by his eyes that he saw nothing before him, for the light had gone from them; they were dull and simple with anguish and bewilderment. His walk was a lurching stagger, he could barely put one foot before the other, and his arms hung loose at his sides. His clothes were ragged and his face was unshaven and his full lips were open because he did not have the energy to close them.

What she was seeing was worse than what she had felt, and she cried out, "What happened to him? This doesn't make sense!"

THE MARE

Ginger: The way I had lived: blank loneliness broken by friendships that would come suddenly into being, surge through the color spectrum, then blacken, crumple, and

die; scene after drunken idiotic scene, mashed-up conversations nobody could hear, rage, tears, ugly laughter
quieted only by the rubber tit of quaaludes or vodka or
something else. Friendship was bad, sex was worse, and
love—love! That was someone who rang my doorbell at
3:00 a.m. and I would let him in so he could tell me I was
worthless, hit me, fuck me, and leave unless he needed
to sleep over because his real girlfriend was—for some
reason!—mad at him. It was not pleasure, it was like a
brick wall that a giant hand smashed me against again
and again, and it was like the most powerful drug in
the world. Paul knows about this but he doesn't know.
Because how can I describe it? It was like being locked
into a nightmare more real than anything until I woke
and couldn't really remember the details or make sense
of it, knowing only that it was terrible and that I would
do it again.

The demon smiled, if you could call it that. And another
picture came, of the young man's smiling, beautiful
face, which, as she watched, transformed into a rigid
mask with a gaping mouth and eyes. The young man
seemed to resist this transformation; Ginger could see
him resisting in his eyes and mouth, trying to stay in the
pleasure and lightness of his earthly self. But he could
not resist, and light pleasure turned into anger, fear,
and despair—and then became a mute totem of those
things. The mask became wooden and then it became
the face of a building, its stiff oblong mouth stretched
to become a door, its stunned square eyes the windows.

And then Ginger was inside the building. She was inside the young man.

Inside the young man, she felt his soul and— Oh! His soul was the beautiful song that Ginger had sensed, and it was not a lie. It was vast and radiant and it was squashed into something small and hard, and it was dying of pain. Valiantly, he tried to bring his soul to life in the small thing through which it had to live, and it was crushed, again and again. Meanwhile, women came flying at him, loving him, swarming like hornets, beautiful with love, drunk with love, near crazy with love, sick with it, buzzing all around him, looking for the beautiful soul they sensed unerringly. Seeking them too, this soul reached longingly through the upper chambers of the young man's heart, and that way he loved the women as he could. And then, when he could do no more, he took each woman down into his basement and, one by one, threw them into that dark cellar, where they were digested and decomposed, one into the other, all the same.

"He doesn't want this!" cried Ginger. "He so does not want this!"

"He dies of loneliness amid this broken flesh," agreed the demon, "though he will occasionally chew some limb or other—wait, aren't those your arms?"

Yes, Ginger saw her dismembered arms, reaching for the poor man, dying to touch him.

"You think you are different," said the demon. "But to him you are just one more."

•

Ginger: "Sex addiction," "addicted to emotion," these were the sober terms by which I learned to describe this dull little hell, and for a while such terms helped me the way crutches help a broken-legged person to walk. They helped, but they did not heal.

I rode home on the train and I looked out the window at the shining dark water with its glowing rim of light left over from the day and I knew: just because I had been in hell, I don't have to be there always. Love is not always a sickness, and I don't need grim, dry terms in order to walk. I have changed. I can trust myself. I love Paul. I love Velvet. I can trust it.

"Where is he?" cried Ginger. "Where is he now?"

"Oh," said the demon. "He must be around here somewhere. Why?"

"I want to be with him, to tell him—"

"That you love him? That's funny—take a look at yourself!"

Velvet: She whinnied and spun in a circle and bucked, her jerking darkness like my mother's fists when she was so mad she'd walk up and down just beating at the air. The hate had gone out of her. Now it was just the *something else*. It was just me in the dark and her hard, jumping body making pain in the air.

•

There is awkwardness in *The Mare*, cultural ignorance manifested in details that are just slightly wrong or, even more, details that aren't present; in some places the tone or *flavor* isn't quite right. I *did* know the girl the character is based on well in terms of her deeper being, how she thought and felt, how she interrogated the world, my world in particular. But I knew much less about how she functioned socially in her own world, and that is important. I could barely know her mother at all. I knew all of this before I started writing. I resisted writing *The Mare* for years because I could see the problem of my own particular ignorance. But I wrote it because I was compelled. I was *compelled*, I think, because finally my knowing of the girl's deeper being seemed more important than the things I did not know. The girl on the page isn't the same as the girl in life. But she shares with her a beauty of spirit that I don't see represented much. Her courage and honesty were absolutely unique. She could be horrible sometimes! But she had real goodness and I saw it especially when she was near animals. That was a heroine to me, a heroine who deserved a story.

Velvet: I went on Friday night after my mom got off work. She yelled at me the whole time, even on the subway. The people on the subway looked at us because my mom sounded crazy, yelling at me about what an idiot Ginger must be and saying I stole out of her purse and I eat too much and I wore her nightgown, dragging Dante along while he talked to himself about killing some people he made up in his head. When we came up out of the train, the wind was blowing trash all over and we had to walk into it. At least that made my mom shut up. Crazy people were all over the place by then, though, so nobody would've noticed her. "Look," said Dante, "there's your stupid woman."

Ginger: And I was so proud of her. I didn't care what that asshole Becca said. I was just proud to be with her, and I told her so. She smiled huge and then, shyly, looked out the window again. She was still quiet, it was still awkward—but it was the awkwardness of people who love each other and don't know how to show it yet.

Velvet: Then she started telling me that she was painting a real picture of her sister because of me.

I said, "Why because of me?"

And she said, "Because you were asking why I didn't do a real picture and I thought maybe I should."

I asked, "Could I see?" and she took me up to her studio.

But the new painting she did was even crazier than the other one. It was *ugly* too, like I wanted to say, *Did you hate your sister?* But I couldn't say that and I couldn't think of anything else to say that was nice, so I just looked around. And I saw something scary: it was a plastic doll, like for little kids, dressed in leopard-spotted clothes that looked homemade with even leopard socks and a hat. It was beat up and it had one of its eyes rolled up in its head. It looked like it was in a Chucky movie, where a doll goes crazy and kills people. Except this doll looked too retarded to kill anybody. I thought, *Is Ginger retarded?*

Ginger: I knew about the box of half-rotted dolls and toys for years before my sister died; she had shown them to me the last time I'd seen her. She was nearly forty then and making one of her failed attempts to get sober, and she was wondering if maybe I wanted my dolls back. The visit hadn't been going very well, and when she held up the moldy and bald (I'd torn her hair out) Glinda, I lost my temper and said I thought it was crazy to keep these things, that she ought to just throw them out. And my biker-chick sister put her face in her hands and left the room, crying. I sat there for a moment, stunned. Then I got up and went to her. She'd stopped crying by then, and when I said, "Sorry," she said, "No, you're right." And I helped her take the falling-apart box out to the dumpster just before I left for the airport.

She must've brought it right back in after I was gone; the box was just about disintegrated when I came across it. I pawed through everything in it— Barbies, old-style talking dolls, troll dolls, Beatles dolls, plastic horses—to rescue Glinda.

Velvet: While we walked at night, Ginger talked to me about self-destruction. She said she was afraid I was destroying myself by not turning in my papers. She said it made her feel bad because it reminded her of her sister who died, because her sister failed her classes even though she was smart. I didn't say anything. It was cold and there were no more bug noises and the smells were deeper and secreter. I thought about Fiery Girl running, her sides all wet and her mouth frothy and her nose open and big. Her muscles were going like the muscles of the world, and her face when she came around was like a crazy skeleton in an old cartoon, blowing hot smoke from her open nose. But it wasn't scary, it was cute. Because her eye was on me like, *See what I can do!* And then something funny happened. When she was starting to slow down, Beverly came out to stand with me and watch for a minute on her way out to her car. She watched and shook her head and pointed at the mare, like *jabbed* with her finger, and said, "That horse is trouble!" And Fiery Girl spun around in like a whole circle and kicked with her back legs—it was like some nasty thing came out the finger and made her spin till she shook it off. Even Beverly had to laugh. She said, "Damn straight!"

Paul: They attacked her and beat her. Not at the party, but later, they swarmed her and beat her. Because of the clothes my wife bought her. She didn't even try to fight back, there were too many of them. Her little brother was there but he didn't help. He actually stood there and laughed.

Between me and Ginger, there was hell to pay. "Leave the girl alone," I told her, "what do you want to do, get her hurt worse?" And she went *nuts*, she beat the wall and screamed that if it wasn't for me she *could* come stay with us and nobody would hurt her again, and I told her she was crazy and selfish and she ran out the door. It was raining and she just ran out into it. I waited and she didn't come back for I don't even know how long. So I went out in the car and found her walking in her sopping pants.

> While I was working on *The Mare* I dreamed I was Ginger. Except that I was not married, I was alone and living with Velvet. We were poor and the house was a mess and we were arguing. But while we yelled at each other, there was a young White girl, maybe thirteen, looking over Velvet's shoulder at me, sad, wanting to support Velvet but not sure how. That is part of how Ginger understands and loves Velvet. Adult Ginger has need of Velvet, need that is tinged or tangled with ignorance and even racism that she has absorbed. The little girl in her isn't about that; she comes from a sincere place. But she is just a little girl, a girl who was also neglected and hurt. She doesn't really know what to do, and still the woman Ginger just keeps yelling and acting like she knows what to do. In my mind Velvet is subconsciously aware of the girl Ginger; that's part of how they can connect. But her mother is very perturbed to sense a child in a grown woman.

Paul: I opened the door; she got in. We drove around up in the neighborhood we'd first taken Velvet bike riding. I waited for her to talk. She said, "Please don't take her away from me. You wouldn't let us adopt, at least let this happen. Can't you see how good it is for me? I want to be normal. If we can't adopt, this is the closest I can come to having a child."

I told her I was willing to consider adoption. She said no. She said, "I love her."

I struggled to control my voice. I said, "If you love her, think about her safety. She's already been hurt. The truth is, she could get more hurt on those horses."

Mother: The clothes that woman bought my daughter! They were nice, too nice, like the woman was saying to me, *What's wrong with you? You can't even dress your kid right!* I know that's not what she meant, but that was my first feeling and my first feeling is always right; whenever I've gotten into trouble, it's been because I didn't follow my first feeling. Besides, when she put them on, she just looked conceited, a bitch royale, and she looks like that anyway. Maybe where Ginger lives girls can go around looking like that, but not here, you're gonna get *hurt* and *I knew it*. But everybody keeps telling me I'm too hard, I yell, I don't understand it here—okay, fine. I can see she hates the clothes I can get for her, she always wants better and more—okay, fine. Let her have it. Let her see. She never wore those things again. But how stupid was this Ginger that she didn't even talk to me? How *disrespect-ful*. Did she think she was dressing a doll? I knew she was silly, but I believed her to be good, or good enough. Was she? There *was* something strange in her eye, es rara, something deep. But it never stayed long enough for me to know what it was. Mostly she looked immature, more girl than woman—a sad girl who was trying to be happy. Una sufrida—what else could she be, married but not one child? I could see the sadness and emptiness of her eyes and I'd feel her, that surely she's been through some real hell. Then she'd stare at me, and the deep thing would pass through, and I'd know she was also something else. But what? She acted so big, walking up to me like she knew my daughter better than I did. But then the next second she'd seem so *lost*, and you'd see this tiny stop in every movement she made. Who was she? Why was she being so nice? No one is so nice for no reason.

I don't know how many people noticed, but Ginger *does* have things in common with Velvet. She has things in common with Velvet's mother. Neither Ginger nor Mrs. Vargas realizes this. But neither really feels like she belongs in her own world: Mrs. Vargas because she's in a foreign country, but also because, like Ginger, she is . . . not normal. When I was involved with Caesar and Natalia, it was striking how alone their mother was; even though she had some relatives in the city, she rarely seemed to spend time with them or with anyone else. Maybe she had been hurt by people, maybe she didn't like that many people, maybe she worked so hard that she was just too tired to socialize much. But for whatever reason, she kept to herself. This independence gave her a kind of unreadable dignity and made me respect her. But it must've been very lonely.

The mother's unusual loneliness didn't surprise me. But I was surprised to realize, much later, that her daughter was that way too. She didn't seem that way as a girl; even though she was clearly not popular in school and apparently had treacherous friendships, she still seemed very attuned to social language and could connect to many different kinds of people. She could be shy but she could also be charming. I was surprised to hear her say to me, as a twenty-four-year-old adult, that she'd always felt like she couldn't fit in anywhere.

Velvet: I got her to the mounting block and worked to make the girth right, over and over thinking, *Beg a mare, beg a mare.* Then I worked to get on—first just standing with my left foot in the stirrup, then both feet in, sitting very soft, just sitting, no legs on. Finally walking, thinking, *I won't beg, I won't beg,* and then wind came through the arena, and she spooked, and I couldn't turn her fast enough, and her head came up, she reared up under me. I grabbed her mane and prayed forward, my feet out of the stirrups, her body wilding under me like a snake, like Joker swimming. She came back down and I was ready, I turned her hard, right into my thigh. We went forward again, walking, trotting, walking. Each feeling where the other was, except it kept moving and changing. Was this what Pat meant by "begging"? Because that's not what it was, it was like *finding*—no, not that either. It was . . . I tried to think what it was so hard that my mind grew like a forest with everything in it: my mom and Dante and school and Dominic's eyes, Shawn's hands, Strawberry so close in the closet, Ginger. My grandfather said, *You can walk your path better than that lady ever could. She loves you and you should respect her love. But she doesn't know your path. You can walk it. She can't.* And somebody else was there too, a twisted-up face coming at me sideways through a crack in the forest floor: Manuel, my father's friend who lived with us. *Walk your path!* The forest closed up and I was just on my mare, and for a long moment, I found her.

Mother: *I* rode a horse when I was six. Because my father was friends with Mr. Reyes, the man who ran a store down the street, and Mr. Reyes had a horse. One day my father held me up so I could see the horse's face and he had rough skin but soft eyes. I put my hands on his neck and it felt good. I wanted to get up on him, so my father laughed and put me on his back. And on that horse I saw the world: sky, trees, buildings, streets going in different directions. My life going in different directions. My father was talking to Mrs. Reyes with his hand on the horse, it was right by my leg. But then he turned and his hand came off the horse. And the horse began to move! He walked and then Mr. Reyes yelled and the horse ran, and the world was shaking so hard my teeth rattled. I grabbed the mane and watched the world clatter by, I clattered by my mother running out of the house waving a towel. Somebody grabbed the horse, and he reared up and I fell off. I banged my head; it felt like all my bones broke. I cried, "Mami!" A dark hole closed over me and I fell down into it.

In the hole people were yoked to machines, thousands of people, naked, bent, and pulling, so angry that they bit the shoulders of those before them. Voices said, "You are lazy and selfish"; the voices came from faces joined together in a breathing darkness, one dark, expressionless face made of many faces, a black field of nose-holes, eye-holes, and many mouths; people fell down the slippery holes and mouths and into working guts, they were shit out into dreams of people who did not even know them. And then I was there, with the shit-people. We crawled in the dirt of dreams, the dreams of those who cursed us without knowing us. Above were signs, telling us what we were: crosses, dollars, flashing lights, thousands of quick-moving pictures showing pain and ugliness. But my father picked me up and said, "Don't look there. Look here." And then there was a beautiful girl, riding a horse in green grass, under blue skies and trees. "Remember her," said my father. "She is here for you and you for her." But the horse suddenly got scared, it moved sideways, and the girl fell off and I cried out—

And my mother grabbed me up by my arm and slapped me awake, crying. My father said, "It's not her fault!" but still she got me home and whipped my legs. Later, my father got me a piece of candy.

Now he's gone. When he died I could not even be with him to say goodbye because I had no money to get on the plane. Instead I'm here, pushing through mud. Dante's heartbeat against my chest; he pulls me forward. Velvet pulls from behind. I've got to put her in her own room. Because I don't want to be like my mother. But sometimes I want to reach back and push the girl under the mud.

·

Ginger: On the phone I said, "Listen, I want to invite your mom and brother up along with you around Christmas. I'm acting in a play and I think it would be fun if you all came to see it. It's a children's theater."

"Why are you acting in a theater for children?"

"Because it's fun. Do you think you would want to act in it if you could?"

"I dunno."

"Could you ask your mom if she'd like to come?"

She didn't answer. I felt her like she was next to me breathing.

I said, "I'm thinking if she had a chance to look around up here, it might make her think about coming here to live."

Paul: We walked to the theater in silence. I thought I saw Mrs. Vargas looking approvingly at the Christmas lights. I saw she'd put lipstick on. The boy's shoe came untied and she made Velvet stop to tie it. I asked, "Don't you know how to tie your shoes, young man?" He said, "She does it for me. I'm only seven." I said, "A seven-year-old man needs to tie his own shoes, and before you go home, I'm going to teach you."

The boy looked down. Mrs. Vargas gave me a sharp look, and I thought, *She understands.* But we were at the ticket booth by then, and there were people with their radiant children. Her sharpness deserted her; she put her hand on the boy's shoulder. The boy frankly looked the other kids up and down. Velvet led the way upstairs; she looked back and smiled at me. There was a burst of happy voices and then children running up and down a hallway in half-costume, rosy families getting out of their coats, a vibrant little girl handing out programs amid papier-mâché castles and trees with brown trunks and balls of green sitting atop them. A girl recognized Velvet and spoke to her. Mrs. Vargas sank back into herself.

"Hola! Bienvenidos!"

Mrs. Vargas blinked and looked up. Bearing down on us through the crowd was Ginger wearing pajamas and a bonnet with a man in blue face paint holding out his arms and gesturing at his heart like to a long-lost friend.

Body and eyes, Mrs. Vargas rose to the welcome instinctively. And then she sagged back, bewildered. The blue-faced guy put his arm around her shoulders and began talking to her in Spanish. She talked back, but her body inwardly sagged. Ginger was talking to somebody else in a bonnet. Dante was slowly wandering forward, looking with great interest at plastic knight's armor, assorted masks, and weaponry.

Mother: Painted people came out onstage; Ginger led little girls around making faces, singing, like weird prayer cards come to life. A little one forgot to sing, just looked at us, smiling—sweet. The old lady I dropped on the floor has whole walls covered by tacked-up prayer cards, pictures of grandkids, crayon drawings, and presidents, a mass of faces, real and unreal, yellowing away or bright as Easter. Saint Clare with full ruby lips, Saint Lucy with her eyes on a plate, a snowman drawn in orange, a boy, a dog. I close my eyes and disappear in the wall of pictures.

"*Mami!*" Velvet jabs me; I jab back. Boring, an old man is on the stage eating from a bowl. The pretend clock is striking. This lady keeps her dishes in the oven and her refrigerator full of disgusting dry cakes like they sell from a food truck. I scold Velvet and pinch her. The old man looks up; someone is moaning, rattling around. I pinch myself, wake up. The old man shouts, "*Who's there?*" The old lady thinks the neighbor boys are coming to steal her pantyhose, but she's got her purse open on the table. She wants to know: "What kind of person would take your pantyhose?" I hold my tongue, wash her scabby ass. "Easy, easy," she whines. The old man clutches the other man in pretend chains, begging. She says the same thing every time: came to New York, job at the candle factory, lost her husband, had a child, lost the child. The stage goes dark. Music starts. I feel my head drooping. There's music on the subway, people singing and begging. Velvet jabs me. A girl stands in the spotlight, holding a doll and crying out, trying to sound unhappy, but she obviously has no idea what it is. People, singing and crying in rags, crawl from behind the black curtains. The subway beggars tell their stories, play guitars; one man has cats riding his shoulders. They do tricks, their faces smart like people . . . wait, that's Ginger's face, she's on the floor, crawling, making a face that is—well, that is funny, worth coming to see. Now she's holding up play money, they're all giving play money to the girl with the doll, but she won't take it, doesn't see it. She screams, "Help, help!" but doesn't take the money— what in hell is this thing about? In the subway I saw a man with no legs stuck in the door. Somebody took him there to beg and now he's stuck in the door—how did he get there? I try to turn around and help him, but it's crowded, they push me in. I look again; he's not there. The stage goes dark again. Velvet and Dante press near me. A lot of people *do* steal from the old ladies. But I don't. Not unless they leave it right out on the table. That's just stupid. The light goes out, the subway goes into the tunnel. I speed along on my belly. Above me, they carry crosses and dollar signs. Above me, there are songs of love; the ugly woman is transformed by love. I speed on my belly down the side of the road. Leave it on the table, that's not even stealing. That's— Suddenly I am lifted up. My love is here, our hands are about to touch—that's not even—but I don't remember who he is.

And Ginger saw that she was no longer a little girl but an old woman, naked and visibly withered, feeble and dry. Ginger was so outraged by this low trick that she actually stamped her dry little foot and cried, "I don't care! I just want to see him!"

The demon laughed and stamped *its* foot with such mocking glee that fire jetted out its leathery ass. "That's rich!" it said. "All right then, here he is, your love!" And it tossed a large black spider at her.

Mother: *"Mami, you snore!"* Dante pokes and I sit up among strangers. The old man is singing alone in his pajamas. As he sings he turns the crank on a little music box; his voice is beautiful and broken. Three young girls in white gowns turn with the music like they are inside the box; they face one another, turn away, face one another, step away.

I looked at Velvet, shining with her eyes, picking at her nose. My poor daughter. My poor, worthless girl.

Paul: "Human love is the vilest thing in the world."

"What's wrong?"

"I just said it."

"Why?"

"Because she loves them. I can tell she loves them. But when they were getting into their night-clothes, she made Velvet come stand out in the hall in her gown and she talked at me. And Velvet translated. She said, 'My mom wants you to look and see how ugly I am.'" Ginger breathed hard and slow, like she was pushing with all her might against something that would not give.

"Maybe you'd like to see your mother and father," said the demon. "They're both here too."`

"They can't be, they're still alive!"

"Oh, they're here, and I think you saw them already on your way down."

Velvet: She put on this tape of old music called Shangri-Las. She said it was the name of a place where people didn't get old, and there was a story about people getting lost there. Life was so perfect there that it made them crazy, so they couldn't stay even though one of them fell in love. They tried to go back over the mountains, but a huge snowstorm came and the Shangri-La woman who came with them turned old and died in front of her boyfriend while he cried. I asked if that's what they were singing about, and she said no, it was just the name of the group. We were quiet for a while, and I tried to like the music, even though it was corny. We drove into fog and everything got weird-beautiful: the red taillights on parked cars and numbers flashing on mailboxes, and sometimes deer eyes. Ginger started singing, really soft. Her drunk voice was embarrassing, little and pinchy like a funny bone. But still, my neck tingled like when my mom did my hair. I said, "Can we drive a long time? Can we get a little bit lost?" And she laughed and said, "Honey, we already are a little bit lost."

And again they came before her, the driven people. Once more she saw the one next to her with his terrible eyes and bared teeth. Dumbstruck, she covered her heart with her hands; it was her father. It was her mother, her grandmother, her sister, and they were driven with countless others into a grinding machine that crushed them and remade them, over and over, into faces and postures and emotions that Ginger recognized and held dear, but were now revealed as stiff and terrible maskhouses with unfeeling eye-holes and mouths in shapes of meaningless happiness or pain. Ginger cried out and covered her eyes. "Life on earth!" cried the demon as it worked the machine. "Yes, life on earth!" Ginger tried to get away, crying and stumbling. The demon laughed and ground the wheel of the machine with pleasureful spite.

Velvet: And then it all happened: Beverly saw me and spun so she damn near hit herself with her own whip—just before Joker reared up on her from the back and she fell down. Then Fiery Girl took off almost out from under me, running down the trail toward the water. I couldn't control her. I could barely stay on. Was Beverly dead? The mare went off the path into the neighbor farm's orchard. The trees came at me with black claw-arms and rushed away, green leaves and rotting fruit. I put the reins in one hand and grabbed her mane; she took me through. I yelled, *"Whoa!"* but she didn't even slow. Everything was flying past and I would go to jail, my mom talking forever about what shit I was. I took the reins again, felt for her mouth, but it was no good, I was already slipping when I saw the fence coming. I screamed, *"Whoa!"* and pulled the reins hard. She came up on her back legs, and I saw nothing but sky that went forever until I slammed down on my back so hard my head bounced. The sky blurred and black came in on the edges. I pushed it back and made myself sit up. My horse was trotting slowly alongside the fence. I felt vomit coming. Ginger's voice said, *Our relationship is over.* I called to my horse; she ignored me. My eyes blurred; my horse blurred and then she was gone. Dominic was there, his arm around Brianna. We were outside the school. He was walking with her, and at first I thought he didn't even see me because he turned his back to me, both their backs were to me. But then he turned his head back around and looked at me that same way he looked a long time ago, when he was with Sondra, and turning to look at me, joking and serious. But it was horrible now. Because he had touched my breasts and my lips and his eyes mentioned that while he turned away to be with someone who hated me. Alicia saw. Other people saw. I was all of a sudden a tiny hurting center of something huge that had nothing to do with me.

I felt dizzy. Grass and trees stretched away. Now I was not at the center of anything. I wasn't anything. Grass and trees stretched away from me, not touching me. The mare ate grass, ignoring me. Far away was a road with cars and people that had nothing to do with me. The sky was like the ocean, full of things I couldn't see. Birds flew, hunting for invisible things to kill. People said this was beautiful, but it was not. It would kill you if you were alone in it, and I was alone. I was alone everywhere. There was nothing to stand on, nothing to hold. My mother wouldn't even hit me because I wasn't worth it. I bent over and vomited.

The next time I saw Shawn, I went with him and I did what he told me. I wanted Dominic to hear and be mad. When I finished, I don't even know why, but I said, "So you love me?" He said, "Sure, you cool." The next time I saw Dominic he was with another girl, a friend of Brianna's named Janelle. He didn't even look at me.

Any man could have her and who would want to?

Beverly would say it about me if she knew. It wasn't true. But she would say it. Maybe even Pat would. Why? Why did they talk that way about somebody? I bent over again, but instead of vomit pain came with a sound that was horrible to me. I fell onto my knees and the sound became words. I hit myself and said them: "Ugly, stupid chicken-head bitch. Worthless, stupid. Nobody wants you. Even the horse doesn't want you, you're worse than shit. Even the horse knows. You're not worth it."

I wiped my mouth with my shirt. The black closed in and then parted; the grass was so green beneath me. I felt her breath on me. Then her nose against my shoulder. The grass was so green. I lifted my face and she lipped my hair. I almost laughed because she had come back, but then I saw she was scared. She was scared, but she still came back to see if I was okay. I could not make her more scared.

A voice said, "Enough." The demon hissed.

Velvet: The blackness cleared. I stood up and touched her shoulder with both my hands. I made my hands soft and I talked to her like she was smaller than me. I said I was sorry I said those things, that I wasn't talking to her. I said I would never say those things again. I tried to kiss her and to hug her. She shied away. I tried again; she moved away again, stronger this time, like I was scaring her. I didn't understand and it hurt me. I needed to feel her, but I couldn't make her more scared. Her skin was wet and shining, and her head was up, nervous, even though her eyes were trusting me. I put my head down and moved close enough to put my hand on her shoulder. I felt her blood pounding in her muscles and I felt *her*. I remembered suddenly how it was when I walked to the barn with Ginger that first time, how all the green was too much, too open, and I knew: she doesn't feel safe enough to hug in the open. Like she knew I understood, she put her head down and began to eat the grass. I petted her neck and picked up the reins. I let her eat for a few minutes—it made me feel calm to watch her eat, looking like a little piggy with her big nose and mouth. Then when I was ready I said, "Come on," and pulled her head up. I led her to the fence like it was a mounting block. I climbed up on it. She shied away at first, but I talked her back. She saw what I was doing and she let me.

I sat on her and swung my hair behind me. The sky was huge and bright, but it was touching me now, it was friendly, and the huge brightness of the grass stretched before me. I started her at a walk. This was my place. No one would ever be in this place but me and my horse. No man, not even children; they would never come here with me. This place was only for me and my mare.

Beverly says: Jesus Christ. Even her, the tough Black girl from the city—or Puerto Rican, or whatever she is—even she's been ruined by the Disney-fied horse snot they sell in the multiplex. Love and self-esteem, love and self-esteem— love is good for babies and that's it. Yes, you make a horse good by raising it up with a little love and a lot of discipline. But you make a horse great by making it feel like shit. Because it knows it is *not* shit and it will turn itself inside out to prove it to you. Sure you give it love, just a touch. And then you burn its ass, make it crave the love, make it try to please you for another little taste—it will turn itself inside out to show you it's good. You make that horse prove it over and over, every time. If that horse is worth anything, it will pull up everything it's got for you and it *will* find what it's worth and be more and more proud. It will know it can take whatever you got and sometimes it will give it back. But it will know its worth. And it will do *anything* to make you know it.

Velvet: What if they would never let me see her again? My brain had a bruise on it, that's what the doctor said, because it hit against my skull. "Shit for brains, but she can ride, you gotta give her that." That's what Beverly said. I pictured my brain pressing on my skull and I felt like there was something invisible pressing in the dark, trying to get visible. Was this what happened to my brother when the babysitter gave him the aspirin? I was afraid if I slept I would dream of Hell and I would not wake up. Why did my grandfather tell me to go to Hell that time? Was he in Hell? Alicia said almost everybody went to Hell, it didn't even matter if you were a good person or not. Gare said, "You rode the hell out of that bitch." I said, "Don't call her a bitch." But maybe I sent her to Hell. Because if I couldn't see her, who would take care of her, who would love her? The way she looked at me when Pat put her away in her stall—even though she did not turn her head, I know she looked and loved me with her dark eye. I thought of Dominic, turning to look at me while he was with Brianna. My heart hurt. I held my chest, it hurt.

I thought Pat would talk about it in the car, but she just put the radio on. We drove over the bridge and took a road I didn't know, like a dirty tongue going up a hill with no houses or even trees on the sides of it. The Iraq war was on the radio and people were being blown up. Pat said the war was a horrible mistake; she said it like she wanted to know what I thought. But I was thinking of when I showed Ginger's picture to Shawn. I wanted him to see how nice she was, but he said, "You know why those people can act nice? Other people do the violence for them. That's how they have that nice world." I said, "Ginger doesn't have anybody doin' violence." He just tossed her picture back at me and said, "She must think you some li'l Orphan Annie."

Pat changed the station to a song I didn't know. Suddenly I thought, *I don't know her. And she is Beverly's friend.* Hard feelings banged together in me. *You used to be able to beat a kid that acted bad.*

"Where are we going?" I asked.

"My place," she said. "Where did you think?"

We went up a bumpy driveway. I remembered a long time ago when I rode my bike with Ginger and she said, "Lumpety bumpety!" and we flew.

Pat said, "Just so you know, my place is primitive compared to Estella's."

"What's 'primitive'?"

"I mean there's no toilet in the barn. When I don't feel like walking to the house I use a bucket."

We drove past a little house with tin patched on it and colored plastic flowers twirling in the yard. There was a vegetable garden with wire around it and a barn behind a bunch of pale trees. Two horses in a jellybean-shaped paddock came running at us, then away; they were both light brown, one with a blond mane and low, round, ripply shoulders. "Chloe's the blondie," said Pat. "The gelding's Nut. See the difference in the way they're built?" I looked; Nut looked stronger to me, he was tall and his back was very wide. "She's built what they call 'uphill'—and her back is nice and short *and* she's got a strong rear. See how long her shoulders are, that long neck? Chloe's a good jumper partly because of how she's built, but the main reason is she actually likes to jump."

"Is Fiery Girl a good jumper?" I asked.

"I don't know, I haven't seen her jump. I don't even know if she's been jumped. She does have the build for it, though, got a beautiful neck."

"But her neck's not long like that horse."

"No, it's more what they call 'horizontal,' which is more unusual."

I thought we were going to bring the horses in, but they didn't want to come in so we went to clean their feed and water buckets instead. We brought the buckets out of the barn and ran the hose. It was still hot; plant and vegetable smells spread in the air like invisible color with dark horse-smell underneath. I remembered Shawn in my mouth. I remembered Dominic in front of me with his legs open and soft heat coming from between them. I remembered his eyes when he was holding Brianna and looking at me over his shoulder, sharp like the arrow in the valentine, hitting sharp in my heart, my real heart, like in the science chart of your body, soft, bare muscle in darkness. Soft/sharp. Love.

•

Ginger: Boys liked Melinda. She always knew what to say. She always seemed like she was moving even when she was just standing with her hand on her hip, like her skirt was swinging though it wasn't. When I was in elementary school and she was in junior high, I asked her what happened when you liked a boy. She said, "It's like when you see him you feel this big warmth and he does too. It's like there's nobody else there. Except when you slow-dance together too long and you know you stink and then you wish he *wasn't* there!"

Warmth; stink. My sister was natural. I was not. I didn't feel warmth, I felt painful burning and tenderness so big it made me want to run and hide, because how could something so soft live with such burning? Of course boys didn't like me. Burning and stunned, I hid inside myself, stiff as a glass doll. Melinda went outward, smiling and warm.

Smiling and warm. Why was she hurt? I can understand why I was hurt; glass begs to be smashed. But why her? Why?

Velvet: But mostly me and Chloe jumped. She was different from my mare, lighter, like she never cried in her life. When she jumped she rounded her back so strong it almost pushed me off, and she pulled her legs up into her body so soft and landed on them like a cat. Once she didn't take the jump, she ran around it, and I fell off and banged my head. I got mad and yelled at her and Pat yelled at me. "That was you, not her," she said. "She saw you missed the distance and she wasn't going to hurt herself *and you*, ass over teakettle."

I started loving Chloe. I loved the feeling I got in my legs sometimes when I was on her, like the spot where my legs touched her sides was the best place in the world and we were both in it. I never felt that with Fiery Girl. I didn't know why and it made me feel bad. I didn't want to ask Pat about it because I didn't want to admit it.

I talked to Ginger about it. We were in the car at night, "getting lost" on the same roads we always drove. She said, "It sounds like she misses you. You used to come every day, and suddenly you're not there."

I said, "But I always go away, she's used to it."

"Maybe she knows it's different now. Maybe she knows you're really liking another horse."

So I told her about the leg thing, how I could feel it with Chloe and not with my mare. When I said it, she didn't answer for so long it was like she didn't hear me. Then she said, "Just because you can't feel it with Fiery Girl doesn't mean it's not there. Before my sister died I didn't feel love for her. I didn't even like her. But I did love her. I just didn't feel it."

"How could you love somebody and not feel it?"

"I don't know how to describe it."

I didn't say anything. The same trees and houses went past, slanty and shadowy, the same but still strange. Ginger's music was on, this grown woman singing like she was my age. It was ugly and fake, her making her voice like that, but I didn't care. I was remembering something from a long time ago.

Ginger said, "Before Paul there was a—a . . . boyfriend who I had a bad relationship with. We were bad to each other."

"How?"

"We just hurt each other all the time. It was awful and I always felt bad about it. But I ran into him a little while ago, and I realized there was love between us, even though we acted horrible. I was glad."

The thing I remembered: being in the car with my father. His free hand under my clothes, feeling me all over for money, until he found it and he took it. Because I was lying he kept it all.

"So I'm saying, just because you haven't felt that thing with Fiery Girl yet doesn't mean it's not there. It's just not right on that spot where your legs are."

I was lying—why did I lie? The money was for emergencies. Was the toll an emergency? Was he right not to see me again or even send anything?

"I used to feel something like that," said Ginger. "I felt it when I painted."

"In your legs?"

"No. In my brain. I used to think of it as a radio signal that I had to be alone to hear. I don't hear it now, but I'm hoping it's still there."

"What did it sound like?"

"I didn't actually hear it. I more felt it."

"That doesn't make sense."

"I know." There was a space between songs and I heard her breathe in, then out. The music started again.

I thought, *Did my father love me but not feel it?*

Ginger said, "I wonder if I can't hear it anymore because I'm not alone."

She said it like she *was* alone. That made me feel alone.

"Then I'm glad I don't hear it," she said. "I'd rather hear you."

211

Does Dominic love me and not feel it?

What Shawn said, that Ginger could be nice because people like her got other people to do the violence for them; I didn't understand what he meant, but it felt true. Ginger in the car, talking to me about Fiery Girl loving me and the signal thing she could only hear by herself—that was true too. I knew because now I was hearing it.

The truth of Shawn and the truth of Ginger were both real, but I couldn't be in them at the same time.

Ginger: I poured me some pomegranate juice, mixed it with lime, soda, and a ton of sugar. I went outside and drank it and thought of Michael.

We kissed with our whole mouths, but the feeling was delicate, too delicate for sex. He touched my face and we held each other. I told him I never forgot this dream he had of geometric shapes moving rhythmically in the dark, except they were misshapen, deformed on one side, and he realized that they were him. He said, "You remember that?" and I said, "I remember everything," and he said, "I do too." I sang a song to him, a nonsense song from when we were teenagers, and he looked it up online to see who it was by because I didn't know. It was like a miracle of gentleness, something young springing from inside age, smiling and sweet like I was never able to be in middle school or high school, or when I knew this man nearly two decades ago; in that foolish moment, the hard glass of my girlhood became flesh as if for the first time.

Middle school, where Velvet was.

The phone rang in my lap; I picked it up and said, "Honey, what's going on? It's late, why were you out?"

"It's before ten," she said.

I said, "It's still late for you."

She ignored that and said, "When can I come up there? I want to see my horse."

"You know you can come whenever your mother says it's okay. But your voice sounds different. Why haven't you been talking to me?"

She was quiet a long moment. Then she said she hadn't been going to school, that she thought I'd be mad at her.

"Honey," I said, "why aren't you going to school?"

"Something bad happened."

"Listen," I said. "Something bad happened this summer. You got thrown off a horse and got a concussion and you got kicked out of the barn. But you kept riding, and now you've moved your horse to a better place where you can ride her again. You *walked your path*. You asked me how to do that; now you know because you did it. Keep walking your path."

She listened to me. I could tell. Because I believed my words and she could hear it in my voice. Of course I believed it. If a man who had told me I wasn't worth anything could hold me and kiss me and I could sing him a song, then any good thing might happen. If what I had longed for, blindly and brokenly, and struggled like an animal to find in the most unlikely form, if it had really been there and was now simply, gently revealed—any good thing might happen. Anything.

Ginger looked up into near-blinding light. She shielded her eyes and looked at the demon; it was no longer there. Out of the light came a girl, a dark-skinned girl of maybe twelve, a very dark-skinned old man at her side. The girl came forward and put her arms around Ginger; the girl was warm and gentle, but her body was strong.

"Who are you?" asked Ginger.

"She is my granddaughter," said the old man. "She is the one good thing you will do on earth. She is not your child, but a child you will love. Come with us. We are protected."

They stepped into the light, which Ginger realized was from the headlights of a large taxi. She saw that there were other people already in the car, too many than could logically fit. Some of the people looked strange, somehow misshapen; she hesitated, but the old man said, "Come." And, with the young dark girl, they got into the taxi.

As soon as she sat down, Ginger saw that she was seated next to a young boy with pale blond hair, pale lips, and hazel eyes. "Hi," he said shyly; "Hi," she answered back. The old man and the young girl were still there; the forms of other people were there. But all her attention was on the boy. She reached for his hand; he reached for hers too and they held each other.

"Be careful," said the driver. "We're at the crossing."

Velvet: "Ginger," she said, "somebody I know got shot. This boy who didn't even do nothing."

•

Paul: Ginger wasn't even going to tell me about the boy. She wasn't going to tell me because she thought I wouldn't want to hear it, but it woke her in the middle of the night; I could feel her body pulling against itself as she turned and turned in place like some old animal.

"You're helping her," I said. "Ginger, you're doing everything you can, it's amazing what you've done, it's amazing what *she's* done, and she knows it, and that will hold her in good stead."

I held her close and stroked her heart and felt her slowly become right again: fragile, strangely young, but strong, with the fanatic strength that thin girls sometimes have, more fierce nerves than muscle. I remembered that night she said, "I want to be a woman! I want to be a normal woman!" It was as if her whole body said that now, that she wanted to be a woman, she wanted to protect this girl.

Velvet: When Ginger dropped me at Pat's, Miss Pat waited till Ginger drove away, then she took my shoulders and looked in my eyes. "What happened to *you*?" she said.

"Nothin'."

"*Nothin'*? Then why do you look like you got hit by a truck doin' sixty?"

I looked down and didn't say.

She let go of me. She said, "Make that a truck doin' eighty. C'mon, let's get to work."

And we went and worked on jumping Fiery Girl, who did not want to jump. Chloe and Nut watched from their side of the paddock while we trotted around and around, and I tried to make her go over the jump and she would not go. Pat yelled, "Be clear! You're not being clear! You decide and you get your legs on her and tell what you want to do!" But I couldn't be clear because nothing was clear. There was Dominic's lips on me and an old man crawling on glass and Shawn's crocodile dick and his eyes and Dominic's eyes and my body burning all the time and the noise coming in all night while I lay on the couch, some idiot yelling. I kicked Fiery Girl and told her to jump, but all I wanted to do was look at my phone and see if Dominic texted even though he hadn't even once. The only clear thing I could feel was that Fiery Girl was scared of jumping and she was getting pissed at me, and still I couldn't focus right.

"You know I have love for you. You love me?"

It was late when he finally came. The kids, Rochelle and Jason, were asleep. He came in looking angry, then I realized, no, scared. Something happened, he wouldn't say what it was, said I shouldn't know. He kept walking around. He sat close to me on the couch, but he didn't look at me, he texted. I could smell him, and the smell of him scared me and I didn't know why. I tried to bring back the warm feeling of when he crouched down with his legs open, but this was not like that. His sideways face was hard, his hands didn't care about anything but texting. He worked his phone. I didn't move, but still I went toward him in waves, hurting to touch him. He closed the phone and put it on the table. He looked at me; he started to talk, he stopped. His eyes saw, and I let him see my feelings all the way. He said he had to do something and he picked up his phone again. He opened it and stared at it. He put it down and looked at me. He touched my face with his hand. I had words I couldn't say, but he heard and answered with kissing lips. And with noises too, little baby noises that said, *Please let me close, please let me inside,* and because the noises were so baby, I touched the back of his head like to protect him. He bent and kissed my titties; he kneeled and put his head on my breast. I pulled my shirt up and he touched my titties and kissed them. It felt so good I got scared and my body trembled. He rose up and kissed my face and said, "Damn, I shouldn't. But I gotta see your body, I wanna touch you. I wanna feel you next to me. We can do it, we can make it right. You know I have love for you. You have love for me?"

I said yes by kissing him, and we went in the next room where there was a bed. I touched his chest with my hand and kissed it. I took off my bra and he touched and kissed me. We talked about his uncle and about Shawn and how my grandfather talked to me and what happened that night after I went home. About his sister and how he got split up from her when his mom moved in with this boss up in Washington Heights. Also about Fiery Girl: how I talked to her and she talked back to me and I cleaned her dirty stall. He told me about how he used to want to be an actor; he said he acted at this charter school he used to be at. It put on plays and he was Romeo in one of them. I laughed. I said, "You mean like *where for art thou?*" and he said, "Yeah, you don't believe me?" I said, "No!" just to be that way. And he said the next time he saw me, he'd give me the picture his mom took.

And the whole time we were talking, we were touching everything. I took off everything except my panties and he touched everything.

And they passed into a field of beautiful voices talking and singing together, like flowers with intelligent tongues, growing in all shapes and sizes and changing as they grew, joking with each other, privately and gently, as they spread over the field and beyond, becoming something Ginger lacked the ability to see. She looked at the boy, wanting to speak. But he said, "I have to go," and dissolved in the field of voices; his voice joined theirs.

Velvet: Little Tina lay down again, curled with her nose down almost in her bedding. I went and sat against her body for heat. Out the window, the snow was like the beginning of an old black-and-white movie where they show the outside of the house in the snow and then the inside where everybody's living the story. I took out my phone and looked. Nothing.

Ginger: She stopped leaning against me when we sat to watch TV. When I put my arm around her, she went still under *my* touch. I thought she was rejecting me, then I realized it was worse: she had lost her trust in touch. Not just my touch, all touch. I still touched her, out of habit; my hand on her back, her arm, her forehead when I said good night. She stayed remote. Someone had made touch into something else for her and I could not change it back.

Velvet: That Christmas Fiery Girl took the jumps, not just one, but four in a row. It was cold, but the ground was firm and dry with no ice or slush, and I put my legs on her like *business*, not feeling. Because I was going to get some money, I was going to find a way to be in a competition and win some money and buy clothes and do my hair and go to that club and find Dominic.

That's all I thought about back home, trying to sleep on the couch with people brawling at each other outside and their cars pumping music so hard it pumped up in the walls of my building. That's all I thought about when I was on the mare, and damn, she seemed to get it. The one time she gave me trouble in the stall, lifting her head and resisting the bit, I slapped her mouth and *she minded*. "Real smart," said Pat, "you just smacked somebody that outweighs you by a thousand pounds." But when I took her out, that horse took the jumps better than ever, better than Chloe, fiercer, like she's gonna *eat 'em*. When we were done, she cantered proudly, and I remembered that on the couch, watching lights and shadows tangled on my ceiling, hearing voices and music tangled with pretend pictures of me at the club: Dominic's face when he saw me looking bad—everybody would see it.

I didn't want to walk, I wanted us to ride in the car and play music. But she said no, we're going to walk.

It felt sad because I remembered how much I used to like it, and she still wanted it to be that way. But my mind was different now, and the little things in people's yards, their decorations I used to think were so cute—I didn't care about it anymore. There was nothing going on *at all*, except an old person walking his dog and no music, just some kids' voices talking from somewhere in the park. How could anybody stand it? And Ginger I think even knew it, she was trying so hard. Like we walked over a little bridge and she said, "Remember the time we shined a flashlight in the water and we saw an eel?" And then:

"You're having periods, right?"

"For a year now, Ginger."

"Do you ever get really, really mad when you have your period?"

I tried to think and couldn't remember.

"Because when I first started? I remember sometimes I would get unbelievably mad. I was once so mad at my mom I remember looking at the back of her head and wanting to kill her, and she hadn't even *done* anything. It was scary. And then I started my period and I was like, oh, that was why."

I pictured Ginger staring at her mom's head and wanting to kill her. I didn't know what to say.

"It's normal, if you feel that way. I feel it too sometimes, but in a different way."

I said, "Different how?"

"Because I'm on the other end of it. You're starting to have periods and I'm starting to stop. You're coming up and I'm going down. So I can still get mad!"

And I don't know why, but that made me smile. Not because of her going down. More the way she said it. It made me feel her again.

The next day Pat said she had to face reality. She said she had to do that a long time ago. She said it old and tired, like she forgot I was even there. "I have the ability," she said. "I have the quality animals. But I don't have money, and it's all about money in this business."

I didn't know what to say. But I felt her then too. I felt the dirt and the broken things around us. There was wind and the sound of the furnace. There were all the ribbons on the wall saying FIRST PRIZE and ARIES and HANDSOME. I didn't know what to say, but I was wondering: Why was I at the poor, dirty place? I used to think it was so cool, but now it just seemed like crap—as Ginger would say, *literally.*

To write *The Mare* I had to learn to ride horses. This was hard because I was afraid of horses. I was so afraid that at first I did the research by volunteering to muck out stables and groom horses, basically helping with anything that needed to be done. That was challenging too in a different way: as soon as I walked into a stable I lost my confidence to the point that I felt weak and stupid. I guess this was because my confidence is word based and that was suddenly irrelevant. It was also because the stable was a world in which I was a rank beginner. I had no way of judging anything I looked at, and so I didn't

quite realize that the first stable I walked into—
where Natalia had taken lessons years before—was
actually run by strange, barely functional women. I
also didn't realize that they were very poor and that
their dysfunction was connected to their poverty—
this eventually became obvious, but it took perhaps
longer than it should. All I saw was that Natalia had
liked them and felt comfortable with them; they
were blunt and salty but also whimsical, with an easy
affinity for children. One of them (Cait) believed she
could understand the horses speaking and that they
understood her. (She talked to birds too, but mostly
it was horses.) The other (Sandy) believed that she
could read the animals' minds; she really disliked a
particular mare named Flora for being "stuck up." I
asked why she thought that about Flora, and she said,
"She only wants to go to a show where they have great
big flags." I asked why she thought that was. She said,
"Big flags make her feel important." Sandy was very
pissed off by anyone, human or animal, who thought
they were too important. She once called me a "royal
bitch" based on the way I cleaned a couple of stalls
when a farrier was visiting; she thought I was taking
up too much space and in that way giving attitude to
the farrier. She told dirty stories about local people
(and at least once I heard a local person intimate that
she'd heard some colorful things about Sandy and
Cait). When I asked her if there was a moment in her
life that she remembered with joy, she thought for a
bit and then recounted a time when a woman had
implied that Sandy had lost a jumping competition

because she was overweight; some years later Sandy had the opportunity to call that woman fat and "it was *choice*." But in a different mood she could be good to talk to; she could also be appreciative. Once when I was there, mucking out stalls, I heard her take a phone call from someone asking her when she would be done at the stable. She said, "We're almost done now. Yeah, Mary is here helping out and she's a fast worker, makes a big difference. Yeah, that's the writer. No, no, they don't give her any trouble. Even Cool Cat doesn't give her trouble. She's got a nice, quiet way with them and they just go with her." She would not have said this to me directly, but she had to know that I could hear her.

Eventually I did ride. I even fell in love with a horse, a gelding named Midnight. I did not expect this. Midnight was a beautiful Tennessee Walker with an even disposition, but at first he *did* give me a little trouble. One day when I was leading him out to the paddock to graze, he shoved me with his head, not hard enough to knock me down, but hard enough to make me stumble. Later, on a different day, as I was leading him back into his stall, he bolted in past me so fast that he knocked me into the wall. After that I avoided him when possible, until one day when, because of a family emergency, Cait and Sandy were both away from the barn for the day and I was the only one there in the morning. They told me to just go ahead and take care of "my usual stalls," that someone else would be there in the afternoon. But one of the horses I was responsible for had his stall right next to Midnight's. Normally Midnight would ignore me while I cleaned, but that day he stood stock-still, staring at me fixedly, sometimes even turning his head so he could look at me with one eye and then the other. Clearly he was trying to tell me something, so I went around to the other side of the barn to look at his stall. It was so filthy that he was standing in shit. His mute face said *help me* so plainly it was as if he'd spoken the words. I didn't speak out loud. But I thought at him: *I would like to help, but I'm afraid of you. You shoved me with your head and then you knocked me against the wall.* He continued to stare at me, and again, I understood as plainly as if he'd spoken: *I'm not going to hurt you. I need help. Please help.*

And so I went to his stall and cleaned it. It's generally better to take the horse out of the stall to clean, especially if it's a horse you're not comfortable with. But because I'd had problems when I'd led him, I felt better going in, at least after I'd put some hay in his bucket to get him away from the door. As soon as I entered, I realized I was safe. I cleaned one side of the stall, then gently pushed him to the other side and cleaned that. When I was done I stood with him and stroked his neck. His lips trembled with pleasure; I felt flooded with happiness.

I didn't ride him immediately after that. But I did start cleaning his stall and grooming him, and when I did those things, I felt a milder version of the same happiness. Then one day Cait said to me, "I have a very special request for you. You don't have to accept it, but it is a request." She paused. I listened. She said, "Midnight really, really wants you to ride him." I looked at the horse. He looked at me, inclining his head, all but batting his eyelashes. It was unbelievably sweet and so was the ride. When I dismounted and came around to his front to say thank you, Midnight pressed his nose against my cheek and held it there for a long moment.

Something mysterious: Of all the horses I met I loved only Midnight. But I had my most profound experience with another horse, a mare named Queen. I don't even know why it happened. But one day I was riding her and I suddenly *felt* her where my calves pressed against her sides. It is a hard sensation to describe, but it was beautiful: soft, gentle, *round*. It didn't last long, less than a minute. Because it was so brief I might've thought that I'd imagined it. But Cait confirmed it. She said, "Something different just happened." I asked, "What was it?" And she said, "I don't know. But the mare's eyes got soft for a minute." I still loved Midnight. But that never happened with him. I still don't even know what it was or what made it happen. But once when someone asked me to define real joy, I gave that moment with Queen as an example.

I volunteered and rode at places other than Cait's. All the other places were more orderly and better appointed. The horses were better cared for, and no one would ever have called me a bitch or shared dirty jokes about anyone. But in some odd way I preferred Cait's place, and this was true even before

I bonded with Midnight. Perhaps it was because of
the connection they'd had with Natalia for years
and knowing they'd been good to her. But for some
reason I felt greater depth of being working with these
women, or even just sitting with them in freezing cold
or summer heat, eating our lunch during a break, the
cats clinging to Sandy even as she griped about them.
I looked forward to driving out there in the early
morning and being with those particular horses. I still
had some fear of them, but even so I felt soothed by
them; I felt these things simultaneously rather than
alternately. I sometimes dreamed about the horses;
once I even dreamed of Sandy out in the paddock
with them, half horse herself, like a beautiful female
centaur, luxuriantly promenading, as if finally able to
be her most genuine self.

"The lovely and lovable world which quietly
persists." That is a phrase from a short essay/lecture
that Vladimir Nabokov wrote for undergrads
called "The Art of Literature and Commonsense."
In it, he whimsically assails common sense as the
oafish enemy of art and even of human goodness.
Cait and Sandy were not particularly interested
in literature. They were, remarkably to me, great
believers in common sense. But it was in their barn
with their horses that I felt the strength of that
radiant phrase.

Perhaps that is why Natalia felt good with them
too. The combination of fear, anger, and deep,
abiding comfort could've been very familiar to her.
But under that she could also have felt something

deeper: the lovely and lovable world so present in
the horses and in the smells of sweat and foliage and
manure, the togetherness of lunch, the clinging cats.

Mother: I got home to make food. I had crackers and ginger tea instead of dinner, and for once Velvet didn't act like
a malcriada, sat and read her book in a corner. I lay in bed,
coming in and out of sleep, while street noise patterned up
and broke. Cars, voices, music, lights, subways rumbling in
their dirty holes. Except that sometimes there was a forgotten passage and a crack to hide in, or a flight of stairs, and I
ran down, and there was a young blanca running too. She
didn't see me, and I hid in a crack to safely watch. She ran
through crucifixes, dollar signs, flashing lights, thousands
of quick-moving pictures of pain and ugliness. But she saw
none of it. She was looking for something and she was in
danger and she did not know it. I wanted to warn her but
could not, because in the pattern I was placed against her
and in the pattern you could not change your position.
Street noise filled my ears, good voices forced into vicious
shapes by iron hands—whose hands? Dante came into bed
with me and I held him tight. Where was my daughter?
God, with the White girl! And the White girl walked in a
hall with living heads sprouting from walls, and they spoke
all languages but not one could understand the other and
their talk split our ears. Then I was in the hall with her and
somebody said, "No, no, you're seeing the pattern wrong,
you and she are not opposed," but still she didn't see me,
and then there was a beautiful girl high above us with a
face of dignity and joy shining like it would burst, and then

the mystery would be solved. Except the voices were loud, too loud, and I screamed, "*Callate!*"

Ginger: Like I didn't already know there must be a reason he'd suddenly become so kind and understanding of Velvet and me, a reason he'd stopped with the racial piety about how really, while I think I love her, it's actually "White guilt" or something even more perverted and sick, it can't possibly be what it looks like or feels like to me. Frankly, it was such a relief not to hear that shit anymore that I'd rather he shut up and "cheat" if it meant he would leave us alone or even actually show support and back me up. "Cheat," what a stupid word, like you're playing cards and your partner cheats and the whole deck has to rise up and attack you, both of you, him because he didn't play right, and me because—why? Because I didn't catch him? Because therefore I'm now "humiliated" *officially*? Well, guess what, here's the good thing, the one good thing, *the one good thing* about having been the piece on the side where the guy goes to act like he can't with his main squeeze: you realize it doesn't mean anything much except he feels like doing it with somebody else. The wife isn't "humiliated" or unloved or anything. If that's happening to anybody, it's usually the other one. He says he's not even seeing her anymore, but still here he is with his AA face on, talking about amends and wanting to feel close again—all of it, the piety, the careful examining and blaming of himself for daring to want sex, of me for being—what? A guilty White person who must be doing something wrong? That pious judging is so much more disgusting than his wanting strange pussy, and so are his hard, fake, self-righteous friends.

But I know. I know why they call it "cheating." I hate it but I know. So much of what happens between people is comparable to a game. There is a deep, soft core that everyone longs for, too deep for games or even words. But to get to that, you have to play and play well. And I did not know how. Art, society, relationships, simple conversation—I couldn't understand how to do any of it. I don't know why. I don't know what was wrong with me. I tried, and when I was young and good-looking it could at least sometimes seem like my failure was actually an interesting *artistic* version of some special game. But now the truth is so plain that even Velvet's illiterate mother can see it, it's clear even to her, somehow *especially* to her, that I couldn't even do the thing every woman on the planet knows how to do. I can see her contempt, the question in her eyes: *What is wrong with her, how did she even get a husband?* And still, it was her child, the lovely girl that she *doesn't even want*, the child who I finally loved, who somehow allowed me a way in, who made me feel what everyone else felt; finally I could join, be part of the play—except everybody thought that was wrong too, that somehow I still wasn't doing it right.

Velvet: My mom said about Ginger once that she had a crazy eye, and I always thought, *No, she just looks sad a lot.* But now her eyes shone like an animal's in the dark and I didn't know their expression.

So I went to see the horses. I didn't think about what was wrong with Ginger. I couldn't stop thinking about

Dominic, but for once I felt like . . . He says I'm from *some-place else* and he can't be there—and he's right. He can't be here. Here is like coming back to my country, and not sneaking in like an illegal. Fiery Girl's stall had her carved sign on it, and inside it was *cleaned*, and when I came with the halter she put her head down like *YES*.

Pat took Graylie and we all went out to the paddock. I saw Sugar and Nova running together, and all the others bucking, clowning, and talking loud at each other with their heads and backs and legs. Fiery Girl raised her head and called to them and somebody called back. I could feel her shivering toward the other horses inside herself, but I pulled down on the shank and she lowered her head, sending softness and obedience to me. The air had new smells and sounds, and the horses said it with all the muscles of their backs and legs.

Paul: I saw her ride for the first time. She'd spent the weekend practicing and she wanted us to come. She and Ginger were getting ready to go when she looked at me and said, "Could you come too?" The horse at first surprised me—the way Velvet talked about it, I expected it to be big and beautiful and it was not. It was built somehow a bit strangely, with a narrow chest that from the side was deep in breadth. But its muscles were fine and distinct under its glossy, moving skin and its steps were springy, like it had elastic ankles. Its head was overlarge, but there was something noble, *senatorial*, in its boniness and size. As Velvet rode it quietly around the arena, I guess warming it up, I began to see its personality and to understand; the horse was rippling with nerves, like its basic forward movement contained fierce motion in all directions that Velvet controlled seemingly without effort. Once it broke into a nervous jog, which Velvet smoothly corrected without so much as a glance at us. Then Ginger's lips parted and her face glowed; her parted lips stayed quiet, her smile touched her eyes and cheeks only. I realized with a sharp sensation that she looked like she did when she first loved me. Velvet flew over the first jump and the second, flowing like silk. I made an involuntary noise; Ginger laughed, tiny and delighted.

When she first loved me: her softness emerging as if from hiding, overjoyed to be out in the open, coming to me open-armed. Velvet took the third jump and the horse thundered past us, throwing off heat and breathing with fierce ease. I reached for my wife's hand; she let me. Velvet rode past again, calm and delighted too, her face in a deep expression I'd never seen on her before, oblivious to everything but the animal beneath her.

Velvet: When I was riding my horse in the field there was no nightmare or daymare, nothing but her huge heart with thorns holding me up. Ginger and her strange eyes fell away. Dominic and Brianna's girls were there but floating off to the left side of me like a made-up island. When we went for the jump all of them disappeared.

·

She realized the voices were the poor, crushed, enslaved, and broken beings of earth; as they sang and spoke they were unfolding and becoming whole. They were growing around an ancient, broken machine, helping it to soften and slowly decompose into the earth. Ginger did not know how she knew this, but she did. With gratitude, she kissed the young girl's cheek. As if dreaming, the girl smiled. "How did you come?" asked Ginger. "How did you find me?"

Velvet: I didn't go find him to take him from Brianna, only to talk to him. I couldn't text or call, so I went to the block, the block we first met on and then met on again. When I walked there this time, boys looked but didn't talk to me so much, I guess because it was still cold and my body was covered and my face was closed to them because I was all the time calling him, calling him with my mind. I know I was doing that because he heard me; I know he heard me because he came.

He wasn't alone, he was with another boy—really he was a man, and he had a hard face. My heart opened too fast, and I said his name in a voice you shouldn't speak on the street with a hard man there. And Dominic, he looked at me with his face hard too. His look froze my heart, but I could not close it. "What you want, girl?" He said it like he didn't know me.

I thought of Fiery Girl, her face on mine—I tried to grab the memory of it. Instead I felt the eyes of people who hated me. I remembered the beatdown and Alicia snapping her fingers at my face and Ginger saying, "I'm weak." And my mom saying, "It's not your fault. You have bad genes." For the first time I understood: she said that to make me feel better. From love.

"My granddaughter can't answer," said the old man. "She doesn't know she's here; she's asleep on earth. But I know she loves you. When I saw what was happening, I knew she would want to help you, and I knew it would comfort you to see her face. And so I asked that we be brought here."

"How did your granddaughter come to know me?"

"You lived in the same place."

"Where?"

"Life on earth."

Ginger: There is a graveyard in the next town over that I like a lot. It's small and very old, full of thin, crumbling stones so decrepit the names and dates are worn away, slanting sideways or lurching back, some with pieces broken off. There are few big display plots, just these plain, mostly anonymous stones from the 1880s. The living have worn a path through the grass on their way to the drugstore or the parking lot or the diner on the main street—where I'm going to meet Kayla for coffee.

I walk slow, reading the few legible stones and feeling the gentle humor of the ground beneath me. AS YOU ARE NOW, SO ONCE WAS I / AS I AM NOW, SO YOU MUST BE / PREPARE FOR DEATH AND FOLLOW ME—somebody who died in 1803 wanted his stone to say that. Numbly, I smile and wonder how it will be on my deathbed to remember that when I was fifty I acted in a performance of *A Christmas Carol* with children wearing pajamas and bonnets, and that a Dominican family came from East New York to see it. Where will Velvet be then? What will she remember of our time? She is so aloof now and doesn't tell me anything. When I talked to her about our periods, and I said, "You're coming up and I'm going down," she just smiled, *big*.

Probably Paul is right, everyone is right, the whole coarse world is right, I can't even be her *pretend* mother. I give in, I agree. I'm finished, over. It is what it is. But I can still get her on that fucking horse. I can help her win.

"But *where*?"

"Be still," said the old man. "You're nearly home." As he spoke the taxi driver dissolved in the mirror and with him his car. There was nothing carrying them but the warmth of the old man's arms and the sound of voices. There were no people visible, but Ginger thought she could feel their comforting weight still around them.

Velvet: That night my mom made asopao with chicken, which she knows I love and we don't have hardly ever. But that night the delicious taste hurt, like it was love that wanted to protect me but could not and could be torn away like nothing. It doesn't make sense, but that's what it felt like in my mouth and in the way my mom watched me chew.

•

Ginger: "I *am* really happy that you're going to do it," I said. "Your mom needs to sign the permission, though, like now."

"You can send it, she'll sign."

"That's great. Is she going to come?"

"My parents," said Ginger. "Are they going to Hell?"

"I can't answer."

"Please. I need to know."

"You spoke to a demon. Demons lie."

"And the boy? Why did the boy say he would see me again *back there*?"

"Hush!"

"Please tell me! Is he going to eat my arms? Even though he hates it?"

"Demons especially enjoy metaphors."

"Do you mean that was a lie too?"

"You ask too much."

"Tell me! You have to tell me!"

Velvet: She hit me with her shoe, panting so hard spit flew. I hit too, I cried and hit wild, just to keep her off, to keep her words out of me with knife words of my own.

"Why are you so proud? Why do you think you're so special?"

"Because I don't think I'm shit? Because I don't want to think I'm shit? Ginger doesn't think I'm shit, Pat doesn't think it, only you, my own mother!"

"*Ginger?*" She laughed, and instead of hitting me, she hit herself, both hands on her face, then me and then herself again. "What did I do to make you like this? God help me, what do I need to do to stop you?"

"You've already stopped me, you don't do anything but stop me!"

"Maybe when you're crippled by that horse you'll learn!"

Like a machine that cried tears I closed my bag up. Crying machine tears, I dragged it down the hall. My mom shouted after me, "At least when you're in a wheelchair you'll—"

But I was gone.

Ginger: We had sandwiches for lunch and then Velvet went to practice. I went upstairs and went into her room the way I usually do when she first comes. There was her open bag, her toiletries. There, on the dresser, was a torn, taped-up, wrinkled picture of a beautiful young boy in a costume, holding his arms out and smiling like a lover; there was a real, almost completely dried-out seahorse and something I couldn't identify until I picked it up and felt it: a piece of blue seashell. I held it and thought, *Her mom has to come. She has to.*

Velvet: I walked out and sat on the feed bags on the side of the barn. My mom had called me five times in two hours. The last two times she left messages.

•

My mom did not leave messages. She called and expected you to see it and call back.

I put the phone facedown on the feed bag and watched Chelsea and Tracy get picked up by their moms. They called to each other and waved goodbye as they got in their cars. I called my voice mail.

The first message: *This is what I have to say to you. If you ride in that race, don't bother to come home, because there won't be a home for you anymore.*

The second message: *And don't think your home is there. You are all alone with those people. Trust me.*

I put the phone back facedown. I watched Pat come out of the barn with a wheelbarrow full of dirty bedding, dump it out, go back. I didn't feel anything. I couldn't feel anything. I just thought. I thought about this time when Ginger was driving me back from riding at Pat's: we were talking about tattoos, and I said I wanted to tattoo my mom's name on my one hand and Dante's on the other. Ginger pulled over on the side of the road and said, "Don't do that." I said, "Why?" And she said, "Because your mom's name is already written inside you. You don't need to make it literal." "But why?" "Because when somebody's name is written on you that person owns you. Like you're a slave." And I felt sorry for Ginger when she said it, that she would think like that. Now I felt sorry for me.

Mother: I wiped the windows, mopped the floor. The whole time I'm thinking, *It's no good. We don't belong here. Not in this neighborhood, not in this country, not on this filthy planet. My prayers are worthless, I have no grace. And my daughter does not respect me because some fool woman has made her into a pet.* My son cries, "You think she's going to be crippled but you let her go?" I hit him, but I was thinking, *Yes, I let her go, like I knew she was sneaking out some nights and didn't stay awake to stop her. A good mother would stop her, a good mother*—A good mother wouldn't let her daughter get turned into a pet for a few hundred dollars a month.

The field of voices went silent. Ferociously, Ginger grabbed the old man's arm and shouted, "Tell me!" And the old man let her go.

Velvet: And that's when it happened: I heard the horses talking to me like the first time I came. I don't know if I made it up because of being so sad, but it didn't matter, it made me feel better. *Hello, girl! We know you! Come see me! Have you got something for me? What's the matter?* Fiery Girl, though, didn't say anything. She didn't have to. She just looked at me like she saw me all the way to the bottom, and all her muscles were proud and ready. Like a Jesus heart with fire and thorns inside it.

And I knew: I am doing it for *this.* If somebody asked me what *this* was, I wouldn't be able to tell them. But I knew, I knew.

•

Ginger: Normally when I would compliment her, she'd smile awkwardly and thank me with a full, tender voice. This time she thanked me with her voice and face so measured she looked like a much older person, almost *middle-aged.*

It was much later that I realized: she looked like her mother. Like her mother the fighter. Except that, unlike her mother, she wasn't in a tank. She was out in the open.

Paul: I got there early to pick them up, but couldn't find a spot in the near lot, had to spiral up the parking structure for a space, thinking tangentially of Ginger's sister, whom I had once compared, after her death, to a fictional character named Hazel Shade, an ugly girl who kills herself on being rejected by a cloddish boy. I did not make a direct comparison between live Melinda and the fictional dead girl for Ginger; I just repeated one critic's somewhat quixotically made case that poor scorned Hazel is transformed by death into a Vanessa butterfly, a kind angel who gently guides her father into the spirit world and even comforts the egotistical lunatic (and great rejector of women) who inadvertently drew her dad to his death.

I heard a train pulling in as I hurried down the concrete steps, feeling that strange gladness in anticipation of the lumpen, frowning woman and her odd boy whom I could deliver to my even odder wife, who had liked the comparison between her sister and Hazel Shade, because she felt Melinda had guided her to Velvet and Velvet to the horse. And because she believed in transformation, she did not accept that anything just "is what it is"; she always thought it could be something else, something secretly beautiful and glorious.

Ginger: The stable was open and I walked through it, hoping to find Velvet and tell her that her mother would come after all. But I didn't see her. I asked a couple of girls if they knew her. They said, "Who?" and looked at each other like I must be joking. This bothered me more than it should've. I went to the pavilion and waited to get the attention of the women. The one with the strange face sat back and fixed me with a speculative, quietly malign look that I didn't understand and pretended not to see; did she know me? "Excuse me," I said to the other. "I'm looking for Velveteen Vargas, do you know who she is?"

"The name certainly stands out," she said. "I don't know her personally but . . ." She scanned a list with the help of a swollen finger. "Here she is, she's here with a mare called Fugly Girl."

"Oh," I said, relieved but bothered again. "That's a mistake, that's not the horse's name."

"Well, that's what it says here, that's—"

"Ginger!"

I turned and there was Paul, alone.

"They weren't there," he said. "They weren't at Poughkeepsie or Rhinecliff, I checked there too. I tried to call them several times, I got no answer."

"There she is!" said the swollen-fingered woman. "There's your girl right there!"

•

Velvet: I looked at the bleachers, trying to find Ginger and Paul. They weren't there. Only strangers were there. *You are all alone with those people. Trust me.* Fiery Girl bucked up under me so small it was more like bumping. I pulled her head up and scrunched the reins, turning her head good. *If you ride in that race, don't bother to come home, because there won't be a home here for you anymore.* "Get her out in front!" yelled Pat. "Don't worry about where her head is!" Fiery Girl went like a question mark under me, and I answered her with my legs. I shut out my mom's voice, put my legs on the mare, and went for the jumps. She hit the first one with her hoof, and she knocked a rail off the second one. That's when I heard them say our names, I heard "Velveteen Vargas and Fugly Girl on deck!" And I knew it was time to go for real.

Paul: "Who *is* that little Black girl?" said a woman seated before us.

"They said she's from Brooklyn?"

"Where'd she learn to ride like that in Brooklyn?"

The horse went into a spirited, near-chaotic trot.

And Silvia's face went dark with anger. It made no sense. She went from joy to rage in seconds. Ginger said to her, "I can't tell what's happening, but I think she just did really well!" then registered that Mrs. Vargas looked like she was about to explode. The explosion was defused, though, when one of the two women in front turned around, beamed, and asked, "Is that your daughter?" She apparently repeated herself in Spanish, because Mrs. Vargas rather sheepishly replied, "Sí." The woman said something else, probably "you must be so proud," then turned around. Whereupon Mrs. Vargas looked Ginger in the eye and said something that sounded like a curse.

Velvet: When that voice called her "fugly," a bad feeling took hold of me, like when the branches flew past and I fell off her all alone, up into the sky and then slam on the ground, darkness coming in. Her running away from me. Dominic walking away from me. Everything far away. *You are all alone.*

Mother: My face burned; my heart swelled. I turned to Ginger and said, "If anything happens to her I am going to kill you."

Velvet: Yes, I was alone with her in the hurricane, so alone it didn't even matter when they called her "fugly" again; Pat said, "Go," and I rode her into it.

Then Ginger was running up the same flight of stairs she had run down, carrying the bag of treasure. She came to the trapdoor and pushed it open and came out in her own backyard; her heart flooded with happiness to see the grass in the early-morning light. She went straight to her bedroom and put the treasure under the bed so she would be sure to find it the next day. Then she got in bed and fell asleep, dreaming of what she would spend it on.

•

I originally didn't intend to write from Mrs. Vargas's point of view. There are White writers in the world who know well enough what it's like to live in a foreign country, in poverty, with young children, on one of the lowest rungs of the social ladder— but I'm not one of them. I can imagine it at least basically: everything around you is foreign, the way it looks and feels and sounds. You are poor. Your neighborhood is poor. It seems dangerous, but because you can't understand what people are saying, and they can't understand you, it's hard to know how to assess the danger. The only understanding is that you are all poor. Unlike some people you have no proud posture with which to protect yourself. Because you are not young you have no beauty with which to protect yourself. There is gunfire at night. Mail comes with official messages about bills and legal status and school business, but you can't read it. Your elementary school child has to read it and explain it. And even so, sometimes the lights get turned off. Yes, I can imagine all of this. But life has taught me that even powerful imaging is a distant relation to experience. And so I felt the same way that my dream about the writing of *Veronica* made me feel: afraid of subtly exploiting hardship that I could only understand in my head, and then foolishly *defining* that hardship in a way that real people, if they read it, might find weirdly unrecognizable.

I didn't feel as much fear in depicting Velvet
because she was based on someone I knew intimately
for a long time, someone who grew up with roughly
the same American popular culture, who spoke and
could read the same language as me; as she described
it, her experience of girlhood had big things in
common with mine. I understood her relationship
with her mother at least some because she talked
to me about it and because I recognized parts of it
in my relationship with my father. When I learned
that Natalia's mother told her over and over again
that she couldn't hope to do well because she had
"bad blood," it rang like a dismal echo of my father
telling us, over and over, that "it" wasn't our fault
because we had "bad genes." When I saw Natalia's
mother sneer at pictures of her daughter smiling
triumphantly at summer camp, I thought of my
father remarking, "I don't think your editor really
cares about the book." Still, while I knew what it was
like to hear those things, I don't know what it's like
to *say* them, to feel *compelled* to say them, to someone
you love. I don't even know what it felt like for my
father, though I could sometimes sense it in fitful
snatches of *something* almost impossible to define.
I thought I could sometimes sense it in Natalia's
mother, but even more fitfully and faintly.

In spite of all this, about halfway in I decided
to write from Silvia's point of view. The book's
penultimate scene is between Velvet and her mother,
with her little brother there too; it's one of the
most important scenes of the book, if not the most

important. I did not think it could land right unless
the reader could see what Mrs. Vargas was thinking
and feeling leading up to it well in advance, how
she arrived where she did. I referred earlier to the
awkwardness I felt was inevitable in writing the
book, awkwardness in the form of cultural mistakes,
wrong details, words, tone—as opposed to my trust
in my deeper understanding of the story. In this
scene those oppositions met, the knowing that I
couldn't get everything right, yet feeling the need
and the will to create a world in which mother and
daughter could drop their "weapons" and love in
spite of all the forces against them. Writing the
scene was in a way like following my father through
the house, yelling about having a real relationship:
clumsy and self-righteous but painfully sincere.

When my first book was published, I did an
interview with a (White) journalist at a Detroit
paper who was clearly offended by my portrayal of
suburban Detroit in the story "Secretary." He asked,
sarcastically, "Have you ever even *been* here?" When
I answered that I'd grown up there, he was silent
for a long moment. He probably couldn't believe
that anyone could see his home area in the way that
I had described it, or maybe he even thought I was
lying. His Detroit suburb wasn't the same as mine,
and mine isn't the same as that of another writer; it's
an invention, a made-up concoction of private and
public reality.

Mrs. Vargas doesn't represent Dominican women
or poor people of color as a group any more than

Ginger represents White women (or even me). She, Mrs. Vargas, and Velvet are *characters*, and even if they were inspired by actual people, I did not exploit their "story," I invented it. Or rather I half invented it, half lived it, for this was my story too. The scene between Velvet and her mother at the end is a scene of tenderness struggling to emerge from brutality and pain, wanting to come out and exist. In an essential way the whole story is about that, and it is a story I know, beyond this book or these characters; I know it from my life. Ginger has goodness, but it's warped by emotional injury and stunted naïveté, particularly naïveté about racism and— although she has suffered quite a bit—her own social advantage; these elements in her war without her full knowledge. But although Ginger doesn't know, she can sense that Velvet's mother is warring too, that *her* essential goodness has been brutalized and warped by poverty, racism, and emotional injury, and yet it's there, a *lovely and lovable world that quietly persists*. And in the mother's case the stakes are higher and the courage is more intense, because she's in a more adversarial world where she can't be seen for who she is or *be* who she is, where people don't even speak her language—and because it will affect the well-being of her child. Mrs. Vargas may appear cruel, almost insanely so at moments; in that situation, how would you appear, how would you *be*? The real woman who inspired Silvia Vargas could be cruel too. But when I was honest with myself, I could not think I would be any better in her situation—I might actually be worse.

Yet the children whom she raised had goodness—
not *niceness*, goodness. They had the same kind of
natural softness that I associate with the tormented
girl from my childhood, Emotional; I don't think
they got it from nowhere.

But they were, thank God, tougher than
Emotional. That kind of softness needs to protect
itself lest it be destroyed. Sometimes it protects itself
by being cruel first; the kids learned that from her
too; they also learned to be very forbearing with
that complex blur of injury, love, and cruelty. They
learned it as I did, toward my father and even more
toward the man who molested me, in the form of
pity that I was too young to understand or to keep
myself from feeling. That kind of forbearance is not
something that should ideally be experienced by
young children, but all over the world, in every race,
class, and culture, young children experience it.

I wanted to write a story where that profound
and sometimes tragic will to understand and forbear
could be supported and comforted by a powerful
animal, a reliable and inviolate goodness that Velvet
could feel through her legs, on the warm sides of her
mare's body. I saw that happen in reality, and I don't
believe it's exploitation to depict what I saw and, to a
lesser extent, felt with my own legs.

When she woke in the morning, Ginger looked under
the bed and saw nothing. She was disappointed, but
then she forgot about it. She ate breakfast and went

out to play with her sister. They played in the backyard and ran back and forth over the spot where the trap-door had been. That evening they ate dinner as usual and watched the news on TV. Their father said, "The world is going to hell!"

Ginger remembered what had happened then, and before she got in bed that night, she checked under it to see if the treasure was there after all. Seeing nothing, she got into the bed and listened to her mother sing them to sleep.

But though she saw nothing, the treasure was there. The old woman she had met in Hell was not a demon and she had told the truth. It was there.

Just not where Ginger could see it.

At the date of this writing I am sixty-five years old. I dreamed of going to Hell to steal from the Devil when I was six. The story is not the same as the dream; in the dream I didn't get lost in Hell or meet anybody or see faces on a wall. I just took the treasure from behind the Devil's armchair (where he sat peacefully reading) and ran back up the stairs into my yard, into my home. Right before I put the bag of treasure under my bed, I opened the top drawer of my dresser to see if my underwear and the weird little objects that I collected there were the same; that everything was as usual somehow convinced me that the dream was real, and I went to bed satisfied. I was very disappointed to find that the bag wasn't there the next day.

I had another powerful dream sometime after that, maybe I was seven. I was at school in the big auditorium where we would be assembled for any important announcement or national occasion, like a speech about the meaning of Thanksgiving or patriotism. In the dream the whole school was present and the principal was giving an inspiring speech. But we couldn't concentrate on the speech, because behind the principal was a huge cake that was almost as high as the ceiling. When he was finished talking, we were going to eat the cake and we could hardly wait. He went on and on, but finally the moment arrived and all the kids charged the fantastic cake, which had been conveniently cut into individual pieces. I grabbed a piece and started to take a bite—and then saw that the cake was full of worms.

When I told my husband about this dream he said, "You were realizing at a young age that whenever an authority figure is giving an inspiring speech, there's got to be worms somewhere." That could be; the social nature of the dream is clear in its location in the school assembly room—my locus of official civic life at the time. It is about socially dispensed bounty that is beautiful and appetizing but full of rot not visible from the outside. It is also about greed, the kind of greed that children are punished for in fairy tales, the forever greed of humankind.

My dream of the Devil is about greed too, for candy and the treasure with which to buy it. In the story about the dream, this greed comes from starvation: women are starving for love and the beauty of a young man who lives in a delightful world, a young man whose own starvation transforms him into a charnel house where arms are torn off and eaten, a young man whose soul is a beautiful song trapped in the terrible place where it is housed.

THE END OF SEASONS

The boy stood on the sagging porch of a low-built shack in the middle of a field, shivering and searching his wet pockets for cigarettes. Rain fell on the flickering green weeds and gray puddles that lay in the weedless dirt. A small brown rabbit picked its way across the field in soft, short jumps. The boy could see its eye flash from where he stood. It paused, twitched its wet ears, and nibbled at a wild plant growing from a broken flowerpot. The boy absorbed its smallness and softness, its blunt claws, the piercing shine of its eyes. It made him feel small and soft inside, curled in a burrow of earth. Outside the burrow were thousands of faces and eyes streaking through immensity and violence, but here he was alone with only the smallest and softest of movements and the clarity to know when to make them. From safety, he looked up at the sky; inside the heavy gray clouds enormous light was stirring. Slow and rolling, it pierced the gray with lavender and blue and colors the boy had no words for. A window flew open in his brain. It was a window that looked into several worlds at once. It looked into people, into dreams, into the peculiar webbing where the dreams of different people overlapped. It looked into the past, present, and future. It looked without order.

Whatever it looked out on could slip into it, and sometimes the boy could slip out of it. It was not something he could give words to, but it gave words to him. Sometimes he was conscious of it and sometimes he was not.

Last night, a man had called him an angel. He had put his thumb in the boy's mouth so he could suck it. It had tasted metallic, salty, and a little grainy. "Rafael," said the man. "The funniest and friendliest of the angel flock." They were in a place called the Red Spot, sitting at a red banquette (a lush seat, cracked and taped) that somebody else had just vacated. The table was strewn with smeared plates and dirty utensils, balled greasy napkins, bits of bun and untouched lumps of slaw. The waiters let them sit there anyway—it was packed and they let things go to hell this time of night. Next to them a man with huge denim-clad thighs and an open, hungering mouth kissed a middle-aged woman with her skirt up around her waist and her skinny legs open under the table. She threw her head back and offered him her breasts, the pulpy lobes of her ears, the raised bones of her throat. His gobbling, kissing head came straight up out of his neck, to eat it all like a mouth coming out of a tree. Two fat grinning police with clubs and guns and black devices hanging off them looked on, swapping jokes with the bartender. One of them looked at the man fucking the boy's mouth with his thumb; the man froze. But the police turned away to look at a young blond girl in a silver skirt, her pug nose red from cold. She yawned like a kitten and tossed back her green drink. A dog trotted through the crowd with affable death in its eyes and a rubber bone in its mouth. A song from the jukebox filled the room with mild sorrow and mild joy that evaporated in the air. *If we ever gonna survive we gonna hafta get—* The singer's voice flew across the empty canyon of the song on stately wings. The boy tongued the man's thumb and imagined a flying angel with pure black skin and electric blue eyes. It was not friendly in the usual sense of the word and it was not funny. It was terrifying and it was beautiful. It had nothing to do with the song, it had simply used its emptiness as a way to enter the human world. It was watching everyone in the room. It was sorting and weighing them, for punishments and also mercy. It was finding out how well they were being what they were meant to be, and it was pitying them because it knew in advance that they could not do it.

They could not do it. How hard it is just to be as we were born to be; I think I understood that when I dreamed of Hell at the age of six. I didn't understand it in my mind. I understood it through an obscene onrush of powerful feelings in my body as it was manipulated by a man I thought was my friend, a man who lived down the street with his wife and child but who also lived in hell. A man whose human face transformed into *something else* before my stunned eyes.

The Devil is about forbidden power, or the wish for it. The story of original sin is about forbidden knowledge, and at six I had probably heard that story more than once. But what kind of knowledge or power did I try to steal at that age? Some way to understand what my child's mind couldn't? To understand what no one seemed to know? When I was writing the story, I asked myself those questions without really expecting to find an answer. It wasn't until I was writing this that it occurred to me: I wasn't trying to steal at all. I was trying to take back something that had been stolen from me: my sexuality, my core nature; *what I was born to be*.

This circumstance is crippling. This circumstance is treasure. This circumstance just *is*.

But I wasn't thinking about that when I wrote the story. I was thinking about the dream itself, its willful energy, its combination of mystery and simple childish verve. I started it separately from *The Mare*, but the more I worked on the two pieces, the more they seemed linked, not directly but intuitively: the incomprehensible *stuff* underlying the purposeful striving of life and how a child might try to understand it; the contrast between what is happening on the surface and what is happening underneath. (In life, Ginger seems to be redeeming Velvet; in the secret world underneath, Velvet redeems Ginger.) Then there are the themes of stealing and greed—greed that makes Ginger (who in the "real" world is starving inside) demanding and disrespectful of Velvet's grandfather when he appears to help her in the underworld. Stealing and greed are obvious themes, but it was not until I read the story to an audience of Black and Latinx college students in Brooklyn that I fully felt their resonance. I could feel it in the air of the room: a bone-deep awareness of rape, enslavement, and dispossession as the perpetual drama of life on earth. They were an appreciative audience. But I thought I could feel them wondering what I was really trying to say in my story.

Yes, the story and the novel are more linked than I first realized. The story of *The Mare* is light and gentle on its surface, but underneath that surface people stumble around in hell, suffering and blindly inflicting their suffering on those around them, some trying to give reparation for that which can never be repaid, weeping with pain and remorse, no one able to be what they were meant to be—but still trying, foolishly and futilely, as best they can.

The boy lived in a small town north of New York City. He was sixteen, but he was about to graduate from high school. Until a few days ago he had lived with his mother in a big, ruined house with half its roof caved in, its blinded windows like eyes rolled back in a drunken head. Boarders upstairs hung their laundry off the iron railing around the cupola. The animals ran wild in the yard; Jolly, the German shepherd, tore the leg off somebody's cat and charged old people on the sidewalk. Neighbors walking by yelled, "Chain that thing up, you jackass!" while his mother ran around the yard chasing the dog in her T-shirt and underpants. She was narrow and thin with a long freckled face.

The flesh jiggled on her scrawny, vigorous thighs. She was always boiling and collapsing at the same time; ropey veins popped out of her hands and swollen feet. Her mouth was big and her voice full of sex, the angry, gnawing kind. Still her eyes had beauty and sensible intelligence. She'd drag the dog in by the collar, talking to it gently, her wavy blond hair falling loose around her hot face. She'd give it a dish of ice cream and then stride around smoking and yelling about her boyfriend. She knew he went to the Red Spot at night, but that was okay with her. "You're like me," she said. "You're connected to the dark side—and that's great, the dark side's great. You've just gotta accept that in yourself and you'll be fine."

He gave up on the cigarettes and squatted on the porch, waiting for the rain to stop. Now his mother was in a detox center for six months because she'd smashed her car into the side of a restaurant and then got out to slug the person she'd almost run down. His father had come to take custody of him and yelled at him in the car all the way to the thruway. He sighed, stood up, and turned around to study the shack. He'd come across it in a field of weeds between a fairground he'd walked through and a neighborhood he was headed for. It looked like a stable made into a two-unit pit for humans. It looked like no one lived there now. Soft heaps of rags and dissolving garbage were strewn on the ground around the porch. Plastic sheeting was stapled to the dismally curtained windows, but he could tell it was dark inside. He had an appointment but he was early. He was thinking he should break in and investigate when he heard a muffled rapping sound. He peered into a window and started back: there was a face with hollow glaring eyes and a frowning lipless mouth, shadow rain flying brightly across a sunken cheek into deeper shadow. The plastic sheeting moved and rasped in the wind; light and shadow moved in a solid chunk, and a claw pushed aside more ragged curtain. It was an old lady, looking through life and seeing death, and straining to tell them apart. His heart opened. Her dry little head hung toward her chest and her colorless lips mouthed words. She rapped on the window again and said *shoo!* with her hands. Feebleness and courage came off her, rolling and piercing. She glared at visions crowding her sight in a blur of past and present, trying to separate them from the person on her porch. Her gaze stretched into an unearthly future too big for her mind. The boy understood this without knowing how. He even glimpsed it: bright scenes of life enlarged and perfected in heaven, then blotted by a deep black sky filled with flying stars.

He spoke loud enough for her to hear, but he made his voice high and sweet as a child's. "Can I come in, Auntie? It's cold out."

The old woman's glare became less abstract. She frowned and worked her mouth. The ragged curtain fell. There was a long moment and then the sound of clicking metal. She stood before him, a gentle mass of decay in a housedress printed with red and yellow flowers. She wasn't glaring now. Her eyes were milky blue, intense and receptive as those of a cave animal, lids shrinking on top and sagging on the bottom. The personality in those eyes was weak, soupy and run together; in her spirit too her personality was going loose, viscous and falling off in pieces. He thought of his mother running around in the yard in her underwear. She was middle-aged, not old yet. But it was starting in her body and her personality too.

"Are you Jimmy's friend?" asked the old lady.

"Yes," he said. "He sent me to see if you were okay."

"I'm not okay," she said, "and he knows it! Those people are coming around every night now—they've found a way into the house! I can hear them in the annex, talking and laughing!"

There was femininity in the folds of her crumpled voice and in the air about her, sweet and foul as the odor of a decaying melon. No active flesh to live in, but still present, floating off her body, migrating slowly toward the starry darkness—stopping on its way to lightly touch his face and body, still with affection to give.

His mother still had it in her body, but she was losing it. She was holding on to it with all her might, with her bright lipsticks and tight pants and jiggling earrings, fucking every man she could. But when it got ready, it would go. A hole appeared in the lit world and pouring darkness fell.

"I hear them on the roof too—they spend hours up there jumping up and down, can you imagine?" The old lady stood aside to let him in, then closed the door behind him. "I called the police, but those hoods must've heard me on the phone, because by the time the cops came, they were gone."

In the mudroom of the shack there were heaps of tin cans, boxes, and bottles bristling in the silence and dust. In the kitchen an ancient doll in a filthy, frilly dress presided over a table almost entirely covered with feverish little pictures. The oven was full of neatly stacked dishes;

an ironing board was laden with pots, pans, and yellowed spray bottles. On the wall were crucifixes, framed religious sayings, and faded children's drawings fixed to the wall with rotting yellow tape. He thought of biology class, of Mr. Hannawald discussing decomposition, the conversion of mass into energy, shit fertilizing food. The girls giggled and looked at each other, eyes points of hot light intersecting across the room. What would be fertilized by a decomposing personality?

"What is your name?" she asked.

"Rafe. Rafe Goodson."

"Rafe," she echoed. "Rafael." She tilted her head up and blinked her milky eyes; the visions closed in, then dispersed. "Would you like some sweet biscuit?"

"Yeah," he said, "thanks."

When he sat at the table he saw that the pictures were cards illustrated with deep red roses excreting fat beads of glistening dew and saints with beautiful drugged eyes. They were like the Easter egg picture books he secretly loved even when he was too old for them. The old lady rooted in the refrigerator, her shoulders a hump and her spine a row of rusted knobs. The doll stared with her skewed, dust-blind eyes. He glimpsed bread, blackening bananas, and several boxes of factory cakes, the image of a girl in a blue hat stamped on each box. She turned holding a box of cakes, a smile on her face. The air about her head tingled as if reacting to something unseen. She smiled. He felt softness in the decay and tenderness in preserving old, broken things with no use. Her personality was vacating, but something else was trying to come through the empty spaces—what was it?

"Rafael," she said. "I like that." *The funniest and friendliest of the angel flock.*

The man who said that had eyes like blue coins placed over his real eyes, fleshy jowls, and a high, round forehead with its thoughts balled at the top like a forelock. He wore a yellow pullover vest and a white shirt. His manner was like a smooth lid covering a hole with something in it that smelled. He smiled like he hated himself and loved himself for it. "Call me Boo," he said. "Boo Radley." His voice was melodious, his chest fleshy and heavy, full of chopped-up feelings put back together wrong, like horse legs on a pig. They were strong but they were deformed, and when he embraced Rafe, the boy felt them beating the man on the inside, kicking and punching his heart. His cringing, raging heart kept trying to love, but it was getting kicked and punched too much. Still, love eked out his heart from certain random openings, and one of those openings was boys for money. The man gently bit his ear and whispered, "I'll stick it up your ass till it comes out your mouth."

So they went to the restroom of an all-night gas station. An attendant was watching TV inside, but they didn't need to talk to him because Boo Radley had a key. A flickering bulb soft with webs and gnats showed them the door to their gray seraglio. The light went on with a terrible buzz; broken fluorescent tubes rhythmically blanched and blotted the room. The boy bent over the rough square basin; there was the soft stink of public water. There was the waste can, the crumpled tissue, the dented tin mirror over the sink, the soap dispenser clotted with wonderful shiny pink. The man braced himself on the boy's bent spine and swiped a blob of soap. He touched the boy's asshole like it was a heart, and at this touch the boy opened his heart. The man fucked like the broken light, ramming his personality through a defective wire. The boy moved back and forth, the outer world going dim as huge pictures bloomed inside his head. He moved back and forth as he condensed these pictures into a fine point of feeling, sweet as the highest, purest song. He devoured the feeling, wanting it more and more. The man understood this, and deep inside the fucking they touched together. Then there was no heart. There were no pictures. There was just feeling and force. The boy looked up into the dented mirror. His face was swollen and shrunken, then swollen again, shapeless and broken, like a crying child. The man, featureless now in the cloudy tin, was jerking back and forth from crest to cleft of a huge dent like something trapped and trying to jerk free. The light lit them, put them out. The boy closed his eyes. The child disappeared and so did he.

The old lady brought cups of hot water to the table, a tea bag in each cup, along with a jar of dried milk. She poured the dried milk straight from the jar and handed him a cake out of the box. She grimaced as she sat down, easing her knobbed body into its daily seat of pain. The pain bled into the deep color of the prayer roses and rolled over him. He was pierced by the child's drawing on the wall: square blue house with a pointy roof, yellow sun, green child playing with leaping brown animal. "For My Grandma, Love Jimmy." He rolled the pierced feeling into a knot and sent it far inside himself.

"One night they woke me up singing Italian songs, songs my father used to sing. It was like they were making fun of me."

"Are they kids or grown-ups?" asked Rafe.

"Oh, it's all kinds of people. Never mind the cards, you can push 'em to one side. They're prayer cards, I send 'em to people. But anyway, the one song, that was a man and a girl. It's a love song, you know. My father sang it to my mother—and they mock that! It made me sad. And I wondered, how did they know?"

So hurt and so baffled at someone making fun of her, but at the same time accepting it—looking for it. She picked the bag out of her tea and squeezed it into her cupped hand, licking her palm with a wide, candid tongue as she placed the squeezed bag on the table.

The light flashed on and off like a crazy man baring and covering his teeth. The man said, "I'm going to punish you," and gasped like he was going to die.

I tried to take myself back. I spent a lifetime trying. And I succeeded—almost. Because my "self" wasn't completely mine anymore; it had been infected by knowledge, knowledge that I wasn't ready for, and *something else* that I still don't quite know how to define and that I can only give shape to in the language of dreams and metaphors (of which demons are especially fond!), *something else* moving through the images like the unknown bleeds through the fabric of every human life, mutely signaling in an indecipherable code.

The morning before she went to detox, his mother told him about a dream she'd had the previous night. In the dream, she was whipping a man with no arms and no legs. She wondered why he didn't scream in pain. By way of answer he said, "See how I tell time," and his face turned into a clock.

"Explain that to me," she said to her son. "Because I can't figure it out." She was at the stove, making pancakes in her lacy purple slip and the turquoise wrap that didn't close. Jolly followed her back and forth, tongue out and tail wagging. She brought the pan to the table and slid pancakes onto their plates. The strap of her slip fell and showed a small, loose breast. She didn't notice. She put aside a pancake for the dog and put the hot pan in the sink. "I wanted to save him from the bitch with the whip, but I was the bitch with the whip. So I had to split in two. I picked him up and ran from myself. I ran down this long tunnel." She sat down. "So can you figure that out?"

He ran down a dark tunnel, running from a bitch and carrying a man with no legs. He ran past an old man fishing through a hole in ice. Except instead of fish he was looking for sunken jewels, and instead of worms his line was loaded with boys that he lowered deep into the frozen water to pry loose the gems. If some of them drowned that was okay. There were always others. He lifted his line and Rafe saw choking, naked boys. He ran deeper into the tunnel. There was a hobbling old lady in a black crevice, muttering and picking her way along with a stick. There was his mother at the table with her breast showing, her mouth working and no words coming out. There he was, playing with James Johnson before James was Tod Hannert's best friend. There was James on top of him on the playground, beating him up because Rafe's mom had screwed James's dad. Except there was secret friendship in the beating and in James's crying, laughing eyes. He burst from the tunnel. Now the beating was fucking, and he and the man were fiercely joined. Now there was nothing but pleasure and devouring, and worms with mouths for heads eating, eating, eating at the center of the earth.

Then they sat in the man's warm car, the man holding the boy on his lap. The radio played old songs. "I feel safe with you," said Rafe. The man's silence felt emotional, like the deformed things were quiet now, and for the moment his heart was spared. Music rolled out of the radio, human and warm, with words as strong and tender as your father's hand on your head.

Baby, I need your lovin'
Got to have all your lovin'.

Boo swallowed and said, "You are safe with me. I'm a good guy. Most of the time." Rafe pulled himself free and sat up. "Hey," he said. "Did you know there's giant worms at the center of the earth that eat lava?"

Boo laughed, a surprised, hollow sound coated with benevolence.

"It's true, I learned it in biology class."

He laughed again; despair touched the sound and made it real. "You're sweet," he said. And he kissed the boy, trying to push the real thing through his lips, but it was already gone.

The man in his mother's dream told time by becoming time. In the same way, he was able to endure being beaten by becoming the beating. But his mother just said, "Well, that's obvious! What about *me*?" She must've realized her tit was showing then because she pulled up the strap to cover it. She didn't say anything, and her hand movements were irritated and impatient. But he saw her eyes go deep and sad. Inside, he heard her call herself *stupid bitch*. He had contempt for her then and of course she saw it on his face. She reached out and half stroked, half cuffed his cheek. "Don't give me a hard time," she said. "Not today."

The man turned off the radio and reached for his wallet; the boy unlatched the door and nudged it open with his foot. The seat belt signal fired its vibrant pellet of noise and car light spilled over the gravel lot. The lit stones traveled toward the dark, white, then gray, then gone.

When Rafe was a kid this was a beautiful sight to him: sitting with his dad in the car at night, the door open while they waited for his mom. The gravel bright and revealed, then suddenly void, remote as the moon or the ocean.

He wondered what Boo Radley would think if he told him about this. He was frowning as he sat sideways, counting the money with his legs pinched awkwardly together and his pants bunched at the hip joint. "You're safe with me because I'm a good guy. But not every guy is good, so you'd better start being more careful. Like getting paid before you give it up."

They would go to picnics with other families and his mother would always linger with the other wives. There was laughter, fireflies, and then the crunch of his mother's footsteps on the gravel. Her feet made the moon and ocean into earth and the world was saturated in goodness. He wanted to sit there forever, in the moment before she came, listening to her footsteps on lit stones.

Boo Radley turned so that he could give Rafe the cash without looking at him. "Be safe," he said, meaning *you won't be*. Rafe hopped out and the car pulled away, sweeping the lot with its headlights. Gravel and grasses were caught in the hurtling twin disks of light and carried away. The car wound out the asphalt path to the highway. Rafe took a cigarette from his shirt pocket and lit it. The gas station light drenched the concrete in hot, gorgeous purple. The TV inside it flashed like a jewel. The power of weeds and dirt came up through the bottoms of his feet. *Fuck you till it comes out your mouth*. The weeds and dirt were full of feeling, the dark was alive with singers and angels ready to fill their emptiness.

This circumstance is crippling. This circumstance is treasure. This circumstance just *is*.

So many oppositions together inside us, so
much violence and perverted cruelty; so much love
and procreative force; such innocence and filth,
so much innocent filth. How are you supposed to
walk around like that? How can anyone stand it?
It doesn't make any sense together (at least not as
"sense" has been typically defined for us), but it *is*
together. I would not have thought about that as a
child. But I might've felt it, how the simple desire
for something sweet is never . . . simple, how beauty
and deliciousness and inspiring speeches, even those
that are sincere, are so close to rot and worms; the
bewilderment and hugeness of it. In the face of such
bewilderment and hugeness, one might feel fear and
reverence, or one might just say, *Fuck it, I'm going to
do what I can to get as much as I can.* I have felt both
of those things, at different times. Mostly, I have
felt longing, ever since I can remember and before
I had words for it: longing for unity, integration,
compassion, especially compassion for ugliness and
evil, for those so hurt that they become ugly and evil.
For people to be what they were born to be; for the
soul to come free of the terrible house, even for just a
moment. For a way to decipher the code of dreams,
masks, power, weakness, personality, and the raw
matter underneath; to be allowed to see into our
impossible existence. Even if it's just a flash or a quiet
moment. Of pity. Or grace.

ACKNOWLEDGMENTS

I would like to thank Kelsey Nolan; Chris Heiser; Deborah Garrison; Jin Auh; and With Projects, Inc. for putting so much time, energy, and talent into this project; I would especially like to thank Michael Zilkha for conceiving it with so much respect and care.

I have special gratitude to the artists and writers who helped with conversation, advice, and visual work: Debra Losada, Karen Crumley, Peter Trachtenberg, Alison Elizabeth Taylor, and Gregory Crane.

McNally Editions reissues books that are not widely known but have stood the test of time, that remain as singular and engaging as when they were written. Available in the US wherever books are sold or by subscription from mcnallyeditions.com.